KU-011-789

This first English translation of *The Legend of the Ice People*
is dedicated with love and gratitude to the memory
of my dear late husband Asbjørn Sandemo,
who made my life a fairy tale.

Further titles in The Legend of the Ice People saga to be published in 2008

Witch-hunt
ISBN: 978-1-903571-77-4

Depths of Darkness
ISBN: 978-1-903571-79-8

Yearning
ISBN: 978-1-903571-81-1

Mortal Sin
ISBN: 978-1-903571-85-9

Evil Inheritance
ISBN: 978-1-903571-87-3

LM

The Legend of the Ice People

Book 1

Spellbound

MARGIT SANDEMO

Translated from Swedish
by Gregory Herring and Angela Cook

740006066236

The Legend of the Ice People

Spellbound

The original Norwegian version was published in 1982 under the title
Sagan om Isfolket 1: Trollbundet by Bladkompaniet, Oslo, Norway

First published in Great Britain in paperback in June 2008
by Tagman Worldwide Ltd in The Tagman Press imprint.

Tagman Worldwide Ltd
Media H
Burrel R
Cambri(
Tel: 084!
Fax: 084
www.tag
email: e(

HEREFORDSHIRE
LIBRARIES

623

Bertrams	06/10/2011
FAN	£7.00
LM	

Publishe ... ight to the works
shall be ... ranted.

Copyrig
English

The rigl ... ork has been
asserted ... Act 1988.

All rights reserved. No part of this publication may be reproduced, stored in a retrieval
system or transmitted in any form or by any means, electronic, mechanical, recording or
otherwise, without the prior written permission of the author and copyright holders.

ISBN
Hardcover 978-1-903571-74-3
Paperback 978-1-903571-75-0

A CIP catalogue record for this book is available from the British Library

Text & Cover Design: Richard Legg
Translation: Gregory Herring and Angela Cook

Printed by CLE Print Ltd, St Ives, Cambs, PE27 3LE UK

Tagman   www.tagmanpress.co.uk

Chapter 1

ONE evening in the late autumn of 1581, as an icy mist played with the blood-red reflection of fire in the sky above Trondheim, two young women made their way along the town's streets, each unaware of the other.

Not quite seventeen, Silje was a girl whose deep eyes showed an indifference to the world around her, mirroring the loneliness and hunger she felt inside. She hugged herself to keep out the cold, thrusting her hands beneath her clothes, most of which seemed to be made from old sacking. Strips of hide were bound round her worn-out shoes and her attractive hazelnut hair was covered with a woollen shawl, which doubled as a blanket whenever she found a safe place to sleep.

She stepped cautiously around a corpse lying in the narrow alley. Just one more victim of the plague, she told herself. This plague – she could no longer remember how many outbreaks there had been during the last century – had taken her whole family just two or three weeks ago, leaving her alone and forced to scavenge for food.

Her father had been a blacksmith on a large farm to the south of Trondheim, but when he and her mother, brother and sister had died, Silje had been driven out of the wooden cabin where they had lived. What use would a young girl be in a blacksmith's forge?

In truth, Silje had been relieved to move away from the farm. She had left behind a secret, buried deep in her heart, that she had never shared with a soul. To the south-west lay the strange and eerie mountains she called the 'Land of Shadows' or the 'Land of Evening'. Throughout her childhood their brooding mass had always frightened her, yet also held her spellbound. They were so far away as to be barely visible but, when the brightness of the evening sun lit up the jagged peaks, it gave them a strange ethereal clarity that stirred the girl's lively imagination.

She would gaze at the mountains for ages, in fear and fascination. Then finally she would see 'them', the nameless creatures that lived there. They rose up from the valleys between the peaks, gliding slowly through the air, searching, closer and closer to her home until their evil eyes found her. Whenever this happened, Silje would run and hide.

Except that they did have a name. People on the farm always spoke of the distant mountains in hushed voices and it was probably their words that had first frightened her and excited her imagination.

'You must never go up there,' they would say. 'There is nothing but witchcraft and evil there. The Ice People are not human! They are the spawn of cold and darkness, and woe betide the person who goes too close to their lair!'

The Ice People? Yes, that was what they were called – but Silje was the only person who had seen them riding on the air. She had never known what these creatures were. Not trolls. Oh no, they were not trolls. Nor were they wraiths. They could not be called devils either. Were they some sort of supernatural marvel perhaps, or spirits from beyond the grave? She had once heard their landlord call one of the horses a 'demon'. This was a new word to her ears, but she felt it was a suitable name for 'them'. The strength of her fantasies about the Land of Shadows was such that she would often dream about it while in a restless and troubled sleep. It was only natural that she should turn her back to those haunting mountains as she left the farm.

A primitive instinct had led her to Trondheim, where she would find people – hoping for help now that she was alone and in need. She soon came to realise, though, that none of the townspeople welcomed strangers into their homes, and especially now, at a time when the plague followed in the footsteps of those who travelled the land. What better place for the sickness to spread unchecked than in these overcrowded houses, fighting for space in dirty narrow streets?

It had taken her a whole day to find a way to get through the town gates. When she had noticed some families returning from work to their homes in the town, she followed them and, walking on the far side of one of the wagons, slipped unnoticed past the guards. Once inside, however, she had not found help. Nothing, that is, but a few stale crusts of bread thrown to her now and then from a window, and barely enough to keep her from the grave.

From the marketplace by the cathedral could be heard the sounds of drunkenness and brawling. Once, foolishly, she had gone there, drawn by the promise of the company of others like herself. It hadn't taken her long to understand that this was no place for an attractive young girl. Seeing the mob had been a shock, and although she tried to put it out of her mind, she couldn't quite forget the experience.

After several days of walking, her feet ached constantly. The long road to Trondheim had exhausted all her energy

– and with no comfort to be found there, she felt the consuming pain of hopelessness clawing at her insides.

Rats squealed in the doorway she had begun to walk towards, hoping to find a place to sleep for a few hours, so she turned away and continued on her hopeless wandering. Without thinking, she was being drawn towards the glow of the fire across the hill outside the town. Fire meant warmth. It also meant burning corpses – for three days and three nights a huge funeral pyre had been alight. Just beside it stood the scaffold.

She hurriedly mumbled a prayer, 'Lord Jesus, keep me from the evil of these lost souls! Give me courage and strength, so that with Thy grace I can rest there safely a while! I desperately need warmth, lest I should perish.'

With dread filling her innocent heart and her gaze fixed on the rising haze of warmth, Silje stumbled on towards the western gates.

****

In the meantime Charlotte Meiden, a young noblewoman, had taken to the street on a secret errand of her own. In disgust, she felt her silken shoes sinking into the filthy waste underfoot. Ice had blocked the gutter that ran down the middle of the street, causing this disgusting mess to remain where it lay. Anxious not to lose her footing, she cradled a tightly wrapped bundle in her arms.

Charlotte had stealthily slipped away from her father's imposing residence and was now making her way towards the town gates, quietly humming a slow dance-tune, a pavane, to keep herself from thinking about what was wrapped in the bundle. Progress was painfully slow. Her lips were white and beads of sweat shone on her forehead and upper lip. Her hair clung to her temples.

That she had been able to keep her condition hidden for all these hateful anxious months was still a mystery to her. However, she had always been small and slender, and nothing had really shown. The style of dress she wore had helped, with corsets and flowing crinolines, and a surcoat draped from her shoulders, covering everything. Of course, she had dressed herself, always pulling her corset painfully tight. No one, least of all her chambermaid, had suspected anything.

She had hated the life that grew within her with a fierce intensity – it was the unwanted result of a liaison with a most handsome Dane from the court of King Frederick. It was only later that she learned he was married. One evening of blind passion and this torment had been her punishment, whilst he moved on quite casually to make new conquests.

She had tried every means to rid herself of this intruder in her life – strong potions, hot baths, even jumping from balustrades. Why, she had gone as far as visiting the churchyard one Thursday night last summer and there had performed rites so secret and hideous that she had now banished them from her memory. It was no use. The spiteful being inside her body had clung on to life with the persistence of a devil.

How afraid she had been these last months – and was still. Strangely however, at that very moment she no longer felt the same burning hatred towards the unwanted creature. Instead something else began to stir in her heart – a warm glow, great sorrow and an unexpected longing. No, she couldn't allow herself to think such thoughts. Just walk, walk quickly and avoid the few people out on a night such as this.

It was so cold. Poor thing. No, no!

She caught a glimpse of a young girl, scarcely more than a child, coming down a side street, and slipped quickly into a doorway. The girl, Silje, passed by without noticing her.

'She looks so alone,' Charlotte thought with a sudden pang of heartfelt compassion that she could not allow herself to feel. She must not give way to sympathy. She must not be weak. Above all, she must hurry. She needed to be back in the town before the gates were closed at nine o'clock. The gatekeeper didn't frighten her and, if he should ask, she could account for herself. The cloak she had thrown around her shoulders belonged to one of the servants. No one would recognise the elegant mistress, Charlotte Meiden, dressed like this.

At last she reached the gates, and as expected, the gatekeeper stopped her. She held out the bundle for a moment.

'Just one more dead. I'm going out to …' she muttered.

The man waved her through without a second glance.

She saw the forest in front of her now, the jagged tops of the pines in silhouette against the glow from the fire. Bright moonlight shone over the frozen evening landscape, making it easy to find the way. If only she hadn't been so exhausted. She was in pain now, more afraid, and from time to time she felt a warm stickiness soak into the towel she had used to staunch the bleeding.

The child had been born in the hayloft above the stables. She had bitten hard on a piece of wood to stop herself from crying out and had done her best with the cord. Afterwards, exhausted from her ordeal, she had lain for a long time before, without looking at it, she had bundled the baby up and risen unsteadily to her feet. In her mind, it seemed, she needed nothing to do with this child. She had smothered its weak and pitiful cries with the blanket. It was still alive – she felt it move now and then. Thank goodness it hadn't cried out as she passed the gates.

She was certain she had removed all trace of the event in the hayloft. If only she could be rid of this shameful burden and return home unnoticed. Then she would be free, finally free of all the worry.

She had come far enough into the woods. Over there, she thought, beneath the tall pine tree, a long way from the path. Charlotte Meiden's hands shook as she laid the bundle down on the bare frozen ground. Her chest tightened and tears welled up as she tucked a woollen blanket and a shawl around the small spark of life, and placed a little pot of milk she had brought with her beside the baby's cheek. Deep down, of course, she knew it could never drink the milk, but she could not bring herself to acknowledge that.

She hesitated for a moment, as an overwhelming feeling of loss and despair raced within her, until finally she staggered off, her frozen footsteps taking her back towards the town.

****

Inside the walls, Silje kept on walking, grateful for the moonlight that cast its pale aura over the streets and alleyways, making it easier for her to avoid the bay windows and other strange features on the buildings as she passed. Step by step, one foot followed the other – half asleep, she kept going. If she allowed herself to think, she would feel the cold, the hunger, the utter weariness and the certainty that she had nowhere to go and no future.

Someone was sobbing nearby.

She stopped. She was at the entrance of a narrow alleyway, making her way towards the western gates.

It was dark in the alley; the moonlight did not reach beyond its entrance. The crying came from a yard at the back, where a door stood half open. It was the sound of a child – the heart-rending sobs tore through her. Hesitantly Silje drew closer and stepped inside. Moonlight filled the small open space, which was surrounded by low houses. A little girl, perhaps two years old, was kneeling beside a dead woman. The child was pulling and shaking her mother, trying to wake her up.

Although Silje was little more than a child herself, her young heart was touched by the plight of the infant, but the sight of the woman's corpse held her back. The tortured face and the froth around her mouth were clear signs that the plague had struck again.

Tröndelag, as this part of the country was called, had been overwhelmed by a pestilence, which in reality consisted of two different illnesses. Plague was the common name for all sicknesses, but this virulent illness had come from Denmark. Sometimes known as the 'Spanish wheeze', it was a catarrh that caused fever, headaches and pains in the chest. At the same time, another type of plague had been brought from Sweden, this kind causing boils and open sores, pains in the side and headaches that eventually led to madness. Silje knew the symptoms – she had seen them all too often.

As yet, the child had not caught sight of her. Silje was so exhausted that she could not think quickly, but she knew that she alone among her own family had survived. She had been wandering through the town, amongst its dead and dying, for a long time now without becoming infected and so did not fear for herself. But what of the little girl? She had a slim chance of escaping the sickness and were she to stay here, alone with her dead mother, she would have no chance at all.

Silje moved forward and knelt beside the child, who turned a tearful face towards her. She was quite stocky, but beautiful, with dark curly hair, dark eyes and small strong hands.

'Your mother is dead,' Silje said softly, 'she can't talk to you any more. You need to come with me.'

The girl's lips trembled, but surprise had served to stop her tears.

Silje rose to her feet and pushed in turn at each of the doors that opened onto the yard. All three were locked. The dead woman probably hadn't lived here; she had perhaps just decided this dark alley was a fitting place to die. Silje knew from experience that it was pointless to knock – people would not open their doors.

With a few swift movements she tore a strip of cloth from the hem of her tattered skirt. She knotted it deftly to make a rag doll and placed it in the dead woman's hand, to stop her returning from beyond the grave to look for her daughter. Then she said a silent prayer for the poor woman's soul.

'Come along,' she said firmly to the little girl. 'We must leave now.'

The child did not want to go. She clung to her mother's cape – it was pretty and didn't seem too worn. The girl was also well-dressed; nothing extravagant, but simple and well made. The girl's mother had once been a real beauty, but now her black unseeing eyes stared at the moon.

It would never have crossed Silje's mind to take the dead woman's cape to protect her own frozen body from the cold. The thought of stealing from a corpse repelled her, especially one who had fallen victim to the plague.

'Come,' she said again, feeling helpless as she faced the tired child's quiet sobbing. Gently, she opened the child's hands and took her in her arms. 'We must try to find you some food.'

She had, of course, no idea where to find any, but the word 'food' worked its magic on the child, who resigned herself and, letting out a final tearful shaking sigh, allowed herself to be carried out of the yard. She cast a last agonising glance back at her mother that was full of grief and heartache – Silje would never forget that look.

The child wept silently as Silje carried her through the streets, along the last stretch towards the gates. She had obviously been crying for so long that she was now too tired to be able to resist. Silje had another worry. Suddenly she was responsible for another human being, a child who would probably be dead from the plague in a few days, but until that happened, Silje had to make sure she didn't go hungry.

They were close to the town gates now and, between the houses, she caught occasional glimpses of the glow from the funeral pyres. It had been bitterly cold of late, making the frozen ground too hard for graves to be dug, so the dead were consigned to the flames. There was a large mass grave that she – but no! She could not allow herself to contemplate such anguish now.

She saw a woman leaning against the wall of a building, looking as if she would faint at any moment. Hesitantly Silje approached her.

'Can I help you?' she asked timidly.

The woman turned and looked at her with anguished eyes. She seemed to be a young lady of noble bearing, but her features were deathly white and beads of perspiration were running down her face.

As Charlotte Meiden's eyes focused on Silje, she forced herself upright and started to walk away.

'Nobody can help me,' she mumbled as she disappeared down a side street.

Silje watched her go, but did not follow.

'The plague again,' she told herself. 'There is nothing I can do.'

Finally she reached the gates. Although they would remain open for a while, Silje knew she would not return to the town. There was no relief to be found there, not for her or the child, of that she was certain. She would have to try and find shelter in a barn in the countryside – or in some other place.

'What if we should meet a wild animal?' she wondered, not that wild animals could be any worse than the brutes to be found around the marketplace in the town – those drunken debauched wretches who pestered her whenever she came near their 'territory'. They showed complete indifference to the plague, perhaps because they knew that they would soon be beyond help and were trying to experience all the pleasures of this life before leaving it.

The guard at the gate asked where she was going so late in the evening, but he was less interested in those leaving than in those who were coming in. She told him that they had been turned out for showing signs of sickness. He understood at once and, with a wave of his hand, sent them on their way. He would not worry that they might carry the sickness to others. Oh no, not at all! Just as long as it left his town.

Silje walked faster. The warm glow of the flames urged her on – what would she do if the fire died out before she reached it? First she had to find a way through the pine forest that lay between the town and the scaffold.

Once before, when she had first arrived in Trondheim, she had lost her way and stumbled upon that awful place

11

– she had turned and left as fast as she was able, away from the disgusting stench and in fear of the horrors she had seen there. Now, her desperate need for warmth was making her go back. Just stretching her icy hands towards the flames, turning her back to the fire, feeling the heat through her clothes, warming a body that had known only cold for so many days and nights. It would be a dream come true.

The forest – she stopped at its edge, just beyond the reach of the trees. Like many others who lived in open farmland, she had always been afraid of the forest. It held too many secrets in its shadows.

The girl was becoming too heavy for her tired arms and she put her down.

'Can you walk by yourself?' she asked. 'I'll carry you again in a little while.'

The child didn't answer, but, still sobbing quietly to herself, did as she was asked.

The shadows were very dark amongst the pine trees. Silje's eyes had grown accustomed to the night, but she still could not see what lay between them. She felt she could detect furtive beings with burning eyes hidden in the undergrowth.

She tried to think more clearly once again.

'The darkness is never completely black,' She told herself. 'It has many shades, darker and lighter, mixing into greys.'

The child was frightened too. Fear had quelled her tears and she pressed herself tightly, ever so tightly, against Silje with a soft moan. Silje's mouth felt dry. She tried to swallow, but her fear remained. They had to keep going step by step, and she fixed her eyes on the glow of the fires from the far side of the woods. It helped, but she did not dare turn around, for she could feel shapeless creatures of the unknown tugging at her heels!

When they were about halfway through the trees, she felt her pulse racing and then the blood drained from her face. She was breathless. Then, for the second time that evening, she heard a child cry. To hear that sound again was more than she could bear. Her heart was pounding madly. It was a baby crying in the woods.

Again came the pitiful sounds of the infant. It could only mean one thing – it must be a *myling*. Silje was terrified at the thought. *Mylings* were the spirits of unwanted children, born out of wedlock and left to die without baptism. She had heard so many stories about them and always dreaded the thought that she might meet one. She knew she was in mortal danger – a *myling* would haunt anyone who passed its secret resting-place. Yes, she had heard all the tales of the fate of those who passed too close to such a grave. They told of an infant child as tall as a house, screaming horribly, that followed the poor passers-by, its footsteps shaking the earth, finally clawing at their backs and dragging them into the ground. She also knew a being like this could transform itself – into a black dog, or a child's corpse with its throat torn out, into ravens or reptiles, each one as evil as the other.

Silje was petrified. Her feet would not move, no matter how much she prayed that they would, so that she could run away from that awful place. The little girl, however, still clinging close to her, reacted differently. She muttered something Silje didn't understand. Just one word – a name perhaps? It sounded like 'Nadda' or something similar. Could she have had a little brother or sister who had recently died? That was quite possible.

The girl began tugging at her hand, willing her towards

the cries coming from among the trees, only a short distance from the path that Silje had hoped they were following. Silje held back; she desperately wanted to get away. Again the child repeated the word, her voice choked with tears.

'But it is too dangerous,' Silje protested. 'We must leave, quickly – quickly!'

But how *could* they run away? Would they have a giant *myling* snapping at their heels? Oh no! That would be even worse.

Suddenly, a thought came to her. The souls of the dead children cried out to be baptised and yearned to be reunited with their mothers. How did one bring peace to a *myling*? Did one read the sacraments for them? She was not a priest, but wait! There was an old verse, a liturgy, if only she could remember it. It was something like, 'I christen thee …' Then she thought it better to say all the prayers she knew.

Taking a deep breath, she began reciting every supplication she had ever learnt, Protestant mixed with Catholic, half-remembered fragments from childhood and lessons taught by the priest. Her steps uncertain, and ready to run at the slightest sign of danger, she drew nearer to the *myling*. It was quiet now. The prayers had worked!

Feeling more confident, she walked a little faster, while trying to think of suitable words for a rite of baptism. The girl was pulling her along, to make her hurry. As they picked their way forward, Silje, in a loud but unsteady voice, said, 'I have found thee in the darkness of night. Therefore I baptise thee Dag, if thou art a boy. Thou wast left to die, I know not when. Therefore I baptise thee Liv, if thou art a girl.'

Did that sound so foolish? Would it be acceptable as a rite of baptism? Just to be sure, she added, 'In the name of

Jesus Christ. Amen,' although she knew full well that she had no right to utter such sacred words. Only the priests were allowed to do that.

Was it dangerous to call a *myling* 'Liv'? Perhaps it would become mortal again and rise up with awesome might. No, better not think of such things. She had done her best and could only pray it would be enough.

The girl seemed determined to find the *myling*, which made Silje even more certain that she once had a younger brother or sister. The girl would not be stopped; Silje had no choice but to follow.

It ought to be here somewhere. Bending forwards, she started to search in the deep shadows beneath the tree, her heart still pounding and her stiff and frozen fingers trembling.

Should a human touch a *myling*? What would it feel like? Would there be anything to touch? Perhaps nothing remained but the dry, brittle bones? Or would it be slimy and horrible? Would she suddenly find something taking hold of her wrist in a vice-like grip? She drew back her hand with an involuntary intake of breath – it was all she could do to stop herself from running away.

The child must have discovered something. She was talking excitedly, but incoherently, and then Silje heard a scratching sound like bits of broken wood rubbing together. Again she stretched out her hand, searching blindly in the darkness. Her fingers touched something – something round with a handle. It felt like a wooden pot with a lid. No danger there, she thought, and carried on searching. A piece of cloth – a small bundle – warmer than the frozen earth on which it lay. As she touched it, the weak cries started again. Plucking up all her courage. Silje gently felt inside the shawl. She touched warm skin. It *was* a baby

– and alive. It was not a *myling*, but some poor abandoned child left to its fate.

'Thank you,' she whispered to the little girl. 'Tonight you saved the life of this baby.'

The girl's hands were clutching eagerly at the blanket.

'Nadda,' she said again.

Silje did not have the heart to stop her, even though she was probably carrying the plague. Then she remembered the pot. She picked it up and shook it, splashing some of its contents. Silje stuck her finger into the liquid – it was not yet frozen – and tasted it. Milk! Oh, Dear Lord – it was milk!

For one awful moment she held the pot to her lips, quite ready to drain every last drop. The girl and the infant? She mustn't forget them and she knew that, if she took even the tiniest sip, she would be unable to stop. The girl first – she must have a third. She listened to the deep delighted gulps as the child drank.

It was not easy to take the drink from her, but she had no choice. The girl fought to keep it with a fury that Silje found frightening. To calm her, Silje whispered, 'Nadda must drink, too.'

Anyway the milk seemed to have taken the edge off the girl's hunger – it had not needed much to fill that small belly.

She turned her thoughts to the infant. The babe was wrapped in several layers of blanket, inside which she could make out a gown that reflected a grey sheen in the dark. Silje pulled up a corner and twisted it into a point, dipped it into the milk and put it into the infant's mouth – but it would not drink.

Silje knew very little about newborn babies; did not understand that they were seldom hungry during their first day of life. Nor did she know that they would not all have a strong instinct to suckle. She began to feel helpless and desperate. No matter how she tried, the infant refused the milk. Finally she gave up. They had to move on and she would not be able to carry the pot as well as the children – she only had two arms. Feeling guilty, she drank the remaining milk, although it left a bitter taste, because she knew she had taken the infant's share.

She rose to her feet, cradling the baby, took the girl by the hand and suddenly let out a loud uncontrollable laugh. What on earth was she doing? 'The blind leading the blind,' she told herself. How could *she* possibly help these children?

The milk had eased their hunger and given both Silje and the girl renewed strength. Her fear of the forest had begun to release its grip on her and not far away she could clearly see the glow of firelight.

At the edge of the woods she stopped, her eyes taking in the dreadful sight that lay before her: a huge funeral pyre spewing clouds of stinking smoke in her direction. The gallows, a black silhouette against the flames, stood surrounded by the implements of torture – evidence of the extent of the cruelty the human mind can conceive when the opportunity to inflict pain on others presents itself.

To one side stood the pillory, with a small forge nearby to provide red-hot tongs and swords when called for; there were also huge, vile-looking hooks for piercing the skin of the condemned, on which they would be left to hang. Silje knew there would be thumbscrews, vices and many other grotesque instruments of satanic torture, and shuddered at the thought.

Standing out from the rest, however, was the rack on which the bodies of the unfortunate victims were broken and ...

'Oh no!' she groaned quietly. 'No, no!'

She could see men moving around the scaffold and between the contraptions. She caught sight of the executioner, his black hood covering his severed ears, and his assistant, the most despised and hated man in all of Trondheim, fussing officiously around him while the bailiff's soldiers swarmed about. Some of them were restraining a man. He was young, with wavy blond hair, and his hands were tied behind his back. They were forcing him towards the rack.

'No! Please don't do it,' she whispered.

Silhouetted by the fires, the young man looked so handsome. Her heart sank and her blood ran cold as she thought of the torment he was about to endure.

The group of men stood beside the rack and other equipment with which every bone in his body would be crushed. The executioner – headsman or hangman, it didn't matter what he was called – paced around with heavy determined steps, carrying a large broad-bladed axe in one hand. So the prisoner was to suffer torture before being beheaded.

Silje wanted it all to stop. She had not known many young men in her life, but she knew that this one was special. Who could he be, she wondered? Was he a thief? Surely not, for there were far too many soldiers for that. He must be someone of considerable importance.

All thoughts of the young man stopped suddenly and she started in fear, as a deep voice from the forest behind her asked, 'What are you doing here, woman?'

Silje and the little girl both spun round, the child letting out a shriek. Silje just managed to stop herself from doing the same.

There, among the trees, was the tall shape of a figure who

looked part human and part animal. With considerable relief, she saw it was a man wrapped in a wolf-skin cloak, the shaggy hood resembling the head of an animal. Yet, his shoulders were strange and broad, like those of a bear. Narrow eyes gleamed at her from a face filled with drama, exquisite yet sinister, white teeth reflecting a wolf-like grin. The firelight shone on his features at one moment and the next he was in darkness. He stood motionless.

'Just wanted to warm ourselves at the fire, master,' she answered, her voice trembling.

'Are these your children?' His voice was deep and strong.

'Mine? Oh no, I am but sixteen years, master,' she replied with a nervous smile and shaking from the cold. 'I found both this very night. They are foundlings.'

He let his eyes rest thoughtfully on her for a long time – fearfully Silje lowered her gaze. The little girl was also afraid and hid herself in Silje's skirts.

'You saved them, did you?' Then he asked, 'Do you want to save another life this night?'

The burning eyes made her anxious and uncertain.

'One more life? I don't know – I don't understand.'

'Hunger and worry show on your face,' he said. 'You can pass for someone two or three years older. Perhaps you can save my brother's life. Will you help?'

She wondered briefly how it was that two brothers could look so different. The handsome blond-haired boy below and this creature, with his dark lank hair hanging over his eyes.

'I do not wish to see him die,' she said hesitantly. 'But how can I save him?'

'I cannot do it alone,' he said. 'There are too many of them, and besides, they are looking for me. They would arrest me and that would be of no help to him. But you ...'

From his pocket he took a small scroll of parchment.

'Here! Take this message; it bears the royal seal. Tell them you are his wife and that these are his children. You live hereabouts and his name is Niels Stierne. He is the King's Messenger. And what is your name?'

'Silje'

With a look of irritation, he said, 'Cecilie, you foolish girl! You can't have a peasant girl's name like Silje. You are a countess, remember that. Now, you must slip this message into his clothes unnoticed and then pretend to find it.'

This was a daring idea, she thought.

'How can I pass for a countess?' she asked. 'Nobody will believe me.'

'Have you not looked at the child you are carrying?' he snapped from among the shadows.

Startled, she looked away.

'No, but ...'

As the fire began to burn more brightly, it lit up the area where they stood and she could clearly see about her. The infant was wrapped in a shawl of the finest wool, beautifully woven, with shining threads of gold, the like of which Silje had never seen. The thicker blanket beneath had a brocade pattern – French lilies, she thought it was called – and finally there was a shining white lace and linen sheet, the one she had dipped in the milk.

The man stepped forward to where they were, still hidden by the pines. Instinctively she backed away. He had an aura of prehistoric heathen timelessness about him; a mystical animal attraction, mixed with an irresistible air of authority.

'The infant has blood on its face,' he said, wiping it away with a corner of the blanket. 'It is newborn. Are you sure it is not yours?'

Silje felt affronted.

'I am an honourable girl, my lord!'

His mouth started to smile, but then he turned his eyes towards the scaffold below. The men were not yet ready to begin their evil work – a priest was still trying to persuade this brother to confess his sins.

'Where did you find the infant?'

'In the forest, here, left to die.'

He raised his black eyebrows.

'Was the girl with her?'

'No, no, I found her in the town, beside the body of her dead mother.'

'The plague?' he asked.

'Yes.'

His eyes turned to the children and he said slowly, 'Truly, you have courage.'

'I do not fear this plague. It has been my companion for many days. It strikes those around me, but I have not suffered.'

What could have been taken for a smile crossed his face.

'Neither have I,' he paused. 'So will you go down there?'

She hesitated and he said, 'Having the children with you will keep you safe. They will not dare take a mother with her children. But wait – they must have names.'

'Oh, I don't know if the babe is a girl or boy. But I christened it Dag or Liv. I believed it was a *myling* calling to me.'

'I understand. What about the girl?'

She paused, thinking, and then said, 'They are both children of the night. I found them amidst death and darkness. I think I want to call her Sol.'

Those strange eyes, like long shining chinks in his face, fell upon her again, 'Your young head holds thoughts wiser than most. Will you go down there?'

The compliment made Silje blush and she felt a warm glow inside.

'I cannot deny that I am afraid, master.'

'You shall not go without reward.'

Silje shook her head. 'Money will not help me, but ...'

'Yes?' he prompted.

The needs of the children emboldened her. Looking straight at him she said, 'No one will give shelter to wandering strangers in these times. The children depend on me and I am frozen to the bone. If you could just find us food, lodgings and warmth, I shall risk my life for the young count.'

The light from the fire had died down again, leaving the man's face in shadow once more. He thought for a moment.

'I will arrange it,' he promised.

'Good, then I shall go. But what about my clothes? No countess would be seen wearing these rags.'

'I've already thought of that,' he said. 'Take this.'

From beneath the wolf-skin, he pulled a cloak of deep blue velvet. While it had only covered him to the waist, it reached easily to Silje's feet. She pushed her hands through the slits.

'There! It will hide the worst, but keep it tight about you. And take those rags off your shoes.'

Silje did as he said, then asked, 'What about the way I speak?'

'Yes,' he said slowly, 'that did surprise me. You do not speak like a peasant. Perhaps you will sound like a countess. Just do your best!'

She took a deep breath. 'Wish me luck, master.'

He gave a grim nod of his head.

Silje closed her eyes for a moment, took a few deep breaths and considered what she was about to do. With a firm grip on the girl's hand and cradling the infant, she started downwards towards the place where they were now about to bind the young man to the rack.

She could sense the piecing gaze of the wolf-man on her back, almost burning through her clothes.

This is a very strange night, she thought. But this was just the beginning!

Chapter 2

As Silje emerged from the woods, her steps quickened, so that the little girl was barely able keep up with her. From a distance she shouted out, her voice indignant, 'What in the name of God are you doing?'

She had no need to pretend she was appalled. She truly was, and this strengthened her resolve to risk her young life to save the unfortunate count. To think he was a royal messenger! Well, hadn't she known he was different somehow?

The men turned and faced her. The executioner grunted, tightening his grip on the axe as if he were reluctant to lose his victim.

'Have you all lost your senses, you stupid oafs?' she screamed. 'How dare you treat my husband in that manner!'

She glanced quickly at the man bound to the rack. His pale face held a look of determination, but in spite of this it seemed inevitable that his spirit would soon break. Never had she seen a person hide his horror so well. Her arrival was as much a surprise to him as the others, but he quickly recovered himself.

'No!' he yelled. 'You should not have come here. Not with the children!'

The guard commander, trying to move her away, sneered and said, 'If he is your husband, madam, then you have my pity.'

'Do you not know who he is?' she demanded defiantly. Despite her fear, she was enjoying playing the wife of this young count.

'Know who he is? We know only too well!'

'You say that you know and yet still you dare to treat the King's Messenger so disgracefully?'

The man on the rack called out angrily, 'You have no right to divulge my identity!'

Closer now, she turned to him, and was amazed to see how noble he looked. But his eyes could not hide the fear of death within them.

'No, you would rather die than speak out,' she interrupted angrily, 'without thought for your wife and your children. I have no intention of losing you!' And turning to the guard commander, she continued, 'Sire, I am Countess Cecilie Stierne and this man is His Majesty's Messenger, Niels Stierne. Since my husband hails from this part of the country, it is always he who is called upon in matters concerning this province.'

'Cecilie!' her new-found husband roared.

'Be quiet! I sit at home waiting for word of you, only to hear that some fool among the King's own men has had you arrested and brought to this place. I left home at once! Then to find you like this!'

Stepping closer to the soldier, she whispered, 'He is here on a secret mission.'

'You must not believe her! She lies!' shouted the prisoner.

The soldier was no longer quite so sure of himself. 'And why then has he said nothing?' he asked haughtily, hiding his doubt.

'You of all people must know that a King's Messenger must never, never reveal his true purpose. He would rather suffer death.'

The foul stifling smell of the fires was everywhere. The soldiers' helmets reflected the flames and the executioner stood impatiently, his axe making swishing sounds as he swung it to and fro.

Because Silje's story seemed so believable, the commander was losing confidence.

'We know well who this man is,' he said gruffly. 'His name is Heming, the bailiff-killer, and there is a price on his head.'

On the ground close to Silje lay the thumbscrews and tongs, both covered with unmistakable reddish spots. She fought down a wave of nausea, and moved directly in front of the guard commander. By now she was well into her role, no doubt spurred on by the knowledge that those bestial yellow eyes were watching events from the woods.

'Does he look like one who would murder a bailiff? Yes, he is dirty and unkempt, but so would any man be after a hard ride through the mountains. Look at his noble features! Look at his children, his daughters! Are these the children of a murderer?'

She had said 'daughters' deliberately, knowing that, should they not believe her, they might easily kill the infant. The son of a convicted man could not be allowed to live. Would they want to examine the infant? If they did, she prayed for it to be a girl, otherwise their suspicions would be aroused.

'My small daughters, Sol and Liv – are they to lose their

26

father?' asked Silje after a pause. 'What do you think King Frederick will have to say when he hears of it?'

'And what, pray, is this important mission,' the soldier asked with contempt.

'Sire, I am at a loss! Do you believe my husband would reveal that, even to me? His oath of loyalty to the King silences his tongue and he would die before showing you the message he carries. Is such loyalty to be your reason for killing him?'

'What message?' jeered the soldier. 'He has no message on his person. How could you know that he carries it now?'

'Because he has it with him always – I myself have sewn the hidden pocket where it is kept.'

'But we have searched him.'

'Not well enough, sire,' she retorted.

Silje turned quickly to face the rack and, with the scroll hidden in her palm, she pushed her hand in behind the man's belt and slipped the scroll under his waistband. She fumbled, hindered by the child on her arm, but time was short, so the poor thing would have to suffer being squashed against her side.

The man protested wildly. 'Cecilie, I will never forgive you for this!'

The soldiers were upon her in an instant, but at that moment she ripped the trouser lining and 'found' the message.

The commander tore it from her hand. With one voice the count and Silje cried out, 'Do not break the royal seal!'

'I would not dare do such a thing,' replied the soldier, icily.

He examined the scroll, turning it this way and that, studying the seals and then, with disappointment in his voice, he announced, 'It is genuine.' Whereupon he turned

27

to his men, demanding, 'Who gave this man up as Heming, the bailiff-killer?'

The soldiers pushed one of their number to the fore.

'I could have sworn ...' he stuttered.

'How well did you know the killer?'

'I saw him once.'

'From what distance? Did you speak with him?'

'N-no, Commander. I saw him from above when he rode through a pass in the mountains. I saw the blond hair – and the face, it looked like this man, sir.'

'*Looked like!* Is that all you have to go on?'

The soldier seemed to crumble where he stood, unable to answer.

For some time, from the corner of her eye, Silje had been able to make out a large shadow just beyond the reach of the firelight. She looked at it now – and her legs felt weak as she let out a gasp. From a second gibbet hung a body, turning slowly on the end of the rope, and at that moment its face came into full view. Silje stifled a cry and instinctively tried to hide the girl's face, to stop her from seeing such a sight. The child, however, stared innocently straight up at the grisly figure on the gibbet and chuckled to herself, as though such sights were amusing. Children, Silje thought, see the world very differently.

The commander, clad in full uniform with breastplate and knee-breeches, turned away from the chastened soldier and faced the count once more. 'We are also the King's men,' he said.

'Then why did you say nothing to us?' asked the count.

'Spies and traitors are everywhere,' was the reply.

'Making certain this message does not fall into the wrong hands is more important than my life. Now, if you will be so good as to release me.'

'Of course, My Lord.'

Released from the ropes, the count straightened his aching body and said, 'Perhaps I may now take my wife and children and continue with my duties?'

The commander drew himself to attention and, bowing his head, he returned the scroll.

'We beg your forgiveness, My Lord. This whole affair has been a misunderstanding.'

The young man did not even grace him with a look, but turned to Silje, saying, 'I am very displeased with you! You have revealed my identity and brought dishonour upon me!'

'My Lord, your wife acted correctly,' said the commander with some deference. 'It was the act of a wife of a nobleman. You may be assured that our discretion can be relied on. Such charming children!' he added, patting the girl's head, obviously anxious to find favour with the young count.

The man joined his 'family' and turned towards the woods.

'I must leave at once. This delay will have cost our country a great deal,' he said indignantly, with a hurried glance back over his shoulder.

Silje heard muttering and turned round. The executioner stared at her, his eyes full of hatred, not bothering to conceal his disappointment. She sighed with relief. The soldier had believed her.

It had been her good fortune that the bailiff's soldiers had known so little of the affairs of state of the Danish Court. Had they known more, they would surely have wondered why the King's trusted messenger was Norwegian, and one who spoke the local Trondheim dialect. Although King Frederick II was a just ruler, he was not much interested in Norway. He had visited the country in 1548 when he was the crown prince, but never as its king. His administrators, the bailiffs, sometimes known as lord lieutenants, governed the land in his absence. This had been the practice ever since Norway ceded to Danish rule in 1537. At present, the bailiff of Trondheim was one Jacob Huitfeldt and, if he got word of Silje's bravado and his commander's actions, his rage would know no bounds. No commander could afford to be so ignorant!

Silje was even less aware of matters of state. She congratulated herself on saving the life of an important courier.

Since the Danes had left the governing of Norway to local bailiffs, it was they who had become the object of the ordinary peoples' smouldering hatred. The taxes were intolerable and rents were being driven up all the time. Farmers' produce was weighed on rigged scales and they were forced to sell what goods they had at far below the market price. Administrators demanded 'gifts' in great numbers and the profits from all this corruption and extortion went straight to the coffers of the bailiffs.

Quite naturally, such conditions caused the people to rebel, but these revolts were often too localised to be of consequence. In Trondheim County, six years earlier, Rolf Lynge had led the peasants and farmers against the bailiff, Ludwig Munk, when he had pushed them too far. Now, though, Silje believed things had calmed down, but she did not know much about such things. Her heart was beating fast with excitement at having saved such an outstanding young man and she could not help giving him glances of quiet admiration.

As soon as they reached the edge of the woods he led the way quickly into the trees, but they had not gone far before a large shadow stood before them.

'You blundering idiot!' hissed the wolf-man as he struck the 'count' across the face. At this the young man ran further into the woods.

'Do you strike your own brother?' gasped Silje with alarm.

'He is not my brother.'

'But you said …'

The wolf-man interrupted her angrily, 'What was I supposed to do? Explain everything? There was no time for that.'

'I do not like being lied to,' she said in a low voice as she took back the strips of hide from him and began to wrap them round her shoes again after placing the infant on the ground. She could not bring herself to allow the wolf-man to touch it.

'I had to lie to you.' His voice was harsh and throaty. 'That man had to be saved before he informed on all of us. He has no stomach for pain, and besides, we need him.'

Silje wondered for a moment who 'we' were and then said, 'Then you cannot be a count, since you are not brothers.'

'No more or less than he.' His smile was grim.

'What do you mean? I took you at your word. I believed I would be saving a royal courier.'

'And that was my intention,' he replied warningly. 'Don't be so naïve, Silje. It could cost you your virtue and your honour – or even your life!'

She did not want to hear such troubling words coming from this man, whose aura of sensuality and power continued to demand her attention.

'I am not afraid of losing my virtue,' she retorted as she stood up, her shoes now covered once again. 'I have had to fight to preserve it many times, and I have always won.'

She thought she could hear amusement in his voice when, as she tried to give him back the velvet cloak, he said, 'No, you have more need of it than I. And the infant's clothes – take care of them, Silje, they will be of worth to you one day. Now come, we must go.'

Thinking that he meant her to sell the clothes to buy food or lodging, she started to follow his track in the snow. He seemed like a giant, walking before her in the darkness, but it was probably the wolf-skin that made it seem so. She could not understand how he moved so quickly through the darkness of the forest, but she was not surprised. She would expect almost anything from this man, even that he could see in the dark – just like an animal.

'Please wait, don't go so fast,' she called quietly. 'The girl can't keep up.'

He stopped and waited. Silje could tell he was impatient.

'I heard you speak to that pack of murderers down there,' he said as they drew level with him. 'You spoke like a countess – I was impressed. Now you speak like a peasant once more. Who are you? Indeed, what are you?'

'I am who I am – just Silje. Better that you judge me by my rags than by my words. That I can speak with class, should I so wish, is a long story, but not one that can be told while fleeing through a forest.'

He slackened his step so that they could keep up. Clearly the little girl was tiring.

Silje began wondering about the young man.

'How handsome he is,' she said, captivated by her thoughts, forgetting that he would hear her.

The older man sniffed loudly.

'Yes, girls do find him so. It was because of a woman that he nearly lost his life back there. He forgot to be on his guard.'

She felt dejected. 'I suppose he has many girls?'

'It doesn't matter – he's not one for you,' he said, breaking his stride momentarily and then walking on more slowly. 'All the same, *he* could need someone like you,' he said dryly.

'Someone like me?' Her heart was pounding.

'Yes, a strong courageous woman with her wits about her – and a good heart. Perhaps that would give him the backbone he sadly lacks.'

'I am not strong – or any of those other things!'

In the darkness he turned abruptly to face her, so close she felt the warmth of his body and the fascination of his forceful personality.

'You take care of one child that you believe has the plague and then another you thought to be a *myling*. Without question ,you risk your life for a stranger. Then you played the part of a wife as if you had been one for years. You are either strong beyond imagination or too foolish to understand danger. Now I'm beginning to think that it's the latter.'

He fell silent. They were not heading towards the town, but upward, deeper into the forest. They continued until they came to a road where a wagon stood waiting, its horses snorting in the cold air. A handful of riders also waited quietly nearby.

Here, in the open, the moonlight cast a pale glow and she saw the prisoner's blond hair shining. He did not have a horse, but stood already beside the wagon. Seeing him once more made her heart beat faster. The thought of never seeing this handsome man again had already begun to worry her.

The half-man, for that was how she had come to think of the man clad in wolf-skin, strode up to the wagoner and spoke to him for some time. Then he mounted a waiting horse and rode off, followed by the other riders.

Silje and the children were helped into the wagon by the wagoner and the young man whose life she had saved. They climbed on board and the wheels began to creak as the wagon set off.

Now, suddenly, Silje's willpower seemed to desert her. There was nothing left to sustain it. Despite sitting close to this young man, it seemed as if a spell had been lifted and she was once more the exhausted and lonely Silje she had been earlier, racked with cold and desperately hungry. She would never have dared to take on the bailiff's soldiers feeling the way she did now.

However, she refused to give in to the weakness that was overcoming her. She sat rigidly upright against one side of the wagon, holding the infant close to her, to give it as much warmth as possible – if indeed she had any left to give, although it didn't feel like it. The little girl had fallen quickly asleep, her head on Silje's knee, with one sheepskin to lie on and another covering her. Silje had made good use of the beautiful velvet cloak to cover herself and both the children. She had lost all feeling in her arms from carrying and cradling the newborn, but she would not give up now, even though her eyes ached with tiredness and her body felt like a block of ice.

The journey was swift and bumpy. She had to brace her legs against the other side of the wagon to stop from being thrown around. Moonlight shimmered through the trees as they left Trondheim far behind and headed south.

'Where are we going?' Silje asked after they had travelled for some time. Her lips were frozen, making her speech slurred.

'You are going to a farm,' replied the young man. 'A

farm where the plague has already taken those it wants. I am going somewhere else.'

'Excuse me for asking,' she said, now tired and submissive, 'but there is one thing I don't understand.'

'Only one! That's extraordinary!'

She felt as if he were chiding her, as he would a foolish child, but continued, 'The scroll carrying the royal seal – they said it was genuine.'

'And so it is, but it's very old. We have had good use of it many times.'

'How did you come to possess it?'

'You ask too many questions,' he said, his laugh mocking her. 'Anyway, I should thank you for your help.'

'About time!' she thought, even though she had never expected any gratitude for what she had done. She watched him from the corner of her eye. He sat almost opposite her, with his feet pushed against her side of the wagon. They were in open country now and in the moonlight she saw his handsome young face with round cheeks and an impudent nose. His mouth was curled slightly into a smile, but as she asked her next question, the smile died.

'Who was he?'

He tensed. 'Who? The guard commander?'

'No, no! You know the one I mean. He who helped us.'

He stared at her in the pale light. 'I don't know what you're talking about.'

'The man at the edge of the woods, clad in the wolf-skin. He was almost like an animal himself. He hit you!'

The freed prisoner leaned closer to her.

'There was nobody there.' He was agitated. 'Nobody! Do you understand? Nobody – nobody!'

Silje drew back. 'But …'

'You have had a dream. You have seen *nothing* tonight.

Remember that! Do you think I would allow someone to hit me without revenge? I should knife any man who dared to do so.'

He had spoken in an excited whisper that the wagoner would not overhear. Silje gave up. She could understand him. It was difficult to suffer the dishonour he must feel. Close to execution, then saved by a young girl and finally hit across the face by that wolf-man.

'I see,' she answered meekly.

At once, his tone was milder. 'You must be completely exhausted. Here – let me hold the infant for a while. Is it yours?'

She gave him a dejected look.

'No, for God's sake, it isn't mine! I just took care of them both. There was nobody else.'

She looked down at the infant. She had been concerned for some time, and now she said anxiously, 'I don't know if it's still alive. It has been very quiet since we left… that place.'

In her mind the smell of funeral pyres came to her once more – that awful stench would remain with her forever.

'She's just sleeping,' he said casually, taking the infant from her outstretched arms.

Oh! How wonderful it felt to be able to move her arms without the weight of the baby. She tucked the sheepskin more closely about the little girl, and then she curled herself up under her skirts, shawl and the velvet cloak and rested her head against the side of the wagon.

The moon was directly above the horses' heads. This was a good sign she thought, her eyes following their manes as they swayed. She hoped this foretold a bright future, and then, as the wagon took a curve in the road, she looked up and saw a star glittering brightly. This was even better, because, as everyone knew, the stars were holes in the night sky through which one could see into God's shining heaven. Now God had shown her that He was looking down with extra care upon her and the two foundlings, as well as the refined young man whose life she had been chosen to save.

Silje was somewhat annoyed that, now this wonderful-looking man was sitting right in front of her, she was so tired that she could no longer keep her eyes open. Shaken by the wagon and freezing cold, she sat there, neither asleep nor fully awake, half-aware – and all the while her body ached.

She remembered half-waking briefly, sensing that the wagon had stopped and hearing the sound of voices. Something was placed in her arms, but she had already begun to fall asleep again, seeking release from her worries. The next thing she knew, the wagoner was standing over her, shaking her shoulder.

'Where are we?' Silje wondered, mumbling, unable to form the words.

'We have arrived. I have spoken to Master Benedikt. You may stay in the workers' cottage.'

People moved in the darkness, taking the children from her. The moon had set, so she knew it would soon be morning. The little girl cried and called for her mother. The wagoner helped Silje from the wagon, supporting her because her legs would not bear her weight.

'Who's Benedikt?'

'He's a church painter and a bit strange, but he will give you a place to stay.'

'And the children?'

'Yes, the children too.'

They stood alone beside the wagon and Silje asked, 'What became of the young man?'

'Heming? He left us about half an hour ago. He took another road.'

Heming! Heming, the bailiff-killer? It was him after all. A sudden feeling of guilt and shame came over her, knowing that she had helped a murderer – but he was so young and good-looking!

'I suppose there are many good Norwegians who fight for the freedom of our country?' she said hurriedly.

'I am sure there are, Mistress Silje.'

'Perhaps he belongs to such a band here?'

'You should not be asking such questions.'

That meant that he was, she was sure. She felt calmer. Fighting for his country meant he could be forgiven.

The wagon-driver was very polite when he spoke to her, she thought. Mistress Silje! It was probably because of the fine velvet cloak.

'And the other man. Was he also a fighter?'

'Which other man would that be?'

'The one who spoke to you. The one who bade you bring us here to this Benedikt.'

The wagoner bent down, adjusting a strap on the wagon. 'There were no others, Mistress Silje, only young Heming. I took my orders from him.'

She held her breath, about to argue. Then she remembered Heming's words to her.

'No, I'm probably mistaken. I seem to have forgotten much of what happened last night.'

'It is best so, mistress.'

A tallow torch burned in the small hut and a farmhand was lighting a fire in the hearth as she entered. She heard friendly voices soothing the children. Two older women were taking care of them, undressing them and feeding the little girl something warm.

'She is very pretty,' said one of them, unworried at being wakened in the middle of the night. 'What's her name?'

'I don't know,' replied Silje. 'I call her Sol. How is the baby? I've been so worried … is it still alive?'

'Oh yes. There's nothing wrong with him, even though his umbilical remains.'

'Him! Oh dear, that could have been a problem. You see I told some bad men that his name was Liv to save him from death. Now he'll be called Dag instead. He would not eat before and …'

'Oh, that doesn't matter,' said the woman, 'he is newborn and he brings nourishment with him into the world. We shall wash him and cut his cord, then wrap him up tightly. No harm will come to him, despite entering this world in such an ungodly fashion. We shall bathe him in blessed water warmed with hot coals and we have placed a piece of steel in his bed. He'll be blessed with bread, as is proper, and silver will be placed upon his breast.' She paused, then said,' But the little girl looks tired and weary. We'll take the babe in with us so that she may sleep. Here is some hot broth – it will warm you.'

Silje was beyond caring. The girl Sol lay curled up in one of the beds, her eyelids heavy and almost closed. The delightful warmth of the fire filled the room and Silje could not remember when she had last felt so at ease. She picked up the bowl of soup and drank it down without using the spoon. It was a thin oatmeal broth with small pieces of pork and it tasted wonderful. Soon its warmth began to spread through her body and before the women had left the room she lay back on the bed feeling quite drowsy. She was dimly aware of the women removing her shoes, undressing her and tucking covers around her; but she could not open her eyes. Her body felt as heavy as lead. Then the door closed and Silje fell into a deep sleep.

Chapter 3

Silje had fallen asleep shortly before daybreak and did not wake until the evening. The only light she saw that day was amongst the shadows of dusk, as she lay gazing at a low ceiling and dark rough-hewn timber walls. There was a window – just imagine a proper window with glass! Silje had only ever been used to a window opening, with a wooden shutter. The glass was slightly green and uneven, but it allowed the evening light to fill the room.

'The children!' she suddenly thought. She turned her head and saw that the little girl was not lying in the other bed. Listening hard, she could hear the sound of a child's giggling laughter – playing with someone, perhaps. From further away she heard a baby's angry unending cries. The crying stopped – was the baby being fed? Probably.

The room was very warm, the fire still burning in the hearth. Someone must have … Silje felt the colour rush to her face as a memory came back to her. She had been awake once. Had woken up and pulled the covers back over her.

'There, there,' a voice had said, 'there is no need to worry my dear. We are old men and the fire of youth left us long since.'

She had opened her eyes in panic to find two old men standing over her. She was relieved to find that she was still wearing her linen shift.

'This is the parish barber,' a tall man with a grey goatee beard and long thinning grey hair said to her. He wore clothes of strikingly bright colours. 'He is well-versed in the practice of healing – and I am called Benedikt the Painter.'

He delivered these last words in a manner that made her feel she should rise and curtsy before him. The barber who, as was common practice at that time, not only shaved beards but cured the sick, was a short tubby man with friendly eyes.

'How long have you had these feet, young lady?' he asked.

Benedikt chuckled, saying, 'Since she was born, I expect.'

Silje had not taken her shoes off for a couple of weeks and, raising her head, she looked down at them anxiously. They were unrecognisable – swollen, bruised and covered with blisters. They were also quite filthy, but that would be easy to remedy. The skin was another matter entirely.

'We shall prepare a healing poultice,' the barber said calmly. 'I'll not bleed you just now – you have precious little to take! Your hands are little better than your feet, but I've seen worse frostbite. You'll heal. I come highly recommended of course, with references from those in high places, such as the baron.'

He recited a pretentious list of fine-sounding names in order to impress. Benedikt waved his hand, brushing away the man's boasts, and sat down on her bed. Hurriedly she pulled the covers back over her.

'Now tell me,' he said in a concerned fatherly voice, 'what kind of unusual stranger are you? They tell me that you saved those two children and that wilful Heming. Those deeds alone are reason to care for you. Alas, your clothes tell me that you have known great poverty.'

'They are not mine,' she said quietly. 'I gave mine to one whose need was greater, an old woman who had only a thin smock. She remained on the farm.'

'And these?' With an expression of distaste, he lifted the edge of one of the rags she had been wearing between finger and thumb and quickly dropped it again.

'I made them from things that I found in the barn.'

The painter shook his head in despair. 'I've never heard the like! You gave away the clothes off your back for the sake of an old crone! I hear that you are well-spoken, educated perhaps, but what is your background?'

Somewhat embarrassed, she replied, 'I'm nobody special, just the unruly child of a blacksmith, Silje, daughter of Arngrim. I was driven from the farm when the plague took my family. That I am able to speak well is another matter.'

'Well I think you are someone special.' Benedikt's friendly eyes held a twinkle. 'You have a good heart, and that's rare in hard times like these when people look first to their own needs. That you are protected by such good patronage also means a lot.'

All this time the barber had been attending to her feet, mixing an aromatic brew in the pot on the hearth. Silje had wanted to ask what Benedikt meant by 'good patronage', but her experience this far told her that it would be pointless. They spoke about young Heming gladly, but of the one who was behind him they would say not a word.

Benedikt continued, 'You called yourself an unruly child.' He paused, and then, 'What was it like on the farm? What chores did you perform?'

She looked away, and with a knowing smile she replied, 'I'm afraid they used to despair of me sometimes. Of course I did as I was asked, in the fields and in the master's house, but I was a bit – what shall I say? Absent-minded? I would daydream a lot and spend much of my time making small decorations and ornaments and such things.'

Benedikt's eyes lit up. 'Did you hear that, barber? Perhaps we have here someone who will appreciate my work. In truth, there are few that do. Tomorrow, Silje, you must come with me to the church. There you'll see decorations!'

She gave a broad smile. 'Thank you, I shall be glad to.'

The barber mumbled to himself, but loud enough for them to hear, something like, 'Not on these feet you won't.'

'May I get up now?' she asked.

'No,' he replied as he placed poultices from the pot on each foot and bandaged them well. They were so hot that they almost burnt her and the room became filled with a bittersweet smell of herbs.

'No,' he said again. 'You must rest with these on your feet for several hours. Besides, do you not need to sleep some more?'

'Yes, I think I do,' she agreed. A smile touched her lips. 'But what of the children?'

'Don't worry yourself,' Benedikt said. 'My dear little ladies are taking good care of them both.'

With that they had left the room, and Silje, with a warm body and a happy heart, had fallen asleep once more.

****

Now Silje could tell from the light through the window that it was evening. She sat up and gently tried to stand. Her feet hurt as she put her weight on them, but the pain was bearable and no worse than she had suffered during the past days of mindless wandering. With God's help, it would be over. With His blessing, she and the children might stay with these kind people. She suddenly realised that she had not thanked them properly. What on earth would the distinguished church painter think of her?

Her clothes had been taken away. Instead, a blouse in coarse natural-coloured cloth and a dark waisted skirt had been laid out for her. On the floor stood a pair of large felt overshoes, large enough to take her bandaged feet.

She dressed swiftly and ran a comb through her hair. Her hands were not bandaged, but they had been treated with an ointment that smelt of mint. She desperately longed to soak her whole being in warm scented water – head, hair, everything – and drown herself in cleanliness. Now I am being unreasonable, she thought, smiling to herself. It's easy to get spoilt. Only yesterday I was grateful for a crust of mouldy bread!

The clothes were comfortable, just a bit too big. A striped pinafore had also been left for her, and she tightened its laces round her waist to a snug fit. She did not have the energy to braid her hair, so it hung loose. A straight collared jacket with puffed sleeves, tight cuffs and short tails lay there also, but she did not put it on. She knew that these had once been the clothes of a servant girl.

With halting steps she approached the door. The wide floorboards creaked – a wooden floor! At home she had been used to bare earth or stone floors. She stepped over the high threshold and onto a flagstone step.

The sun, lying very low on the horizon, made her blink. She hadn't realised that it was still so bright outside – the green windowpanes had masked the light. She was in a courtyard, covered by a dusting of snow and surrounded by the dark outlines of buildings. The large main dwelling stood beside her and beyond that a fine beautifully decorated house with a loft, roofed gallery and ornate carvings. There was nobody to be seen. She shivered now that she had left the warmth of the hut. She raised her head to look around. The blood drained from her face, her heart froze.

'Oh dear God – NO!' she groaned.

Feeling faint, she took hold of the doorframe and then, cautiously and fearfully, she took another look. The tallest of the mountains rose high above the roofs of the buildings, but there was an opening between the houses where the road ran up to the farm, and there she could see they soared with compelling closeness. She recognised every peak, every valley and every crevice. The Land of Shadows! The Land of Evening! She had come much closer to the terror of her childhood, the Ice People's dreadful secret lair.

In fact, she found herself almost at the foot of the mountains, separated from them only by a desolate heath. Beyond the heath a wall of mountain rose straight up, unassailable, piercing the sky and defying God in his heaven! Her first thought was to get away as quickly as she could, but then she began to think properly. She was no longer a child, she told herself, and all her childish fantasies of demons gliding through the air were just that – fantasies. She had dreamt them up; they were not real. As for the stories people had told of the dreaded Ice People, well, she would just keep well away from the mountains. Was she about to leave the only refuge she had found for fear of some childish ideas?

One of the old women emerged from the main house and waved at her to come over. Without another glance at the blue-black snow-capped bastions, she limped across the yard.

'Come in, come in,' the woman said pleasantly. 'We are

gathered in the kitchen to eat. You must be quite hungry now, my dear?'

'Yes, I am. But I should like to wash and tidy myself before I eat, please.'

'Of course,' said the woman.

This done, she went into the large cheery kitchen with its huge open hearth and a long narrow table, with benches each side, where everyone from the farm sat eating. Greeting them timidly, she made a small curtsey to each one there. They were few in number. The plague must have been savage here, she thought. Benedikt sat at the head of the table and there were the two women, each holding one of the children, and the farmhand. That was all.

The women were so alike that they had to be sisters. Both wore long black gowns and, always smiling, they tried to make everyone feel at ease. Silje felt that she would learn to like them very much.

To her delight, she noticed that the baby, Dag, was feeding. He was being given pieces of bread soaked in milk that he could suck on. Little Sol greeted her with a smile of recognition, but then quickly turned her attention back to the farmhand who was playing with her, making her giggle.

'Come in, my dear girl,' said Benedikt. 'Sit here next to me.'

She thanked him with a small curtsey, said grace silently and sat down. The painter seemed to be a man of simple tastes, as the evening meal consisted only of three dishes – salt beef, cured pork and boiled cabbage – and large mugs of ale. Compared with the habits of the time this was frugal. Country folk would usually have at least six dishes, while the wealthy would have up to fourteen courses. Adults would usually drink at least six jugs of ale every day; many would drink twice that amount.

To Silje, however, the sight of so much food was like a dream. Helping herself to some, she looked at the children.

'This is the first time I've seen them in the light,' she said shyly. 'They are both beautiful, but so different.'

'The little girl is a wild one,' one of the women remarked. 'Such temperament! One moment she's bright and cheerful, but if she can't have her way, what rage!'

Silje nodded. 'I noticed that last night.'

'She'll be a handful for the boys when she's older,' growled Benedikt. 'What with those green eyes and that curly black hair!'

If she's allowed to live, Silje thought sadly. The next few days would tell. Once again she could see the image of the girl's dead mother.

Trying to put such thoughts out of her mind, she said brightly, 'The boy is unusually handsome for a newborn, don't you think?' She gazed at the tiny face with its halo of fair hair.

'Indeed,' said Benedikt. 'Makes you wonder where he's from. You saw the blankets he was wrapped in?'

'Yes, last night in the moonlight. It's strange.'

'Scandals will befall the best of families,' Benedikt mumbled.

'I was told to keep his things and look after them.'

Benedikt nodded but his expression was serious.

'Yes, you must do so. But did young Heming really have such foresight?'

Why, oh why did her pulse begin to race and colour rush to her cheeks whenever his name was mentioned? She didn't know – but the truth was that she was really looking forward to seeing that handsome face again.

'No. It was somebody else,' Silje answered, her thoughts confused. 'A strange man, almost part man, part beast, but

I am in his debt for it was he who sent me to you. I do want to thank you all for your kindness towards me. Taking us into your home in the middle of the night without question – you are very generous.'

'One can do no less,' mumbled the painter, then, as if trying to avoid further questions, he quickly said, 'anyway, I never thought Heming would be so sensible.' A pause, then, 'So Silje! What are we to do with you? As you see, there are only a few of us left here and we could use an extra pair of hands. Will you stay? We can offer only food and lodging.'

'Yes, thank you so much,' she said, looking down at her bowl. 'I'll try to keep my thoughts on my work.'

'And stop daydreaming?' laughed Benedikt. 'Folk must be allowed to dream, Silje – those such as you and I, even more so.' Then he added, 'My brother and his family, who once lived in this house, are now dead. I beg you not to ask of them, for our sorrow is too great. We that are left behind must try to live on.'

She nodded. 'I have just suffered in the same way, and I understand. We all have those we mourn.'

The women, the farmhand and Benedikt all indicated their agreement; then Benedikt continued, 'I live in the ornate building beside this one and I take no part in the workings of the farm.' To Silje he seemed inordinately proud of his position. 'But see! You have drunk so little. Ale is one thing we have plenty of – you may have seven jugs a day if you wish.'

'Oh! Thank you, but no,' replied Silje. 'I can scarcely manage three jugs in a day.'

'What! That's not enough to keep you alive – but no matter, I feel the same about ale, for as you see, I drink only wine – a drink fit for an artist.'

Silje sat facing the window. Here in the main house the

glass was of better quality, but she had avoided looking outside until now. Encouraged by the painter's friendly tone, she became bolder and said, 'Those mountains – I had the fright of my life when I saw how close they are.'

She began to tell them, as if retelling a dream, of her childhood fears and how, although she had lived far to the north-east, she had seen them clearly and been in awe of them. She made only passing reference to the swirling creatures that lived there, saying merely that the mountains had given her nightmarish visions.

When she had finished, Benedikt said, 'I am not surprised by what you say. They hold a fear for me too. They bear down on you like a great black cloud rising from the land – and all those horrible stories about the Ice People; you must have had your fill of those, I expect?'

'Yes, I did – but who are the Ice People really? What are they?' she asked with some trepidation.

She could not believe that they were all sitting here together talking, the master with the servants. Not many years ago that would have been unheard of. Now times had changed and people sought companionship wherever they could, never knowing where or when the pestilence would strike – and besides, Benedikt was an unusual man, a highly respected artist, and he would do as he pleased.

He had taken a liking to Silje, of that there was no doubt, and she in turn felt that she had found a soul-mate.

'The Ice People,' he said slowly, every eye on him. They had all finished eating, but they remained seated, each reluctant to leave the company of the others. 'The Ice People are just a legend. They were thought to have magic powers and be spawned by evil – I expect that you have heard of Tengel, the evil spirit of the Ice People.'

'Master Benedikt!' exclaimed one of the women, her

voice shrill, as the other crossed herself. The farmhand stood up and walked over to the door, holding his knife, which he then stabbed into the wall above it to ward off evil.

'Ah, superstitions,' said Benedikt. 'Have you heard of him, Silje?'

'Only in secret whispers. Nobody would ever tell me much.'

'Well, I shall tell you about them now, for I am not afraid – not of magic or the Devil! Young Tengel fled to the mountains about three or four hundred years ago, driven from his lands, together with some other farmers, by the new decrees of some long-forgotten king. Tengel swore revenge. He sold his soul to the Devil, Silje, and became chieftain of the Ice People. Tengel, by the way, means chieftain – I don't expect you knew that? And they came to be called the Ice People, because it is thought to be impossible to find a way to where they live – their lair. To get there it is said that one must travel beneath the ice, through a tunnel beside a great river.'

'Was Tengel able to cast spells and work magic before he went to the mountains?'

'We don't know. It is said he was an ordinary man, but that his pact with the Devil left him with amazing abilities. Over the centuries the Ice People's notoriety grew and the rumours spread, because the children he fathered shared his magic powers.' Benedikt paused and lowered his voice. 'And they say that Tengel has no grave!'

Silje was wide-eyed. Unwittingly she peered across into a dark corner where a door led into shadows beyond.

'Do you mean that the Evil One took him? Spirited him away?'

The painter lowered his gaze. 'I didn't say that. I never said that.' He looked up again. 'There is supposed to be nothing the Ice People cannot do – but it is all just talk, Silje. Just silly foolish superstition.'

'So they don't really exist?' she asked.

'I've never seen them and I have lived here all my life. I am honest enough to admit that I will not willingly go up into those mountains, but that is another matter. It's because the mountains themselves frighten me.'

The woman holding Sol in her lap had put her hand over the child's ears. 'Master Benedikt, you should be more careful what you say.' She said resentfully. 'One must not speak of them.'

The farmhand had more courage. 'They don't exist!' he said. 'Maybe long ago, but not now. They probably all perished in the Black Death two hundred years ago, along with nearly everyone else. I have been into the mountains many times and have seen neither people nor their "lair".'

So it was all in my imagination, thought Silje. She was now more relaxed. She would not think about it again and would no longer feel afraid. It was just wonderful to eat her fill, be warm again and wear clean clothes once more – even though they had belonged to some poor girl on the farm. She was elated, and suddenly exclaimed, 'I am so very happy. I don't think that even heaven can compare to this!'

The others all laughed, sharing her joy. Then she thought once more of Sol and the plague. She looked worriedly at the little girl. How long would it be before they knew? She had seen enough of the plague to recognise the signs, but so far the child was bright and cheerful. Only once, while they were eating had she looked sad, her chin trembling and a faraway look in her eyes.

'Mummy,' she had said with an unsteady voice. 'Mummy!'

One of the women had cradled her in her arms, saying, 'She is so young. She will soon forget.' Then the woman had rocked her gently until she was calm again.

They all wanted Silje to tell them everything she had experienced in her travels and especially about the past day and night, when so much had happened. No one could explain who it was who had helped her, but she saw how the two women exchanged expressionless glances. One of them said something like '*Miserere*' and the young farmhand hid his face, looking at the floor.

They all heard it at the same moment, and looked around startled. Horses were galloping up the road and they could hear the rattling of weapons and armour.

'Bailiff's soldiers!' said Benedikt looking through the window into the courtyard where a number of riders had begun to dismount. 'Silje! Were these the men you spoke to last night at the gibbet hill?'

Dusk was falling and the glass was not easy to see through, but she was certain. 'No, I don't recognise any of them.'

'Good, then you need not hide.' He paused, then addressed one of the women. 'Grete you must take away the little one at least and perhaps the girl too.'

The woman took the two children and went into an adjoining room. Benedikt stood up and went outside to meet the riders. The others waited behind, straining to hear every word. In the yard, Benedikt greeted the men and asked them the nature of their business. The officer walked up and stood on the step.

'Have you seen any strangers here last night or today?'

'No, we have not. Who are you looking for?'

'You know damned well, painter Benedikt! That rebellious troublemaker Dyre Alvsson and his men were out last night. They burned the house of one of the King's men. We shall put a stop to his lawlessness. You will not object if we look in your stables?'

'As you wish, if you think my old mares are worth looking at. Surely you don't believe that I ...'

The officer cut him short. 'Believe!' he snorted and turned on his heel.

All the soldiers walked at once towards the same building. They had obviously been here before searching for strangers' horses. After a short while they came back outside.

'And Heming, the bailiff-killer?' called the officer.

'Haven't seen him in ages,' replied Benedikt, so convincingly that even Silje would have believed him, had she not known otherwise. 'I steer clear of that rogue.'

'Best that you do, for your sake.'

Some of the men searched one or two of the other buildings. Perhaps they thought a horse had been taken in and hidden among the cows in the barn. Then they made ready to leave.

'You had better be careful, Benedikt!' shouted the officer over his shoulder. 'Splashing paint on church ceilings does not give you free passage to heaven.'

'Neither does upsetting the homes of honest folk!' Benedikt shouted back.

So now she knew who he was – the man in the wolf-skin. Dyre Alvsson! Hadn't she heard that name before? The Danes' greatest enemy in Tröndelag! He was impossible to find, no matter how hard the bailiffs tried to hunt him down, because the people protected and sheltered him.

There was no obvious hatred towards the King. Farmers and peasants cared nothing for who ruled the land. When the Swedes had taken control fifteen years earlier they had been well received as the new masters. When they left Tröndelag again, the Danes returned without much fuss from the inhabitants. Copenhagen or Stockholm – either one too far away – others could govern the country. As long as they had their daily bread, they didn't much care what the King was called. Farmers only complained about taxes and other matters close to home.

There were only small numbers of rebels who were continually active. The most notable of these at that time was Dyre Alvsson. He was the most daring and the most admired. Silje had not known until now what he looked like, how old he was or where he came from. Still, even though she knew, she would never inform on him! It was not surprising that nobody wanted to speak about him when she had asked.

She wondered about Heming, that warm feeling taking hold again. Yes, he was a rebel; she had already guessed as much. Benedikt obviously supported them. So maybe she would have a chance of seeing Heming again. Oh, she could see that teasing glint in his eye, his shapely nose and his mouth with its ready smile – and that golden hair that shone in the moonlight!

Silje's innocent young heart was filled with new emotions. This was an infatuation entirely based on appearances that would be normal for any sixteen-year-old girl – the unquestioning adoration that is only found in the spring of youth – idolising someone, always blind to his faults, endowing him with the virtues, feelings and interests that he ought to possess, but may not.

That day was not a long one for Silje. The farm was soon made secure and the people prepared for their beds. The women, being kind-hearted, insisted on keeping the children with them for one more night.

Silje did not think that she would be able to sleep again so soon, but she was wrong. Dreams came and went. She groaned quietly in her sleep, her arms and legs twitching slightly as if she was trying to escape from something. She was lying in the pasture below the farm where she grew up. The Land of Evening was visible far in the distance – the peaks, jagged and broken, with hidden valleys behind and below them. The sky was a burning crimson.

Something rose above the mountains; ghostly images in black with great wings spread wide – her demons. In her sleep, Silje shielded herself from them. There were not many – only six or eight perhaps – but they were dangerous. Gliding through the air, searching; but she knew their eyes were already upon her. They were just pretending not to have seen her.

With a start, she realised that she was naked, but it didn't matter. It meant nothing, because she knew nobody could see her except these spirits from beyond. She found this knowledge quite satisfying and stretched out on the grass, flexing her limbs with sensual pleasure.

They were getting closer now. Her heart started pounding. She could see them clearly. They too were naked – all of them male, and their devilish faces held a provocative attraction. Long talons on their hands, their bodies a fusion of man and beast. Indeed, these creatures had been created more like beasts than men – they were so muscular and graceful.

They saw her and they desired her. Still they did not come to her. They circled above her, keeping their distance, as though holding back, waiting for something. She saw the face of one of them. It was beautiful and noble, despite being twisted and grotesquely deformed – the face of a young man framed in golden curls, with the antlers of a stag. She knew him, and trembled with ecstasy at seeing him again, but even he did not dare descend. The lower half of his body was that of a stag, but his arms had become wings with a mighty span. For some reason she wished he hadn't been naked – she felt ill at ease. It was his face she adored. She wanted nothing more. Then together they began to move away from her.

Up from the Land of Shadows soared yet another creature, bigger and more dangerous than the others, but he remained where he was, silhouetted against the fiery sky. Even though the distance was so great, in her dream Silje could see who it was. She recognised his face – attractive yet repulsive, with the sneer of a predator, enticing, tempting – black hair spiralling across his forehead, eyes blazing. But no matter how hard she tried, she could not see his body. She wanted desperately to see into the dark shadows hiding him, but all she saw was a contoured outline that reminded her of a faun or satyr.

Her body felt tired and heavy and she could not catch her breath. She was strangely ecstatic, and like the creatures she waited, writhing in the grass, drawing her legs up slightly, anxious, afraid, fascinated. His wings moved with a slow beat as he glided towards her. Then she awoke with a scream.

She lay gasping for air, both relieved and disappointed that the dream had ended so abruptly. It was a shock for her to feel the heat of her body, in a way she had never done before. She was confused and shaken, and covered herself with her hands to conceal the shame and the burning inside. But her hands fanned the flame – there was no way back.

Exhausted, she lay there, thinking she might die from the shame of the indescribable rapture she had just experienced. Simply and naturally Silje had become an adult.

****

Benedikt was not painting the local parish church – he had done that long ago and every inch of the vaulted ceiling was decorated. It was but a short distance to the

56

neighbouring parish, whose church he was presently adorning, and late that morning – Benedikt was not an early riser – he took Silje with him in the pony and trap. Silje noticed his blue-veined nose, a sign of the importance he placed on enjoying strong drink.

Silje had been sure that everyone would see in her face what had happened last night, but she was mistaken. No one appeared to notice anything different about her and they all spoke to her quite naturally, as though nothing had happened. How odd! It had been a transformation for her and she had felt so disgraced that she could have died. The fact that she was attracted to the wrong man did not help matters.

Benedikt, lightly holding the reins and guiding the old mare, chatted all the while as they rattled along in the trap, with Silje sitting beside him. He told of his great artistic moments and all the church paintings that he had created. He cursed aloud the priests of the Reformation, who had decreed that all the old most beautiful paintings should be whitewashed over because some of them were considered indecent.

'Indecent!' he fumed. 'There's no such thing as indecency in love, Silje. Everything is natural and beautiful. It's the minds of those bigoted old men that are indecent!'

His words comforted her a little, but not enough.

'Fortunately, there were sensible priests as well, who managed to halt this moral hysteria with the words of Gregory the Great, who said, "Through pictures shall they learn, they who cannot read the Scriptures." He understood what ecclesiastical art was worth! Wait till I show you my Judgement Day angel, Silje. Oh, what a masterpiece! I used Heming as my model.'

Her cheeks reddened. 'I'm sure he was an excellent model,' she muttered.

Benedikt laughed. 'His body, yes, but hardly his soul! Anyway, how would you like to be the model for my Fallen Virgin – in the Judgement Day scene?'

'No!' she replied fiercely.

'Oh, please! With your lovely golden-brown hair you would be perfect. Naturally, you would have to remove your clothing!'

'No – certainly not!' she gasped.

He laughed again. 'I was only teasing you, my dear. Though you may have the soul of an artist, you are far from broad-minded enough – a parochial upbringing?'

She was not going to listen to any more of this, so she clasped her hands firmly and expressively in her lap and stared down at them. If she had turned her head only slightly she would have been able to see the mountains. But she did not look, even though they enticed and called to her – today more than ever. Perhaps the creatures were hovering there in the sky. Maybe the largest of them was …

'Is that the church over there?' she shouted, too eagerly.

'Yes, it is. But it's nothing to get worked up about.'

'No. I was just …' She didn't finish the sentence. She could not describe her imaginings and yet now, shamefully, she began to feel moist again – just as she had last night.

As soon as she could, she jumped down from the trap and wandered idly about inside the church, avoiding the stands and ladders, admiring Benedikt's work. Some motifs were subjects she recognised – the Four Horsemen of the Apocalypse, for example. Another pictured a wandering group of plague victims and another, the ravages of war. To one side, a half-finished figure of Death. And there! Oh yes, there was Heming, the Judgement Day angel – somewhat stylised, but there was no doubt it was him. She sighed wistfully.

She was full of praise for everything she saw and her honest admiring comments delighted Benedikt.

'Look at this – look at this!' he said excitedly, ushering her along. 'What do think of this one?'

'Well … yes.' She hesitated. 'But why have you drawn a woman churning butter? And a devil behind her?'

Benedikt sniggered. 'They always want something like that! A little naughty fun is allowed. The priests, vergers and the congregation all enjoy a bit of fun.'

'I don't quite understand,' she said naively.

He stared at her, open-mouthed. 'Do you mean you don't understand the symbolism? Have you never watched someone churn butter? Never done it yourself?'

'Yes, of course, but …' At that instant she felt her cheeks begin to burn bright red and she quickly turned away from him. It was so common – so vulgar!

Benedikt was full of remorse. 'You are a puzzle to me, my passionate young maiden. Yes, you're certainly passionate; anyone can see that!'

They walked in silence for a few moments. 'Perhaps you would like to help me paint?' he asked, his generosity a response to her previous words of admiration. 'You can colour in this vine. Have you painted before?'

She hadn't, but she was itching to try. He showed her the colours. Caput mortuum was a red-violet colour, lamp-black was to be used sparingly or the picture would be drab, and she was on no account to mix it with the other colours. Yellow ochre, white of lime, copper powder that turned to blue-green, and ultramarine that became light blue – she was allowed to mix all these, so long as she did not mess up his pigments.

Anxiously she took hold of the brush. It took her a quarter of an hour to colour in the first vine-leaf, because she was so worried about painting outside the shape and spilling her colours, but after that she worked more quickly. They chatted enthusiastically about art, while all the time Benedikt was suspended beneath the vaulted ceiling working on Adam and Eve, who were both protecting their virtue behind large fig leaves. Gradually Silje made progress with her vine. She knew nothing of painting, so Benedikt took the role of teacher, one he seemed to enjoy.

Suddenly he asked, 'Am I boring you?'

'No, no!' she replied excitedly. 'This is really interesting. I have never known such conversation.'

He grinned. His almost unbroken monologue could hardly be called a conversation.

Finally he came back down. The day's work was over – and they had completely forgotten to eat the food they had brought with them.

'Now just look at that!' he said admiringly. 'I knew you could do it. You've really brought the leaves to life. How did you know about shadows?'

'I didn't.' She was puzzled, but very proud of her efforts. 'I just tried to remember what they looked like.'

'You must come with me tomorrow as well,' he said eagerly. 'The old women can take care of the children, they know what to do.'

As he strode out of the church ahead of her, she wondered how she had grown so fond of this old man in such a short time. Most importantly perhaps, she had found something inside herself. Silje, the black sheep, not suited to life on the farm, had found a different world. Maybe this was where she belonged.

Chapter 4

Silje was unable to return to the church the following day because one of the sores on her feet had become infected and she was told to rest. Instead she spent the time playing with Sol and doing small jobs that allowed her to remain sitting and talking to the two old women.

Sol was a funny child, very impulsive and straightforward. She was also unpretentious. When she was angry, she was very angry, but equally, when she was happy, it showed and she ran to hug them each in turn. No one could understand a word she said, but they thought that she could not be more than two years old.

The next morning Silje's foot was looking better and she accompanied Benedikt once again, but this time, to unburden the women, they took Sol with them. The girl ran wildly around in the church, her unbounded energy driving them to despair. Time and again Silje had to fetch her down from the pulpit or the gallery. Time and again the child tried to climb up to where Benedikt was working. In the end they decided to tether her with a rope in the chancel, which lay empty.

As before, they painted apart from each other. Silje was

given a slightly more difficult task this time, that of painting the halos around the heads of some of the angels. She did them well.

'You've got it in you,' Benedikt said. 'Come, you can see what I did yesterday, while you weren't here.'

She followed him into one of the side chapels. Under the small vaulted ceiling, he had painted some scenes from the Day of Judgement, but Silje knew at once what he had wanted her to see. It was a half-finished image of the Fallen Virgin. She blushed and turned away.

Benedikt laughed loudly. 'Yes, she's a good likeness of you, isn't she? Her face, I mean. I had to imagine the rest of course, but it wasn't difficult.'

Silje was lost for words. She felt affronted. The woman in the picture did not look like her. Her stomach was much flatter and she had more above the waist than that – thing!

'I look nothing like that,' she yelled.

'You've only got yourself to blame,' he chuckled, good-naturedly. 'You didn't want to be my model. But I'm happy to change it, just you tell me where I've gone wrong.'

Of course the right thing would have been to turn and walk away with a show of indignation. Yet she could not bear the thought of her face perched on top of that pear-shaped body, so she made a few swift, embarrassed gestures over the painting. Benedikt looked her up and down, comparing her with his painting.

'Yes, you're right. You're one of those full bosomed maids, slim from the waist down. That's easily changed. Then we need a devil behind you as well. No matter, it'll have to wait while I finish Field Marshall Death!'

Silje went to the church every day, despite her foot not being healed. Sol was not allowed to go with them because she was far too difficult to look after. Every day she wore her fine blue velvet cloak. On one trip, Benedikt remarked, 'You caress that cloak as though it was a lover.'

She was startled. 'It's only that the velvet is so soft.'

'It's the way you wrap yourself in it – breathing in the sensual fragrance of it – has that anything to do with the quality of the cloth?'

She drew herself upright. 'I have never owned such a beautiful garment, that's all!' she mumbled, embarrassed.

On the fourth day Benedikt told Silje that he thought her painting was so good that he would give her a more important task. There was only a little time left in which to have the church ready, as services were soon to be held there once more. He would not be able to finish it all by himself. Could she paint the devil seducing the virgin, if he drew the outlines?

She was lost for words. Was she to be allowed to do a complete figure? Yes, she knew she could. She had known all her life that she had it in her to draw, but had never had the chance.

'Yes – yes please! I think I should like to try,' she stuttered eagerly. 'But what if it's wrong or not good enough?'

'Then we'll paint over it. But I'm certain you can do it.'

Silje threw herself into her task with heart and soul. She was working alone now, in the side chapel, and they could only shout occasionally to each other. However, she was so deeply engrossed in her work that she frequently forgot both Benedikt and her surroundings.

Towards evening he came down from his labours. He had looked in on her once about midday to see how she was progressing. Now she had almost finished, with only the devil's hoof that showed from behind the woman's legs left to paint.

'You haven't eaten a thing all day,' he called as he came through the nave, his footsteps echoing. 'Daylight's fading. We'll have to stop now.'

He came to a halt suddenly and she stood to one side so that he could see what she had done, anxiously awaiting his verdict.

He stared. 'In God's name, girl, what have you done?'

At that moment she realised what she had painted, seeing it through his eyes. The devil stood behind the woman, as Benedikt had sketched, but she had done much more. The claw-like hands clasped the woman's breasts and her head was thrown back against the devil's shoulder. His long tongue stroked her throat – and his face …

'Oh!' she gasped, putting her hand to her mouth. 'I hadn't noticed that!'

No one who had ever seen the man in the wolf-skin would ever be in doubt as to where the image had come from.

'We must get rid of it,' said Benedikt with alarm.

Silje was about to paint over it, but then he took her hand, saying, 'No, don't. I've changed my mind. It's far too good to be destroyed. You're no master painter and much of this is clumsy, but you have given it such power! Let's hope the King's soldiers never have cause to enter here.'

Then, his voice sounding shocked, he continued, 'Young lady, I would never have thought that you, who seem so virtuous, could create a coarse and vulgar picture like this. Look at the devil's greedy grasping hands! Look at his stance! It is as if you yourself knew what was happening behind that poor woman's back.'

Silje was aghast. 'I can't understand it. I never realised I had painted it like that. It must have created itself!'

'Either you are under a spell or quite simply, you have

the soul of an artist and you have been working as if in a trance. Yes, that's what happened. An artist is often unaware of what he is doing once inspiration takes hold. But I thought you had lost your heart to young Heming!'

So he had discovered her secret.

'And so I have!' She was angry and confused. 'I have! I cannot understand how *this* face has come out of the wall.'

Benedikt began to laugh, softly at first, then more heartily. 'Well, you couldn't have chosen a better specimen to copy! Dear Lord, what a thing to happen! Momentous! But no one must know of this. It's good that it is dark in this corner.'

They set off homewards. It was warmer now, and the small amount of snow that had fallen had melted away. The sky was grey and oppressive. They well knew that this warmth was deceptive. For the sun rose later with each day and winter was tightening its grip, its frozen claws digging ever deeper. This had been a wretched autumn.

****

Silje had been at Benedikt's farm for ten days before Sol became ill. Flushed with fever and crying, she lay on her bed in their room. Silje sat with her the whole day, changing her clothes and keeping her warm.

After taking a look at the child the barber, who was one of Benedikt's drinking friends, gave his verdict. 'No, there's no doubt, I'm afraid. You must keep the infant away from her. We others will be all right – we have survived so far. Has she been baptised? It would be well to ask the priest to call.'

'He is dead,' said one of the women. 'A new one has not yet come. Alas, he was a good man, our last priest. He visited all the sick before he himself was taken. But the girl is so big she must have been baptised.' She choked back a tear – they had all grown to love little Sol.

After the barber had gone, Silje sat with Sol once more. Despair cut through her like a knife. She had become so close to the child that she almost thought of her as a daughter.

'Help us,' she whispered. 'Help us, help us! Do not let her die, for she is so full of life. In the name of heaven, do not take her from me. Please let her live!'

The girl's fever did not break – quite the opposite. Silje could do nothing but wait for the next fearful sign. When at last Sol looked up, her eyes were glazed over.

'Please get well,' Silje begged her. 'I can't bear to see you in pain. I need you so much.'

Sol's eyes widened. 'Thilea needs Thol?'

'Yes, I need Sol. You and I belong together. We have little brother to take care of, as well. It's no fun when you're sick. I love you, Sol.'

A gentle smile lit up the child's tired face. A little hand – burning hot – rested in Silje's. At that moment Silje knew for the first time that Sol really had taken to her, loved her and had a sense of belonging. Until then, their relationship had been based more on necessity.

She had referred to Dag as Sol's baby brother. This might have been unwise; especially if they were all forced to go their separate ways, but it had come from the heart and felt so right. She did not want to be separated from either of them – and she didn't want to see this lovely girl lying in a cold coffin.

Later that evening she heard the sound of a visitor arriving. Benedikt had a rider with him when he returned from the church. Silje did not know what had passed between them, but suddenly the guest stood at the door of the little hut.

'Leave the room, Silje,' he said, his voice low and hoarse.

The room was in shadow and he was not wearing a wolf-skin this time, simply a dark brown hooded tunic, but still she knew him. Her hands were shaking as she rose from the bedside. Sol moaned and reached out to her.

'Should I not stay?' Silje wondered vaguely, forcing herself to meet his gaze, quite certain he could see right through her. She could see now that the strange eyes were like pieces of pale amber nestling between eyelashes as black as coal.

'You're fond of the child, aren't you?'

'Yes. Very, very fond.'

'Then leave! Wait in the kitchen with the women!'

Reluctantly she obeyed, trying to ignore the child's tears. No one in the kitchen spoke. The atmosphere was peculiar, the air charged with tension – but from what? Anxiety? Fear? Obviously, it was not a good idea to have the rebel leader visit the farm. It was dangerous, perilously dangerous.

Benedikt was ill at ease and stood rigidly at the window. The farmhand sat twisting his cap in his hands. Both women sat quite still, then one of them began to pray quietly.

'Stop that!' Benedikt spat the words unthinkingly.

'Of course, forgive me,' said the woman. Her name was Marie – it was she who had taken care of Sol most of the time.

Abruptly, Silje stood up. 'He's been in there for a long time. I shall go and see what's happening.'

Strangely, nobody tried to prevent her. Somewhat hesitantly, she opened the door to the hut. The man was bent over the bed. He straightened and turned to her, showing neither anger nor surprise that she had come back.

'The child is strong,' he said in his unusual hoarse voice. 'She will live, but ...' he paused.

'Can that be true?' Silje was disbelieving, not wanting to hope in vain. 'How do you know?'

He gave a wry smile.

'There are many smitten with the sickness that live. You know this. Just stay with her so she will not feel alone.'

'I shall.'

Sol lay resting; looking at them with a tired feverish smile on her face.

'Why do you limp?'

He gave Silje a searching look.

'It's nothing. Just that the frostbite on my foot will not heal.'

'May I look at it?'

'No!'

She was ashamed that she had spoken so harshly. He just waited, an amused smile playing on his lips. Resigning herself, she sat down on the bed with legs stretched out and, without a word, he sat at her feet and removed her stocking. As his warm hands first touched her skin, it felt to her like the sudden lash of a whip. Impassively, he glanced at her and then gently covered the sore foot with both hands.

'You have been walking on it too much,' he said, as she felt an unusual pulsating warmth radiate up her leg. Then her foot began to feel as if it was on fire.

'Was this what you did to Sol as well?' she asked with a quick look at the girl, who was now sleeping peacefully.

He didn't answer her. Instead he removed his hands from her foot and took a small wooden box from his tunic.

'Rub this onto your foot tonight. It will draw the pus from the sore.'

He stood up, and the room suddenly seemed too small and too hot.

Silje thanked him and then asked, 'Did Benedikt ask you to come?'

'No, it was not Benedikt,' he said. 'But I did find him at the church.'

'At the church! Good Lord, no!'

He had read her thoughts, 'Yes, I saw it.'

No comment, simply a statement of fact. Silje was relieved to be putting on her stocking; otherwise she would not have known where to look or what to do with her hands. She wanted the earth to swallow her up.

He was making ready to leave. Quickly she asked, 'The infant – the boy; will he be smitten?'

He hesitated, then, 'Let me see him.'

As he passed her in the doorway, she sensed the same weakness in her body that she had felt in the dream. The evening sun's rays caught his face for a moment. She had only ever seen him in shadow or half-light and now she realised how wrong she had been about his looks. The poor light must have been what made him seem so awful, so old and haggard. She saw a relatively young man – not a youth, a man in his prime – but still a lot younger than she had imagined. The beast in him was there too. In the eyes, the mouth, the teeth that flashed in a teasing smile and the elegant cat-like movements.

She followed him across the yard, watching his tall upright figure with its wide shoulders, seeing him stride confidently through the mud in his deerskin boots. On the doorstep he stopped and waited for her to open the door.

When they entered the kitchen, the women, frightened, got up and went quickly into another part of the house. The farmhand moved to the other end of the room. Only

Benedikt remained unaffected by their entrance – although Silje did notice an odd guarded formality about him.

'Well?' asked Benedikt. 'What is the verdict?'

'The girl will be well,' Silje beamed. 'But he wants to see Dag also.'

Benedikt shouted for Grete to bring the boy.

From the other room her muttered protest could be heard, 'He has not been baptised yet!'

The imposing man from the wilderness answered her, 'Silje said words of baptism when she found him and that is enough for now.'

'Of course it is,' said Benedikt. 'Grete, remind me that we must fetch a priest to the children as soon as we can. We have neglected their souls for too long already.' His voice was high-pitched in a strange way that Silje hadn't heard before.

Grete appeared at the door. 'Yes, Master Benedikt,' she said accusingly, 'and what if they had died? Their poor souls would have gone to …'

Grete went quiet, casting a timid glance at their visitor. Then she disappeared again and returned with the boy, but refused to cross the threshold into the kitchen. Silje took him and placed him in the man's arms. He gave her a strange melancholy look and said, 'You have a trusting soul and for that I shall do my best. But I need to be alone with him.'

As they left the room Silje looked quickly over her shoulder. It was touching to see this man-beast, large and brooding, holding a tiny human figure in his arms. The boy was almost invisible. Then he looked up at the man through sleepy half-closed eyes and let out a scream. Silje began to wonder if she had done something terribly wrong, but the child was soon quiet again.

Benedikt, Silje and the farmhand waited in the porch silently, not looking at one another. When the man came out to them, he handed the infant to Benedikt, saying, 'New lives will protect themselves. The pestilence does not settle easily on them.'

He said nothing else. Silje followed him into the yard, believing this was what he wanted, since he had given the infant to Benedikt and not to her.

'I know who you are!' she said suddenly.

'You do?' His expression showed amusement and some scepticism.

'Yes, but I shall never betray you. You will always be able to trust me as you would a friend. If ever you should need my help – but you wouldn't, of course.'

His tone became serious. 'You know, Silje, one day I may very well need your help. I believe you understand why I live apart, alone, and how few people I can rely on.'

She nodded eagerly, full of devotion and understanding. His face creased in a smile.

'Are you happy here?'

'Oh, yes! I couldn't wish for better. Thank you for sending me here and thank you for … well, everything!'

His hand moved gently back and forth in the air, a gesture that could have meant many things. It was as though he was chuckling to himself.

'Silje, Silje,' he said slowly, 'you are but a child. But now you are looking much better, and not such a scrawny creature – more like the flower in bud that you truly are. If you should need me again, do not wait to send word.'

With that, he mounted his horse and was soon gone.

Silje stood still, a puzzled look on her face. 'Again?' What had he meant by that? She went back inside to Sol and was surprised to find Marie with her. She had caught sight of a shadow crossing the yard, but had been too engrossed in their visitor to think more about it. Looking ashamed, the woman got up from the floor where she had been crouching beside the child's bed, mumbling an apology as she stood up and left.

Sol was sleeping comfortably and, although she still had bright feverish colour in her cheeks, there was sweat at her temples, matting her hair. The fever was breaking!

Silje was curious to know what Marie had been doing. She leaned forward to Sol and, as she put her weight on the bed, noticed at once that it rocked very slightly. There was something under one of the legs; a coin in fact had been placed there – a silver coin marked with a cross. Silje knew that this was intended as protection from all devils. After a moment's hesitation, she let it remain where it was.

Without her wishing it, her thoughts that evening kept returning to her recent dream and her imagination took over again. If she hadn't woken when she had, what would have happened? Why hadn't she dreamt that it was Heming who was coming for her? Why had the beast-man awakened her slumbering womanhood? She had wanted it to be Heming – yes, she had. If only she could dream the same dream again, but this time with another – she was almost afraid to think the word – with another lover!

As soon as she had admitted the thought to herself, a fire began to rage within her. Heming's image had faded. He was not the one she could see and Silje buried her face in the pillow, moaning helplessly.

When she awoke next morning the first thing she noticed was that her foot no longer ached or stung as much as it had. Over in her bed, Sol was wide awake and wanting to get up.

'No, no, my little one,' said Silje. 'You need to stay in

bed today – you don't heal that quickly – but I will be here with you all the time.'

Silje noticed that her feelings towards the mountains seemed to have changed. Several times she had found herself looking expectantly up at them, as though hoping that, from above the broken mass of granite, those awful creatures would appear, led by their master. Then straight away she felt ashamed at having such daring and childish thoughts.

A day or so later Sol was out of danger and Silje was able to go back to the church. She was working alongside Benedikt now, but he no longer allowed her to paint human figures.

'Nobody knows what you might get up to!' he had said.

They worked quietly and thoughtfully together for a long time, then Silje said, 'He has the power to heal, doesn't he?'

Benedikt, working high under the vault of the ceiling, realised at once whom she meant.

'Indeed he does!'

'Then why is he not better known?'

'One calls upon him only when all else fails.'

'And is that because he must remain in hiding,' she persisted.

'You could say that. He seldom shows himself. I have seen him no more than a couple of times in my life, but he seems to trust me, for some reason. It is strange that he should turn up so often of late. No doubt he has his reasons.'

'How old is he? I've often wondered.'

'And I! He is of every age and yet none at all; exactly the age he wants to be at any moment, it would seem.'

'He told me that he came here to the church.'

'Yes. He asked if all was well at the farm and when I told him of our sick little girl, he returned with me.' Benedikt hesitated for a moment, and then continued decisively, 'He has taken a liking to you, Silje. Be very grateful for that – but be very cautious as well.'

'But why?'

'Don't make this difficult for me,' he begged.

'Please, I would like to know.'

Quiet but determined, she waited for his answer.

'Ah!' exclaimed Benedikt, throwing his arms wide, causing a few drops of turquoise paint to fall on the church floor. 'Wipe that up, Silje. Uh! Well, I would not want to be his enemy – that's all. You will have to learn to tread a fine line.'

'The soldiers are his enemies,' she said with a smile, not taking in his full meaning. 'I expect they have felt his wrath?'

An absent-minded Benedikt answered, 'Ah, yes! Yes indeed. That they most surely have.'

****

In an impressive nobleman's residence in Trondheim, Charlotte Meiden lay awake for the fifth night in succession. It had only been in the hour or two before dawn that she had succeeded in getting some troubled and fitful sleep.

Her heart was as heavy as a stone; her eyes wide and dry. Her empty gaze took in the room, which she kept constantly lit by a single candle because, of late, she had become so afraid of the dark. Her cherished old pieces of furniture were still there, but she no longer noticed them. The sideboard was the work of a French cabinet-maker, the armchairs from Spain always reminded her of the Inquisition, and there were the most beautiful tapestries. Yet none of these seemed to matter any more.

Confused, her thoughts were of the spring, when the air would be warmer. Spring would soon arrive – after Yuletide – and everything would be much better. Nobody would be cold any more.

Her parents were deeply troubled. They no longer understood her or her irritable manner. Her refusal to travel outside the town to visit friends and relatives on the estate and get some fresh country air left them at a loss. Charlotte's uncontrollable outbursts when her older sister came to visit, bringing her young offspring, could not be explained. The children seemed to upset her beyond measure and she would lock herself in her room, refusing to come out as long as they were there.

How had she become so wayward, she who grew up so cheerful and full of life? Their youngest daughter had always been light-hearted, almost frivolous at times – perhaps sometimes even superficial – but she had great charm and was blessed with a quick wit. Being in Charlotte's company had always lifted the spirits, even though she may not have been graced with the best of looks.

Now, though? It should be said that she had not been her usual self for quite some while – more than six months, certainly. She had seemed strange and overwrought. Now she was simply impossible!

Charlotte stared at the lightening shape of the window. She could feel everything continuing to build up within her and threatening to burst forth, no matter how much she tried to withstand it.

'If only I had gone out again that same night.' This was the thought that kept creeping up on her, burrowing inside her, and she was helpless against it. 'Or the morning after ... you can't get out at night ... or the next evening ... or the morning after that. I nearly did once! Put it off, though – afraid, indecisive, uncertain – perhaps things would have been all right then. Now it's too late!'

Oh, dear God! The thought kept returning, no matter how she tried to suppress it.

'Too late! Too late! Too late!'

She took a deep breath and tensed every muscle in her body, as she lay trying to fight the rising hysteria, but the tide of emotion could not be stopped – it had been held back for too long. Thirteen days had passed. Nobody on earth could put up with this torment for thirteen days!

In her mind she saw the tiny bundle beneath the pine tree, the covers soaking wet and starting to rot, and inside them … motionless, unmoving. No more cries – quite still!

From deep within, a desperate tide began to engulf Charlotte, rising up to her throat. Now she screamed out her agony, her hopelessness and her despair – all the emotions that had slowly grown ever more powerful since she had set the baby down and walked away, thinking she was free. No – it had begun even before that – while she was still carrying the small life in her arms through the streets of the town.

A completely uncontrolled fit of crying, heart-rending and unstoppable, racked her body. Her lady's maid, filled with horror, a nightcap pulled over her plaited hair and with only a shawl covering her nightgown, rushed in. She had never heard anyone sobbing in such complete desperation.

'Miss Charlotte! What is it? What's wrong?'

The anguished crying would not stop. It could be heard throughout the house.

'What shall I do?' The maid was completely at a loss. 'Shall I fetch Her Ladyship?'

'No! No!' sobbed Charlotte.

'But what is the matter? Are you unwell, Miss Charlotte?'

The answer may have sounded like, 'No, not at all,' but it could have been anything.

The maid, who had always kept a dignified respectful distance from her mistress, perched hesitantly and anxiously on the edge of the bed. Charlotte sat up at once and threw her arms around her.

'Help me! Oh, help me!'

'What is it?' the maid asked awkwardly, forcing herself to remain sitting. Such intimacy was not something she approved of.

Charlotte, who had wanted to ask her to go out into the forest and look for the baby, sensed the maid's unease and the request remained unspoken. The fit of crying continued unabated.

'Its too late! Much too late! Oh! Dear God, please turn back time, turn it back.' Her cry echoed round the room.

If only time could be turned back, she thought – if only she could acknowledge the child, hold it, keep it warm and take all the disgrace, the contempt and social banishment that would surely follow.

At that moment the door opened and her parents entered, while many curious faces waited outside.

'My dear child!' said her mother. 'What is going on? Have you had a nightmare?'

'Oh, how I pray to God that it were a nightmare,' sobbed Charlotte, catching her breath so that nobody understood what she had said. The mother and the maid changed places, one of them relieved, the other unaccustomed to the situation.

'What has happened, Elspeth?' the mother asked quietly.

'I don't know,' answered the maid. 'All she will say is that it is too late.'

'Too late, Charlotte? Too late to find a husband, do you mean? That's silly, you are only twenty-five!'

'No! No! I do not want to marry,' Charlotte yelled. 'Never! Never! Never!'

Her mother was perplexed. 'You spend too much time indoors, my dear. Tomorrow we shall take a walk in the woods. That will ...'

These words brought forth a mindless scream of terror from Charlotte. Her arms and legs flailed wildly about as she gasped for air, until finally she fell back, helpless and without hope, onto the beautifully embroidered pillow.

'Shall we send for the healer to bleed her?' asked her father. 'Perhaps her blood needs to be purified from evil spirits.'

'No,' gasped Charlotte, exhausted. 'It is over now. It was merely a nightmare.'

Worried and concerned, the others finally left the room, but Charlotte could hear her mother's voice in the corridor, 'It's nothing but the sort of fit that ladies suffer. It'll soon be over.'

Charlotte herself, though, knew that nothing would ever be over, except her outburst. She had come to understand that her whole life would be filled with the aching regret she now felt. It would become a festering sore in her heart and these thoughts would continue to gnaw at her, entering her lonely night-time hours with the pitter-patter of a tiny child's feet.

Chapter 5

In the time that followed, Silje was allowed to work at the church three days each week. Benedikt would have preferred having her there every day, because people had begun to pester him, asking if the work would soon be finished. He raged about the 'ignorant, uncultured barbarians' who didn't understand that 'an artist cannot work under pressure'.

Silje wanted to spend time with the children as well, so that she did not become distant from them and also because she felt she ought to help the old women in and around the farm. Nonetheless, they had chosen a child each and were only too pleased to see her leave for the church.

'Poor old maids,' said Benedikt. 'This is like a second spring for them.'

'But still, Sol can be very tiring,' she replied, concern in her voice. 'They are not my children, but I am fond of them and well, yes …' She was a little sad that she took so little care of Dag. Grete had taken possession of him and, while she was always friendly towards her, Silje noticed how she guarded him jealously and kept a watchful eye on her, if ever she was permitted to tend to him.

'Leave them to it,' laughed Benedikt. 'This church will be finished soon enough anyway.'

'And what then?'

'Then you must return to your share of the chores on the farm. I have been engaged to work some distance away and unfortunately you cannot come with me.'

She didn't reply. A wonderful period in her life would soon be over.

****

'I cannot find the right colour for this tunic,' complained Benedikt one day, suspended just below the ceiling, studying his work and looking as if he was about to break his neck. 'I've got myself stuck, fool that I am. Every colour in the rainbow borders this tunic, so what is there left to choose?'

Silje climbed down from where she was working and looked up at his art with a critical eye.

'Brown,' she said simply.

'Brown? Well yes, you're right. You're a genius.'

'Not at all, but I can see it better from down here.'

He grunted his appreciation, swore lightly because his brush was too hard, then apologised for cursing in church. He had been drinking a little too freely the night before and, whenever this happened, he was always a bit tetchy the following morning. Silje knew his mood by looking at his well-worn velvet cap. When it was pulled down over his forehead, he could stand no loud noises or bright sunlight. When it was perched on the back of his head, feather pointing at the sky, he was his usual self – or he had already had a tot or two! Out of respect, he did not drink in the church, but Silje was well aware that he had something hidden in the trap, because he found excuses to go outside to it every so often.

She climbed back up to her workplace and they painted in silence for a while. Then Benedikt giggled.

'What are you thinking about?' Silje asked.

'A couple of old parishioners were here yesterday looking at our work. They saw your devil over in the alcove and became both shocked and excited by it. They stayed in there for a very long time.'

She blushed. She had not wanted to go and look at the wretched thing since she painted it. Reluctantly and after some thought, she said, 'He – you know who I mean – said he had seen it that time he came here. I didn't like that.'

Benedikt looked decidedly guilty.

'No. It was a … an accident. He happened to go in there and then he asked me about it. I had to say that you were the painter. I couldn't tell a lie, here in the church.'

I'll wager you're lying now, you old fox, Silje thought. You probably couldn't wait to get him here to see it.

Out loud she asked, 'What did he say?'

'Nothing. He seemed thoroughly overwhelmed, taken aback. So I said that we would have to get the girl married off sharply, as she paints such lecherous paintings.'

'Did you really say such a thing?' she moaned. 'What did he say to that?'

'I don't know. He seemed a bit put out I think, but that was probably because I'd said, "We old ones should get her married off", or some such. He did not want to be considered as old as I am. He left a short while later. I believe he was a little hurt that you had painted him as a devil, but what can he expect?'

'Oh, no – he shouldn't have seen it.' Her voice was quiet.

'It was foolish, I must agree,' said Benedikt, 'and I was quite afraid afterwards.' Then, to get away from the subject he added, 'But Silje, you have never told me how it is that you are able to speak so well. You are not from a learned background, are you? We all know that roses grow amongst thorns and on mounds of manure, but you are remarkable. Do you read and write?'

'Just a little. One of the young sons of the manor where I lived spent much of his time with me. He grew attached to me and I became a sort of nursemaid to him, helping to look after him. He wanted me to go everywhere. I was with him when he had tuition as well, and I took the chance to learn all that I could. I was like a wilted plant, Master Benedikt, thirsting for knowledge. I wanted to learn everything! I copied their speech; I borrowed the boy's books – all because I knew that I had been given an opportunity no other girl had been granted. Of course I missed a lot because I was not there all the time, but I managed to get some things into my dullard's brain.'

'Wait! Stop a moment. To embrace learning as you have done requires intelligence. Where did you get that from?'

Silje looked thoughtful. 'My mother knew many things and her father knew how to write. I mean he was a writer; composed writings for other farmers. He carved beautiful things in wood as well.'

'There we have your artistic gift! Thank you, Silje, for explaining several of your riddles to me. What was that?'

They both listened again. Heavy footsteps could be heard from the church tower. Silje looked anxiously at Benedikt; he stared back at her.

'Is this place haunted?' she whispered, and the whispers echoed round the vaults.

'Nonsense!'

They climbed down from their working platforms. Silje had no desire to hang defenceless between heaven and earth while all the spirits of the underworld came marching down from the clock-tower. She resisted the urge to run and hide.

'Who in the world is hiding up there?' whispered Benedikt. He took a step closer to her; she was not sure whether it was to protect her or to be protected by her. They waited in suspense, Silje clenching her hands tightly. With a great creaking sound, the door to the tower opened and a man, gaunt and unshaven, came towards them.

'I am awfully hungry, Benedikt. Have you got a crust to spare?'

'What? So this is where you're hiding! You've scared my apprentice out of her wits.'

'Aha!' Silje thought, she was supposed to be the only one who was frightened, was she?

'Yes, of course we have food, we are always forgetting to eat. Silje, fetch the box!'

She ran to the trap and returned with the box, opening the lid so that the man could help himself. Middle-aged, he was heavily built and wearing typical peasant clothes. His eyes were piercing, though, and it was clear that he was no usual peasant. His tunic was modern and his legs were clad in knitted hose.

'I need enough for two,' he said, taking plenty.

'Is there someone else with you, then?' asked Benedikt.

'Oh yes! Heming is up there fretting.'

'Fretting!' said Silje, dismayed that a sudden blush would give away her feelings.

The man laughed. 'Yes! He hasn't had a woman for three weeks, so he's in a bad way. Why don't you go up to him, girl – I mean with food, of course!'

'No – don't let Silje anywhere close to that blackguard,' said Benedikt, quickly. 'She finds him interesting.'

'Oh, I'll be able to take care of myself,' retorted Silje at once.

She desperately wanted to see her hero again, even

though the gossip about the women irritated her. Of course she didn't really believe all the talk. A young man such as he, so good-looking and clean-cut, could never be other than noble and courteous to women. She hoped the disparaging remarks were caused by no more than the envy of old men, trying to ruin his reputation.

Although she hadn't seen him since the night she saved him from a fate on the rack, she had not been able to put him out of her mind. Her greatest wish was to see him again, and she had worried a great deal over what had become of him. And now, he was here! Carrying the box, she began to climb up the steep flights of worn steps. Eventually she reached a landing in the tower, where shutters allowed a little daylight to filter in. Above her, she heard sounds of movement, as if someone was trying to hide.

'It's me, Silje,' she said breathlessly. 'I've brought you food.'

'Silje?' He seemed to be trying to remember the name. Her expectant smile died. Could he have forgotten her already? 'Ah yes! The little saviour of men.' She heard his voice and then a hand appeared to help her up the last step. Silje was filled with expectation at seeing him.

'Good heavens, what a sight!' she thought to herself. His clothes were dirty and torn, the blond hair matted, black with dirt and in need of a wash. He was covered in a layer of dust and grime – but his appearance did not seem to bother him at all.

'Silje my sweet angel. You must have been sent from heaven. Have you appointed yourself as my permanent bodyguard?'

She lowered her face, beaming with joy, although she did not like him making fun of her.

'Come on now, eat! Help yourself – there's plenty.'

'What have you got in here?' he asked. looking in the box. He wrinkled his nose. 'Salmon again! Can't peasants ever find anything other than salmon to eat?'

Nevertheless he took all that was there and ate with a hearty appetite, leaving Silje feeling a little offended. The kind-hearted farmhand would bring salmon from the river every day and was always proud of his catch. Although their diet sometimes lacked variety, they were always grateful for any food they received.

Silje herself had not eaten at all, and watched with dismay as the contents of the box disappeared – but Heming needed the food more than she did.

When he had finished eating, he glanced up and for the first time really looked at her. She saw surprised admiration in his eyes and felt a warm glow within herself. Heming, who was well acquainted with the psychology of women, realised at once that he would get nowhere with bravado and jokes. Here stood a serious-minded innocent girl – a virgin he was sure. He'd be amazed if she were not. He'd soon change that when the time was right, but just now he had more important things to worry about – like staying alive.

Heming gave her another glance. Yes, taking this budding young flower and helping it bloom could prove a rewarding experience. Her appearance was appealing and she smelled quite clean, apart from a hint of paint. She had warm brown hair, violet-blue eyes and fresh white teeth behind tempting rosy lips – and she did seem to have quite a passionate nature.

'Sit with me a while, Silje,' he said in a tired voice. 'I feel so weary and I need to talk to somebody sensible.'

She hesitated, then sat slightly apart from him against

the wall, hugging her knees and smoothing her skirt primly down over them. Her instinct told her that this was an awkward situation. She had already saved him from a horrific death, watched him have his face slapped and be called a damned idiot, yet was now coming to his rescue again by bringing food to this sorry-looking bedraggled wretch. Intuitively she realised that she should do something to restore his dignity.

'You, er, you're with the rebels, aren't you?' she was full of shy admiration.

He swallowed the last of the ale they had brought with them for refreshment each day.

'Well, I'm one of their leaders, I suppose,' he said, with deliberate nonchalance.

'Ooh!' her eyes widened, impressed.

This reaction encouraged Heming. He studied his nails indifferently – they were filthy.

'You know what it's like. I get the most dangerous missions. That's how I was taken prisoner that time, risking my life for the others.'

This was not exactly the story her mysterious benefactor had told her. He had implied that it had more to do with a heedless visit to a woman, but that was not something Silje wanted to remember.

'Your master is a powerful man, isn't he?' she said absently. 'He came to help me again when the little girl was struck by plague. I do not know what he did, but he cured her and healed my foot of frostbite. His hands were like fire.'

Heming stared at her.

'Who? Oh, you mean *him*! You're wrong,' he exclaimed belligerently. 'He is not my master, I don't know him and I've never met him!'

Silje understood now that perhaps she had gone too far.

No one was supposed to speak of Dyre Alvsson, the rebel leader. One slip of the tongue could send him into the arms of the bailiff's men. Better that he did not exist. She had forgotten for a moment and wasn't surprised that Heming had been angry.

'Was he alone with you?' he whispered – a strange question, since he had virtually denied the man.

'Of course!'

Heming made the sign of the cross, hastily and carelessly.

'You are mad – mad! Did you have salt and bread with you?'

'What are you talking about?'

'Sprinkle salt; that helps. Salt and bread! And the little girl – you are a heathen! How could you? Did you make the sign of the cross above her? Do you have a silver coin with a cross on?'

Silje's expression had frozen.

'Marie, one of the women on the farm, placed such a coin beneath Sol's bed.'

He relaxed with a sigh.

'Oh, thank God, then things should be all right. The infant? What about the infant?'

How kind of him to show such interest in the little ones! Silje was still unable to take her eyes off him. He was so attractive, his well-formed features so perfect, that she felt a rush of joy just watching him.

'Little Dag is well, thank you – almost too well, because Grete spoils him and feeds him too much. I am almost never allowed to see him.'

'You are taking good care of the blankets he was wrapped in, aren't you?'

'Oh yes! *He* said that ...'

Silje stopped short – she had mentioned Dyre Alvsson again.

'Are you sure no one can take them from you? They are valuable – you know?'

'No, no one can take them.'

'You have hidden them well?'

'Yes, in the chest under my bed.'

'I hope they will be safe there. I must leave now, Silje. Many thanks for the food. Will I see you again?'

She blushed. 'If you want to.'

Heming got up and went to her, putting his hand under her chin. He was very close.

'You're very pretty, Silje. You know that, don't you?'

She averted her eyes and shook her head. Her pulse was racing, the blood pounding in her ears, rushing to her cheeks.

'Oh, but you are. May I come and call on you?'

Silje looked terrified.

He smiled, 'For the most honourable of reasons, of course. I only want to make pleasant conversation with you. You're so sensible.'

No matter how she racked her brain later, she could not remember saying anything intelligent at that point. A jumble of mindless exclamations was all she could manage.

'I won't be able to come for some time. We are being hunted and must stay away. It's a lonely life, believe me, but as soon as the soldiers start searching elsewhere, I'll return.'

The touch of his hand on her chin felt strange. No man had ever touched her like that. She had suffered several attempts of rape, of course but, because she had been determined to defend her virtue until the right man came along, she had reacted with spirit and was always left unscathed. Heming's hand did not bring forth the burning excitement that another's touch had done when it had held her foot – such a gentle strong hand – but that was different; *he* had been healing her. But why, oh why, should she think of *that* man right now? *Heming* was the one touching her, his wonderful blue eyes looking into hers, a melancholy, almost sad smile on his face. Poor boy, having to live on the run and so unhappy!

'Of course you may come and visit me at Master Benedikt's,' she said in a throaty voice. ' I shall ask them to prepare a wonderful meal in your honour.'

'No – no!' he whispered. 'No one must know. There are traitors everywhere.'

Then Benedikt began calling from below in the nave, so they made their way back down the steps.

'I thought you'd started to grow roots up there, Silje,' said the painter, giving her an inquisitive look.

Her answer was a beaming, deeply embarrassed grin, which seemed to depress him.

'You look like a cat that got the cream,' he said bitterly.

Silje sniffed back a tear.

'Now you're being unkind, Master Benedikt!'

The two men melted away from the church to pursue their lawless exploits, leaving the painters to return to their work.

Suddenly Benedikt said,' You have many fine qualities, Silje, but you seem to lack a sense of humour.'

She thought about this. 'Perhaps you're right,' she admitted. 'I used to enjoy a joke. I'd see the funny side of almost everything. But it was only a few weeks ago that I lost all my loved ones, so I find it hard to laugh and my sense of humour has died.'

'Of course, my dear girl,' he said, regret in his voice. 'I didn't think of that. It must seem as though I only think of my own sorrow. Happiness will return to you, you'll see. But – well, you need to be a little careful when it comes to that young man.'

'I cannot be sure,' she answered, 'but I don't think he's as bad as people say. Maybe he's just unhappy. He seems gentle and pleasant, and very understanding.'

'Yes,' sighed Benedikt. 'That's exactly why you should be careful.'

****

The work at the church came to an end and Silje returned to her chores on the farm. But she did so reluctantly.

There are those who believe that people have three special powers within themselves: the power to create, the power to preserve and the power to destroy. There are those people who are the perfect embodiment of one of these powers and there are professions that also use only one of them. The work of the housewife is one that embodies preserving and maintaining things as they are. Poor Silje had almost none of this excellent quality. Naturally she carried out all her tasks, dutifully and properly, but she felt nothing for the work. She had tasted the thrill of creating as an artist and knew that was where her future lay. Nothing else would do. She was not a great artist, but the fire was there, the same fire that had tormented and inspired artists since the dawn of time.

Because she was unhappy doing the chores around the farm, she tended to demand even more of herself. She hated seeing a beautifully prepared table reduced to waste after a few minutes' eating, or an elegantly decorated dessert just disappear. She loathed the sight of the scrubbed kitchen sideboard, weighed down with pots and pans yet again and knowing all the time that this would happen over and over and over. Continually repeating the same kind of work in the house, the barns and the stables tormented her more than she dared to say. A creative person will usually do something once only and then never again. Repetition takes away some of the power, the driving force. Baking a cake or knitting a colourful garment every now and then was not enough, yet these were almost the only creative works any housewife was allowed to do.

Silje knew that she would have to force herself to do her daily chores. If she relaxed for a moment, she would soon stop tidying and cleaning, downhearted because she would be doing it all over again in no time at all. She could easily become trapped in daydreams once more and she didn't want to let that happen here, with these warm-hearted people. She remembered the many times she had been called lazy – and that was how most people regarded the creative artists and dreamers of the world.

Benedikt, though, had understood her.

'You have an artist's blood in your veins, Silje', he said one day, 'even though I doubt that painting is your forte and that your strengths lie elsewhere. You just haven't found your path yet. It's unfortunate that you were born a girl, because there will be little opportunity for you ever to do so.'

Silently she railed at this. It would have been more unfortunate to be born a boy. Young girls' dreams, like her dream of Heming, were far too sweet to be missed.

Benedikt continued, 'You'll have to marry money and have lots of servants, and then you can create as much art as you like – either in secret or for the world to see, it doesn't matter. Yes, a good marriage is the best you can hope for.'

As soon as he had uttered these words, a sadness about the reality of what he had advised came over him.

Silje had smiled, saying that she doubted that she would find a wealthy husband. However, she had promised him that she would do her share of the work, so long as she was with them at the farm.

There was one good thing about being there all day – she could spend far more time with Sol and Dag. They all took turns with the children and it was her job to look after them from time to time, while the others were busy with their own work. She would do small jobs around the house as well, when they did not need her full attention.

She was beginning to understand Sol's unusual way of talking a little better – she was learning new words all the time and speaking more clearly. But the girl was as impetuous and unruly as any wild animal. Her green eyes flashed mischievously and she could be as stubborn as a mule when she set her mind to it. Sometimes, too, she would get a faraway look in her eyes that frightened Silje. What was the girl thinking then? What was it she could see?

Dag was growing fast; his little body still swaddled tightly every morning by Grete, as was the fashion. Later in the day, Silje would loosen his clothes and then he would stop crying so much. His hair was blond, but he was still too young to show his own personality. Silje loved this young infant she had found abandoned in the forest on that strange night not so long ago.

The routine and pace of life was the same, day after day. Now it was winter, folk stayed in bed until five o'clock in the morning before rising to rake the fire in the hearth back to life, finding their way around with the light from a taper, held firmly between the teeth. Then followed a breakfast of bread and ale, sometimes with some salmon or salted herring. By about ten, the work in the barn and stables would be completed and they ate the midday meal. Hard work continued for the rest of the day until four or five o'clock when they sat down to the evening meal. They were all in their beds by nine.

****

The winter days wore on. When the time came for the slaughter of animals in preparation for Yuletide, Silje escaped to the forest – she could not face being present when that happened. It would mean the end for many of those animals she had cared for fondly and had come to know. It was all too much, so she took Sol with her and wandered unhappily about over the bare frozen forest floor each day until the difficult time had passed and they could return, safe but sad.

On one occasion, while making her way between the snow-covered pines, she had stopped – suddenly a little uneasy. Sol looked up at her, questioning. They were in the heights above Benedikt's farm, in an area they had not explored before. Silje stood looking around, unmoving, for a considerable time, and then carried on walking.

'It was nothing,' she said quietly.

There was something, though. She couldn't say what it was. A sound – a feeling that someone was close by – her own imagination, perhaps? Probably just an elk. She knew that there were no predatory animals in the area this winter, otherwise she would never have dared venture out with the little girl.

Benedikt was away for several days at a time, staying in a distant parish. He drank much more than before and no longer seemed as happy.

'I wish you could be with me, Silje, he told her on one occasion, 'We had great fun, didn't we?'

'Yes, it was incredible,' she agreed.

'But in the church I'm now working on, it's not possible. I'm staying in a terrible little hovel, and you could never share it with me.'

Of course, she understood.

Benedikt let out a sigh that came from the very depths of his soul.

Another evening he came to her room, very drunk and in a philosophical frame of mind. Although she had gone to bed, knowing who it was, she had let him in. He was the master of the house, her father figure and a completely unthreatening example of humanity. Besides, she thought he might want to discuss something important with her.

She soon realised that she had done herself no favours. After endless drunken ramblings, which she tried her best to answer while still sitting in her bed, he became emotional and sentimental.

'I'm a lonely man, Silje. Lonely an' old. I need your youthful warmth to comfort me. We undershtand eash oth'r, don' we?'

He sat on the edge of her bed, his face coming nearer to hers. He was close enough for her to see his hazy unfocused eyes and every pore in his leathery skin in the warm light of the fire. He dribbled slightly as he spoke.

'Yes, of course we do,' she muttered. Her knees were pulled up to her chest; her hands clasped round them under the bedcover. 'But perhaps it's best that you ...'

'You are a wonderful woman, Silje! I could see tha' from the shtart in th' church, when you shtood painting. D'ya wan' a drink? S'pose not ... I saw the shape of your breasts – I keep an eye on sush thin's, did y' know that? I can shtill shpot a boot'full woman, an' I knew I weren't all old an' wore out. My breeches can still ge' too tight! Silje!'

'I'm very sorry, Master Benedikt, but we should not

wake the girl and I must be up early in the morning again. Maybe it would be better for us to talk about this then.'

'An' so I shaid to mysel' tha' Silje would be kind t' poor ole man.'

His hand groped for the edge of the bedcover to get under it, but he slid forward and almost fell to the floor. Silje leapt up, feeling very uncomfortable, and led the proud old painter to the door, his hat dangling at a rakish angle somewhere behind one ear.

'Don't forget that we must talk some more about this tomorrow, Master Benedikt. If people see you visiting me this late they may talk. I'm sure I don't want to lose my reputation and I wouldn't want yours to suffer either.'

Benedikt giggled softly. He was a happy soul, not one of those who become belligerent when they are drunk. Meekly, he allowed himself to be shown outside and she shut the door noisily after him.

Silje stood for a while, shocked, with her back against the door, until she heard the sound of his muttering move away and the door to his painting shed finally closed.

The next day he had completely forgotten the whole incident – and he argued loudly with Grete about the presence of footprints in the snow outside his door. Grete assured him that they were his own.

'Oh, yes! I suppose I've been out running errands,' he mumbled. 'That's the trouble with taking a glass or two. What goes in must come out again, at the most inconvenient times!'

Silje breathed a deep sigh of relief.

Chapter 6

The cold dry air of winter had finished off the plague. It needed moisture, warmth and decay to thrive. They heard of an occasional case, but then it disappeared, like the morning mist.

The mountains beyond the farm still had the same strange thrilling hold on Silje, but fear was no longer her overwhelming emotion. Without her knowing it, they had become linked in her mind to one certain person and now, whenever she looked up at them, coy and feeling guilty, she moistened her lips with the tip of her tongue and her heart began to beat faster.

She had no more dreams, strange or otherwise, than anybody else. She had forgotten them almost as soon as she awoke. But there was one forbidden dream, much like that about the spirits from beyond, that did return. It was different, but no less shameful for that, and she awoke from it lying on her back and powerless just as before.

She could not recall how it began, only that she stood between soldiers and bailiffs with weapons drawn. The headsman and his helper were there too. She stood accused, but did not know the charge – only that everyone was raging at her. In desperation, to quench their hatred, she did the only thing she could think of – she started to undress, quickly, garment after garment. In response, they all lowered their weapons, stood and stared at her, expectant, with distorted sweaty faces.

But the bailiff said, 'That will not help you. You are still going to die.'

At that moment, almost as one, the mass of people moved aside and the man in the wolf-skin stood there. Everyone made way for him. Bulls' horns grew from the shaggy hair on his head, his face shone and his eyes burned like fire, even though he tried to hide his lust by half-facing away from her.

Slowly he turned back to look at her nakedness, stretched out his hand towards her and then scooped her up and carried her with him to a hilltop. There, where all could see, he caressed every part of her body – but all she wanted was for him to remove the wolf-skin cape.

He turned her around and stood behind her, exactly like the devil in the church painting, and as everybody looked on, he laid his hands across her breasts. The knowledge that everyone could see this filled her with languid coarse excitement. Yet somehow she knew this was only a dream, and she could abandon herself to her desires, unburdened and free.

She felt his long firm tongue glide slowly over her, licking her neck, her shoulder, her cheek. He turned her round to face him and went down on his knees in front of her, letting his tongue flow over the contours of her thighs, until they were almost paralysed with an overwhelming fiery sensation.

And then she woke – panting quietly, her lips barely parted – her mind in turmoil, moaning with desire and shame, full of despair that she could not hold back the passion, the craving, that raged inside her.

****

As the days passed, Benedikt went to great lengths to bring home a couple of young men from nearby farms because, he said, she needed to meet people of her own age and not spend so much time thinking of Heming. When she muttered that she didn't think of him at all, Benedikt simply laughed and told her that he had seen that pining, brooding look in her eyes again and she should meet nice normal boys.

The boys were indeed nice. Young and awkward, they found it difficult to make conversation, and each tried to outdo the other in polite behaviour. They only succeeded in being clumsy, treading on each other's feet and dropping things. Eventually, when one of them took his courage in both hands and whispered that he would like to pay her a night visit next Saturday, she was taken aback. She knew that such visits were common in rural areas, of course, and that she would have to be fully clothed. In his turn the boy was allowed to lie on her bed beside her, also fully clothed except for his shoes.

Although it was all done properly and decently. Silje, had never had a 'night-suitor' before, and felt neither inclined nor ready to receive one. So she signalled to Benedikt for help and, with great understanding, he ushered the boys out, admitting that it had not been a successful experiment.

Then Heming arrived. He came one day while Benedikt was away and the farmhand had taken Grete and Marie in the trap to visit friends. They had asked Silje if they might take the children, their pride, and she had agreed.

The soft knock at the door made her jump, but on hearing that he was there, she opened it at once.

'Welcome. Come in, come in!' she said, her face lighting up. He bent forward slightly and stepped through the low doorway.

'What a nice room!' He sounded impressed. 'Heather, growing in a pot. It's so inviting and homely. Did you weave that rug? And you've done some wood carving as well? You really do have artistic talent, Silje.'

She smiled, blushing. To call that little woven square a rug was exaggerating, she thought, and although she had decorated everywhere she could, it was no more than anyone else would have done.

'Will you not sit? The farmhand will be returning soon, so we will be chaperoned. I don't want to deceive Master Benedikt.'

'Unfortunately I cannot stay for long, Silje my little one, so your honour will be spared – this time at least! I'll be back in a few days, though.' He laughed lightly. 'No, I spoke in jest – I am a gentleman and I did not mean that. But I am very thirsty and would be grateful if you could offer me some ale.'

'I shall fetch some at once,' she said eagerly, and ran to the main house as though she had wings on her feet, returning with a brimming quart-pot.

He was sitting at the table and she saw that he was elegantly dressed this time. Was he going to visit some of his more distinguished friends, perhaps? Of one thing she was sure: Heming was not of ignoble birth.

She sat down opposite him and asked shyly, 'May I ask an impertinent question?'

'Ask what you will!' he replied, looking at her with a twinkle in his eye. 'But this I tell you at once – that I am not wed, that I love you madly, that I shall keep myself only for you.'

'Please do not toy with me.' She was desperately embarrassed. 'I just want to know why they call you the "bailiff-killer".'

He shrugged his shoulders.

'Because that is what I am. It is an old story and the reason I am outlawed. You understand that a man must fight for what he believes in, and I fight for a free Norway. But you must not think that I lay in ambush and attacked him from behind. No, it was him or me – and I won.'

Silje nodded. She felt light-headed. 'Was it not – horrible?'

'Yes, wager your life that it was!'

'And you are now Dyre Alvsson's right-hand man?'

There was reverence and admiration in her voice.

'You could say so,' he answered indifferently, but she could tell that he was proud of the fact. This time he hadn't denied his leader's existence either. Silje took this as a good omen. He was beginning to have confidence in her.

'And the royal scroll, the letter, with its seal and everything? How did you come by that?'

'You have asked me that before, Silje dear girl. But as you will – it was my first exploit with the rebels. We needed such a scroll. A courier came riding through … well, we had our scroll.'

'And the courier?'

'He is no more. But I must tell you that we have had good use from that letter, indeed we have.'

Silje took a deep breath to stave off the feeling of nausea. Smiling faintly, Heming leaned back with his arm stretched along the backrest of the bench.

'You see, Silje, I am quite important to the rebel movement, for many reasons that I cannot disclose here.'

'No, I understand.'

He drank the rest of his ale and stood up.

'Do you not wish for something to eat?' She wanted him to stay. 'I can fetch some food.'

'No, not now. My time is short. But I will come back soon – very soon.'

The last words were a whisper and before she realised what was happening, he had kissed her, quickly and gently. Then he was gone.

Silje stood running her fingers over her lips, dazed. He had kissed her! The most beautiful man in the whole world had kissed *her*, Silje Arngrimsdotter, a worthless peasant girl! Hadn't he behaved impeccably! Of course it was not proper for her to take a man into her room, but from Heming she had nothing to fear. He had told her himself that he was a gentleman – and he was!

Still, for some reason, the episode had left her feeling uneasy. She had not liked what he told her, even less the manner in which he told it – but he was so young that one should try to make allowances. She turned to look out of the window and her leg scraped on the hard edge of something. With a squeal of pain, she bent down to see what it was. The chest? It was carelessly pushed under the bed, so that one corner jutted out – but she knew that she had not touched it herself in a long while.

She heaved the chest out and opened it. There lay her apron, her jacket and … her hands shook. Her heart sank. The blanket and clothes in which Dag had been wrapped when she found him – each and every one was gone. Heming's wide cloak would have concealed them well. So this was why he had seemed concerned, asking her diligently if she had taken care in hiding them securely. She had walked straight into his trap and told him exactly where they lay, safely in the chest under her bed. Interested in the children's welfare? Not him!

Sadness and disappointment welled up inside her. No, it couldn't be true, it couldn't! She rushed out of the door. She could still see him on his horse, galloping down the road from the farm – he had almost reached the country highway. Silje, in complete despair, lost all self-control and ran blindly after him.

'Wait!' she cried, but her weak voice was lost across the snow-covered fields and pastures. 'Wait! Please!'

She ran the whole way down to the highway, but by then he had long disappeared in the direction of Trondheim. She carried on, not stopping to consider how pointless it was to follow him – consumed with rage and disappointment that Dag had lost the only things he had owned in his short life.

'At least bring back the shawl!' she shouted at the empty road, sobbing pitifully. 'It's so beautiful and it's his! How could you steal from a child?'

Some time ago, she and the others on the farm had examined all Dag's things. The linen, which turned out to be a pillowcase, was daintily embroidered with a swirled pattern. Benedikt was sure that he could make out the letters 'C.M.' in the artistically interwoven coils and loops. Above them was woven a crown that Benedikt said was a baronial motif.

Only when she had reached the end of the open fields and faced the great pine forest did she waken from her pain-filled disappointment over Heming. The highway suddenly fell into the shadow cast by the craggy tops of the dark mountains. They seemed so brooding, almost overpowering, and she found her mind turning to the myths of the Ice People, as the stories came flooding back to her.

She recalled what Benedikt had told her once about the madman, Tengel, who had kept watch over the people of the valley from these very peaks, using his powers of sorcery and magic to bring misfortune to all those who had driven him from his land and his home. He was only capable of evil deeds but, in return for those services he performed for Satan, he was rewarded with great personal wealth. Benedikt tried to explain, in an obscure way, that even though he may not have become immortal, he had become a sort of wraith-like presence in the spirit world.

Silje was sure that it was the evil shadow of Tengel that engulfed the highway – and that he was sitting up above her on the mountaintop watching her, with a demonic smile on his lips. With great effort she shook off her fearful imaginings and, although her pace had slowed, she continued resolutely and hopelessly northwards, her breathing heavy and her knees giving way. How could she ever explain this to Dag if, one day, he were to ask what had happened? She had to get all his covers back – or at the very least his wonderful gold-embroidered shawl.

Very quickly the forest closed in around her. Yet some instinct drove her on and her thoughts continued to whirl in her head. Heming! How could he? Deceiving her like that – and to kiss her as well! 'I'll come back soon.' She wouldn't wait for that to happen. He certainly would not show his face again – but if he did, well she would kick him out herself. Tears of bitterness and humiliation rolled down her face, the chill almost turning them to ice on her cheeks. No matter how many times she wiped them away, there were always more.

Dusk had crept up on her, she realised suddenly – the slowly changing daylight had been deceptive. But she still continued her meaningless trek. Then she heard the sound of horses' hooves in front of her. Looking up, she dried her eyes once again to see more clearly. Had he felt a pang of remorse? A glimmer of hope began to glow inside her.

But it was not Heming. With a start, she saw it was his leader and master, the one whose existence he had denied, the one whose name had caused him to cross himself, the one everybody feared. It was the man who had helped Silje before – and he had never been far from her thoughts no matter how hard she tried to be rid of them. She had met him only twice and briefly, yet still he pursued her even into the most secret of her dreams.

He reigned in his horse. Silje ran and grasped the saddle.

'He took it!' she sobbed. 'He took everything!'

The man sat tense, 'What has he taken?'

'The only things that Dag truly owns – inherited from his mother. The fine shawl and the other covers that he was found wrapped in. Those you bade me look after. He deceived me, tricked me into leaving the room and stole them. What am I to do? They belong to Dag!'

Exhausted, she rested her head against his thigh; even through the thick winter clothes she could feel his warmth. Did she imagine that he had relaxed slightly when she mentioned Dag's things? What had he been expecting her to say?

He looked down at her thin neck, saw how her shoulders shook with resigned sobbing, and for one moment he held his hand above her head, as if to stroke her hair then, changing his mind, withdrew it.

She thought she heard him chuckle and raised her head. He leant over his saddlebag.

'I have them here, Silje. I met Heming on the highway and made him give them to me.'

He lifted the covers out to show her, all three of them.

Her face was a study in contradictions, streaming with tears and beaming with delight. 'You have them! Yes, these are the ones!'

Then her smile faded, replaced with worry. What if he wanted to keep them?

He looked at her and shook his head, as if he had read her thoughts.

'They are yours,' he said. 'You must look after them for Dag. Just lock them away more securely in future. Now climb up here with me and we'll ride back to Benedikt's farm.'

He helped her up in front of him, seating her side-saddle, as was proper for a young lady.

'Why are you out on such a cold winter's day and not wearing warm clothes?' he asked in his deep, throaty voice. 'Bareheaded, no hood. You are fortunate that it isn't too cold. There, my wolf-skin cloak covers us both. You can take Dag's shawl to cover your head.'

She protested, strangely disturbed by his closeness. 'I couldn't do that, it's much too nice.'

'Not for you, my young friend. I cannot think of anyone more worthy of it.'

He drew the thinly woven shawl around her head and shoulders properly, and she was surprised at how much it warmed her. She realised her ears had become painfully cold. With a flourish, he swept his cloak around her and she felt cosy and secure, sharing the warmth of his body.

She asked timidly, 'May I ... er, hold on to you, sire?'

'I really believe you should,' he grinned, 'or you will likely fall off.'

Carefully and anxiously she placed her arm around him and grasped the back of his shirt. She could tell he was well-built and muscular, but she knew that above her hand were those unnaturally powerful, brooding shoulders. At first she tried to keep a distance between them, but it proved impossible and, with a sigh of relief and pleasure, she rested her head on his shoulder. She felt his jaw against her temple and breathed in the warmth of his neck.

'Are things so bad for him that he must steal a sad child's clothes?' she asked angrily after a while.

'Dear Silje, have you not yet understood?' said the man, his voice vibrating against her cheek. 'Benedikt told me of the crest with the letters "C.M." – and the infant was found close by the town gates, so it would not have taken much effort for Heming to discover the name of Dag's mother. He would almost certainly have blackmailed her, perhaps for many years. I can't believe he would ever have handed over the garments – which in themselves don't have a great deal of value.'

'How underhand!' gasped Silje. 'To think of taking advantage of that poor woman's circumstances in such a way! Did he know about the letters "C.M."?'

'Not exactly, but he knew that one item had an embroidered motif. I suspect he was going to examine them in private.'

Silje wriggled herself back into a comfortable position – it was easy to slide off the saddle.

'I know I've condemned Dag's mother many times for abandoning her defenceless child, but should I have judged her so harshly? What do I know of her reasons?'

The man stayed silent. It was warm and comforting for her beneath the wolf-skin; only the tip of her nose was visible. Then, to her dismay, she became aware of another warmth beginning to glow within her and pulled away from him slightly. He didn't appear to notice – he had been quiet for a long time. She felt the beat of his heart against her shoulder – fast and strong.

'How did you find Heming?' she asked. 'I mean, did he tell you that he had taken Dag's things?'

'That is not important now, Silje. Anyway, tell me how things are with you.'

Silje was acutely aware that her hand was resting on his chest, of the warmth tormenting her body and the rhythmic movement of the horse, but she managed to answer him, truthfully, that she was very happy living on Benedikt's farm.

'But you would really like to paint with him again, wouldn't you?'

'Why, yes. How did you know?'

'He told me so himself.'

'Oh, so the two of you do meet to talk.'

'Yes, sometimes.'

Silje let his words sink in. 'May I ask you one thing? Where do you live, that is when you don't need to stay hidden?'

He laughed. 'When I do need to stay hidden, I live in an abandoned cottage up in the forest.' He pointed in the general direction.

She frowned slightly. 'I walked up there not long ago. I must have been quite close.'

'I know. I saw you with the little girl.'

'Aha, then it was you who … you were close by. Were you watching us?'

'Did you sense that?' he asked. 'I saw you stop and look about.'

'Yes, I did. Why could you not let me know you were there?'

'Because I did not want to disturb you.'

'It would have made me happy,' said Silje.

He drew a sudden deep breath, almost as though he had

been in pain. He forced himself to speak with a normal voice.

'You were distressed at that time, weren't you?'

'Yes, because of the Yuletide butchery. I was sorry for the animals.'

She felt his head move as he nodded silently, seeming to understand. Then softly, he asked, 'You are not afraid of me, then?'

'No, why should I be?'

'Has nobody told you?'

'Ah, I've seen their foolish reactions. They simply do not understand. Why should there be something wrong, just because you have healing powers?'

He threw back his head impatiently.

'My dear child! Healing powers? Silje, whatever you do, you must never, never tell another soul that you know me. It could mean your death! Believe me, I am a dangerous friend to have – no one, no one at all wants to admit they know me. You yourself have more learning than is usual for someone from a peasant family, and Benedikt has explained to me why this is so. Hide your knowledge, Silje. Only a few years past a woman was burned at the stake as a witch because she had more book learning than most.'

Her reply was almost a whisper, 'There is so much evil around us.'

'Yes, and the worst of it is that so much of this ignorant evil comes from those who should show mercy and understanding – the clergy. In their determination to rid the world of Satan and his misdeeds, they have committed insufferable acts, torturing and killing their victims – equal or worse than the deeds of those they seek to destroy.'

As she listened, Silje realised how much stronger and more mature he was than Heming – and more disquieting!

Changing the subject, she said, 'Heming was certainly elegantly dressed today.'

There was a touch of bitterness in her voice and her companion sniggered, 'Yes, he would be. One of his lovers had generously donated her husband's clothes to him!'

Silje shook her head. 'How on earth could I have found him attractive? I must have been blind.'

The man answered calmly, 'He *is* attractive. That's his greatest asset and he uses it without mercy – and you are very young and inexperienced in the ways of the world. I hope he ...,' he searched for the words, 'didn't take advantage of you?'

'No more than I have told you already. I would never have allowed anything else.'

The rider fell silent, but she could feel against her temple once again that he was smiling. Was he amused by her innocence? No, she thought, the sigh that followed was one of relief – or was he just aching from the ride?

Then, suddenly, the horse stopped. They had reached the farm without her noticing it. The farmhand came outside, but remained at a respectful distance. Silje was disappointed because there were so many things she had wanted to ask, but not had the time. The man dismounted and stretched out his arms to help her down. She happily allowed herself to be embraced by them and for one moment his face was so close to hers that she could look straight into those shimmering green and yellow eyes. What she saw in them left her dismayed. There was sorrow, a deep and painful sadness so great that she felt uncontrollable tears well up in her own eyes. Angrily, she wiped them away.

He placed her gently down and handed her Dag's linens.

'Thank you for your trust,' he whispered, so quickly and quietly that she almost did not hear him. He bade her farewell, remounted the horse and was gone, Silje's eyes following him until he was out of sight. But the pulsating, aching warmth in her body would not subside.

'Have you been out?' asked the farm lad cautiously.

'Yes. Someone stole these and I tried to run after him. Dyre Alvsson helped me.'

The lad frowned. 'Dyre Alvsson?'

At that same moment, Benedikt's wagon drew into the yard and they had other things to talk about. Then, while they were unhitching the wagon, Silje retold her story.

'Dyre Alvsson?' repeated Benedikt, when she had finished. 'But that cannot be! He's not here now, is he? Was he really here?'

The farmhand shook his head in warning. Benedikt understood, and turned to Silje. 'You saw Dyre once in the church. It was he who had been hiding in the tower with Heming. Has he just been here?'

She stood and looked at them in disbelief. 'Was *that* Dyre Alvsson?'

'Of course.'

She considered this for a moment. 'But I thought … so who is the person that was just here? The man I painted as a devil, who always comes when I need him.'

'I know of whom you speak. I met him on the highway and he was looking downhearted. That is never a good sign.' Benedikt took a deep breath and exchanged a glance with the lad. 'How badly do you want to know the truth, Silje?'

'I don't know,' she replied, 'but I want to know who he is. I am tired of vague answers and frightened looks.'

'You should not judge folk for their fear! Do you really want to know the name of your terrifying guardian?'

'Yes – for heaven's sake! Yes!'

'His name,' said Benedikt in a low voice, 'is Tengel – Tengel of the Ice People!'

Chapter 7

Tengel of the Ice People? Icy tendrils of fear snaked down Silje's spine and horror began to creep through her veins. Her mind was filled with memories of all the past remarks and warnings.

'Tengel has no tomb.'
'He is whatever age he chooses to be.'
'He seldom allows himself to be seen.'
'He can manifest himself at will.'
'He sold his soul to Satan.'

'No!' she gasped. 'No – it is not possible!'

'Of course he is not the old Tengel,' Benedikt said quickly, chuckling, trying to reassure her. 'Only superstitious fools still think like that.'

Silje said nothing. She was sure she had detected a tremble of uncertainty in Benedikt's voice. The farmhand, scared almost out of his wits by the bold words of his master, also raised his voice in protest.

'In that case everyone is a fool, Master Benedikt. You know full well that creature has powers that are … unnatural.'

Silje recalled how the man would always come to her aid

when she needed it; how he could sense her mood – whether she was down or sad or angry. He was obviously very perceptive. Then there were his powers of healing, and the heat from his hands. What about the first time she had met him? She was exhausted and ready to die, not thinking clearly, and then suddenly she had been able to perform so well in front of the bailiff's soldiers, managing the almost unimaginable task of freeing the prisoner with such ease. Later, when the man in the wolf-skin had left her, her willpower had died like a spent candle. Perhaps it had not been *her* willpower at all. Above everything, however, were those unbelievably vivid dreams of him as a spirit from beyond, from the Land of Shadows.

Silje let out a small cry and hurried away. She stumbled into her room and threw herself headlong onto the bed, pulling the covers completely over her head and body. She still lay there, curled up like a frightened mouse, when Benedikt and the lad came in.

'Silje,' pleaded the painter, 'you must understand that it is not Tengel himself. It is just one of his descendants.'

To herself she said, 'No, please don't call him that.' She felt the ache of cramps in her stomach. Out loud she demanded, 'Where does he live then?' but her voice was muffled by the covers.

Benedikt shrugged. 'No one knows. He just turns up among humans and then disappears again – never leaves a trace.'

She let out a long wail, not wanting to hear more. Benedikt believes he *is* the old Tengel, she thought to herself. No matter what he says, just like everyone else, he does believe it. He had said 'among humans' – how could it be clearer?'

'Is he not with the rebels?' she asked quickly, almost defensively, as she peeped out from under the covers.

'I wonder about that. I don't know,' replied Benedikt.

'But the night I met him, he rescued Heming!'

'I have never been able to find out how he came to be associated with him.'

'Well, who is Heming, anyway?' she asked, relieved to be talking about someone else.

Benedikt and the lad exchanged searching glances.

'We really don't know,' said Benedikt. 'He arrived here in Tröndelag about two years ago; since then he has been playing fast and loose amongst the womenfolk.'

This observation left her cold. She had no feelings left for Heming now. He was nothing more than an extraordinarily handsome face. But when all was said and done, he had never been more than that to her.

'Ah, I can see you've decided to forget him,' Benedikt continued. 'That's good. Young maidens often confuse admiration with falling in love. They fall for the good looks, only to learn with age that the beauty of the one they hold dear grows out of their love for him, and not the other way about.'

He paused for a moment then returned to the subject in hand. 'Heming lived for some time with a farmer in this parish until he became involved with the rebels. Since then he has had no fixed dwelling. He is no more than an adventurer, completely lacking in character, if you ask me. I don't think that he believes in the rebel cause particularly – he simply uses it as a way to make himself a hero. He is probably more hindrance than help to the others. The next time you meet, you will have to ask him yourself where he lives.'

'No, thank you – I will have no more to do with him. He's a thief!'

Benedikt looked satisfied.

From that day onwards Silje knew no peace. She was continually preoccupied with the mystery surrounding Tengel, both by day and night. She woke from nightmares, screaming. No matter how hard she tried to force herself to think rationally, she did not always succeed and disquiet grew within her. With mixed feelings of dread and secret longing, she looked towards the ridge, sometimes able to see smoke from a fire, while at other times it looked cold, quiet and dead. At those times she feared that he had left and she would never see him again. Then the wisps of smoke returned and she would grow angry, wishing he would disappear from her life forever, or better still, that she had never met him.

The Yuletide season was nearly upon them; the quiet sad days passing swiftly. No one felt the usual happiness or the urge to celebrate this year. Christmas was the time for sharing with one's family and during the past year they each had lost someone dear to them. Everyone felt painful reminders of loved ones who had gone. Each person tried to hide these feelings from the others and even from themselves. Family gatherings of other Christmases came to mind – with all the friendliness and cheerfulness around the table, laid for a feast, and smiling faces that were no more.

Benedikt, Silje and the others all did their chores in silence, walking disconsolately among the buildings, often with tears in their eyes. Had it not been for Sol, then they would not have made any preparations for Yuletide at all.

Then, three days before Christmas, their lives were suddenly turned upside down, and it was only at that moment that they realised fully what a wonderful time they had been having that winter, sharing each other's company.

A coach drew up in front of the steps and an imperious

woman alighted, her ample bosom announcing to the world, 'I am here!' followed by a jutting chin that reinforced the message. She was dressed in the latest fashion, with a ruffed collar, knitted bonnet and a dress sporting puffed sleeves and pleated skirts. She was followed by a boy, about fifteen years old, who looked surly and spiteful.

'Oh damnation!' muttered Benedikt. 'My nephew's widow! What in the fires of hell is she doing here?'

Yet one more person appeared. This time it was a young girl, who seemed to be carrying life's woes with her. Silje thought that she may have good cause, as fat as she was.

'Abelone!' Benedikt called a greeting to his relative. 'What a surprise. What brings you here?'

'My *dear* Benedikt!' said the dominating woman. 'I heard news of your tragedy – that your dear brother and all his family were taken by the plague. I just knew that it was my *duty* to come and offer my support, now that we only have each other. You and me – and my dear children.'

'There must be a food shortage in Trondheim,' he muttered. Then in a normal tone added, 'You know that you're welcome to celebrate Christmas here with us.' But the words sounded as though he had just rinsed out his mouth with vinegar.

'Christmas?' Abelone laughed. 'My children need country air and you need a woman to run your household. My dear man, we have decided to move in with you. It is my duty to take care of you. You are getting old now and should be spending your last days in peace and quiet.'

Benedikt was speechless – appalled and terrified. In silence, he watched as they began to climb the steps to the grand house.

'Good day, Grete. Good day, Marie,' said Abelone graciously, and then nodded curtly at the farmhand.

'And who is this little girl?'

Sol hid at once behind Marie's skirts.

'This is Sol,' said Benedikt proudly. 'And this is Silje. They and little Dag live here with us now.'

Abelone's eyes slowly turned to ice. 'Are they family?'

'No, but they are as dear to us as if they were.'

The farm lad and the two old sisters nodded their agreement solemnly.

'Is that so?' Abelone's reply was terse. 'We'll see about that!'

Life changed from then on.

Abelone would not hear of a quiet undisturbed Yuletide.

'The dead are gone and shall not cast a shadow of discontent over this season,' was her attitude. She was officious and bossy towards the servants, and especially to Silje, for whom she had an instinctive hatred. She would not allow Dag in the house and Sol was made to keep out of her sight. Benedikt was furious and drank and swore more than ever.

Abelone always had a bombastic answer ready for anything.

'As you know, my son is the only heir to this farm,' she would say. 'Things will need a shake up around here. He cannot be allowed to inherit property that has gone to ruin – including the workers and servants!'

'I'm telling you, Abelone,' said Benedikt forcefully, 'Silje and the children are here as my guests. As long as I'm alive, they shall continue to live here. Nothing more is to be said on the subject!'

A dejected mood stifled the farm – there seemed no chance of happiness now. On that Christmas Eve morning Silje went and stared up at the ridge, as she had done so many times before. A thin wisp of smoke was rising through the snow-laden trees and she gazed at it wondering – would she dare? She had often wanted to go up there, but fear and a regard for etiquette had restrained her. Now, though, she felt compelled to go. A force within her urged her on.

Abelone and her children were upstairs rummaging through the dead family's clothing, when Silje entered the kitchen where 'her' people were sitting, looking sad and downhearted.

'May I go and visit someone?' she asked cautiously. 'I should like to take some food to someone, in the spirit of the season.'

They all looked at her with surprise. They knew there were many poor hungry souls in the parish, but none that Silje was acquainted with. Nonetheless, she was allowed to go and Grete and Marie prepared a well-filled basket, with all the best Yuletide foods, sausage, ham, fish, buns and apples. A small flask of Benedikt's home-made spirit, *brännvin*, found its way in as well.

At that moment Abelone came in and walked straight up to the table. 'What is going on here?' she demanded.

Grete tried to explain. 'Silje is going to visit.'

Abelone began to remove things from the basket. 'Nothing leaves this farm, nothing! We have only enough for ourselves. And this Silje has no right …'

Although, even at this early hour, he was quite drunk, Benedikt rose to his feet with an ancient majesty. 'We have *more* than enough! *We* have given this food to Silje and you would do well not to try my patience. I can easily disinherit that worthless progeny of yours!'

Abelone gasped indignantly, 'You cannot do that!'

'No? There are ways and means.'

Abelone was not a fool and she well understood what he was implying. The look that she gave Silje was so filled with hatred that even Benedikt was taken aback. She left the basket without a word and stamped back upstairs. A door slammed and everyone knew that they had not heard the last of the matter.

'You go, Silje,' the old painter said gently. 'Nothing will harm you or the children – that I swear.'

With a tender smile, she thanked them all and left. It was a clear day and, although there was no bright sunshine, the snow reflected the light from the indigo-blue sky, dotted with clouds. She had to guess where the path to the ridge lay, because the last time she had been there she had merely chanced upon it while wandering aimlessly. The snow was not very deep, barely to her ankles, and she was wearing boots with long leather leggings. As she had hoped, she soon reached the narrow forest path, and her progress became much easier.

There were no tracks on the path, but, as it had snowed two nights earlier, this meant little. She climbed steadily for half an hour, then found she was becoming weary from the constant uphill trek and stopped to catch her breath. The village lay below her – she could see the church, the farm lad's salmon stream and Benedikt's farm. She could even see Marie hurrying to the barn.

Silje was standing directly opposite the Land of Shadows now and she thought how different it looked from up here. She had been told that the mountains did have a name. Local people called the jagged peaks the 'Barren Mountains', and it was a fitting description.

She turned to carry on up the path, then let out a startled cry. She had almost bumped into him, as he stood leaning against the trunk of a large pine. The snow had muffled the sound of his approaching footsteps. She looked up at him, fear in her eyes, her heart pounding. This was almost the same as when they had first met. He seemed just as noble, as strange and feral – his eyes still glowed, even in the bright daylight, but this time they held a warning. This was the fearful creature she had dreamt about with such intimacy! Had she lost her mind completely? Silje hid the fear that was coursing through her body. If he were flesh and blood, then he would need food and company.

Somewhat confused, she offered him the basket. 'I have some food for you, sire. It is Christmas and … Glad Tidings,' she added hurriedly.

He reached forward to take the basket from her.

'You should not have come here, Silje,' he said tersely, his expression unyielding and reproach shining in his eyes.

At once she turned on her heel to go.

'All right. It doesn't really matter. I've done what I came to do,' she said in a subdued tone.

He looked at her, his expression unfathomable, then grasped her arm tightly.

'Well, you're here now and you look frozen. I must make sure that you get yourself warm. Follow me,' he said curtly, gesturing for her to carry on up the path towards his home.

They walked on in silence, retracing the footprints he had left when walking down the path. She suddenly wondered what would have happened if those tracks had not been there. In truth she would probably have turned and run, screaming, back to the village. Still, she did not dare look at him. It was frightening, humiliating and degrading that she should still be attracted to him, that her chest tightened and she found it hard to breathe whenever his arm rubbed against hers. It hurt that he was so angry with her for coming there.

'Do you have visitors?' he asked.

At least he was still talking to her.

'Yes,' she sighed, 'things are not good.'

As he obviously expected to hear more, she babbled on breathlessly about Abelone and her children and all the changes on the farm. Nor did she did forget to tell him about the argument in the kitchen earlier that day.

'What did you think Benedikt meant when he said he would disinherit Abelone's children? I don't understand,' he asked impatiently. 'Has he thought to marry *you*?'

She gasped in surprise, 'Oh, no! I'm sure he didn't mean that!'

'Well it sounds like it. How else could he disinherit Abelone's children?'

Silje thought about this.

'He did come to my room one evening and ... well, he talked a lot of rubbish. But he was drunk and I gave it no heed. I got him to leave before he had made a fool of himself. It may be that he has some vague plan, I suppose.'

Her companion was quiet for a long time. She cast a furtive quick glance up at him. He had clenched his jaw so tightly that his lips had lost all colour.

'You've changed, Silje. You are filled with anguish. Tell me what's wrong.'

She took a deep breath and blurted out, 'I've found out your name. Your real name this time.'

He said nothing for a moment. 'And still you came?'

He sounded almost aggressive and Silje wanted to disappear into the ground.

'You have never done me harm,' she said in a subdued voice, 'and besides, you also said that you needed me.'

'Did I? That was reckless of me. Almost as reckless as you coming here.'

Silje wondered what he meant, but didn't dare ask. She was deeply hurt and disappointed, but put on a brave face and said, 'Sire, now is the time for me to confide in you. Life has become very difficult on the farm and this thing ... with your name. I am confused and uncertain – completely at a loss. I must know more, sire, please.'

'Perhaps that would be no bad thing. But first of all I think you should stop calling me 'sire'. You know my name and also that I am no lord or nobleman.'

They walked on through the silent forest until they came to a clearing where a small low cottage stood. The weathered timbers had turned grey from years of ravaging by the sun and the harsh winter weather. Attached to the cottage was an outhouse. Smoke was still rising from a simple skylight on the ridge of the roof.

He opened the low door and, bowing her head, Silje went inside. The instant the door closed, a strange mood overcame them that she was unable to explain. Had he been more congenial, she would have called it an affinity or even intimacy. But he showed no sign of such feelings.

It was a simple log cabin rather than a cottage, with the hearth in the middle of the beaten-earth floor, very like the one she had grown up in. She had only enjoyed the more up-to-date advantages of floorboards and glazed windows at Benedikt's farm. Of course she did not count the manor house where her father had worked. That had been part of a social class so far above her as to be in a different world.

Everything here held a certain familiarity. Against the log walls stood benches, rustic dressers and cupboards, and a small high-sided bunk. It was not an especially cosy home, but at least she wasn't choking, because he had managed to arrange the fire so that the smoke collected in the rafters and went out through the skylight, which also happened to be the

121

only opening by which daylight could enter. Its cover had been made from the caul, or foetal membrane, of some animal, stretched over a frame, which now stood slightly open. Under the roof, spanning the building, a rough-hewn beam supported a chain from which an iron cauldron was hanging.

Silje warmed her frozen fingers by the fire and avoided looking at him. After a moment's hesitation, he lifted her cape from her shoulders, and seeing that its hem was damp from the snow, he hung it to dry.

'Your boots?'

'They're dry. I think I'll keep them on.' She spoke in a strained low tone, still fearful of his anger.

He nodded and motioned her to sit on a wide bench covered with a sheepskin, then sat down on a similar bench opposite her on the other side of the fire.

'Would you like something from the basket, sire?' she wondered.

His tone was cross and severe. 'Yes, thank you, in a while. First I need to speak to you.'

He placed a kettle of water on the fire, seeing that she needed something to warm her, as she had walked so far. Silje reflected on the strained atmosphere in the room, although perhaps she did not need to. Instinctively she knew that her own feelings were largely to blame for it.

'I thought I had asked you not to address me by any title.'

She lowered her eyes. 'I don't believe I can do that. It would be presumptuous of me, and besides, I'm not sure I want to.'

'You want our relationship to remain one of master and servant?'

'Words alone cannot bridge the distance between us.'

Although she did not look up, she could feel him gazing thoughtfully at her.

Abruptly he asked, 'What do you think of me, Silje? Do you believe me to be Tengel – the Evil One?'

She looked across at him through the shimmering flames. He sat with his back to the wall, knees drawn up to his chest, his arms resting on them. In the uncertain light of the fire, his face did indeed have a demonic look about it.

'I cannot believe that,' she said, choosing her words with care. 'It would be so … grotesque. You are a passionate man! But there is much about you that I do not understand, sire.'

A bitter smile played on his lips. 'I imagine there is. Do you really want to hear my story? The Ice People's story?'

'That's what I came for,' she replied with childlike sincerity. 'That, and because I thought you might be hungry.'

'A ghost never gets hungry, which means that you didn't believe I am the evil Tengel.'

'No! No, I did not.'

'Nor am I!' he said angrily. 'How can people think such nonsense.'

She lifted her feet onto the bench and pulled her skirt tightly around her legs. He looked away quickly.

'You know …,' she hesitated, uncertain, not wanting to anger him again. 'No, it was nothing.'

'Come now,' he said sternly, 'what is it? Finish what you were going to say.'

For a moment she was overcome with the memory of that last dream. What if, in desperation, she were to try and calm his anger by undressing, just as she had done in front of the men who threatened her in the dream? How would he react to that? He would probably feel only contempt and disgust for her, and throw her out headlong into the snow. Her dreams were the result of her own desires, not his. It was a hard thing to have to accept.

'No, it was just a silly feeling I had,' she said, her mind quickly returning to what she really wanted to say. 'It meant nothing. It felt as if I have been waiting for this moment all my life.'

'To hear the story of the Ice People?' His tone was sceptical and that saddened her.

'Now you're mocking me, sire. I realise that I spoke out of turn. Forgive me for being so bold.'

'Then tell me what you meant.' There was impatience in his voice.

'I meant only that I felt I could be close to you, because you see things the way I do – you understand me. With you, I'm not afraid to reveal my emotions and I know that whatever I say or do will remain a confidence. But forgive my impertinence, sire, naturally you share no such feelings. I had better leave.'

She stood up without daring to meet his gaze.

'Sit down!' he yelled. 'Do you want to hear what I have to say, or not?'

'Yes – please,' she answered, startled.

'Then stop all your nonsense.'

He waited until they had both calmed themselves, then said, 'Do you want the whole story, right from the beginning?'

'Yes, indeed,' she said in a hushed voice.

'You don't need to whisper. You behave like a fledgling cornered by a snake. So! Where to begin? I have never told this wretched tale to anyone before.'

His face was thoughtful, but resigned. Silje, her heart pounding, eased herself into a more comfortable position on the bench, ready to hear the legend of the Ice People.

Chapter 8

The pensive man sitting on the other side of the fire from Silje drew a long deep breath and began his tale.

'You have heard of the first Tengel, haven't you? How he took his kin, together with other families, and fled up to the Barren Mountains? All this took place in the thirteenth century, and exactly what my infamous ancestor did, I do not know for certain. However, it is said that he entered into a pact with Satan in order to survive the harsh conditions in the mountains. I believe it's more likely he was already a wizard of sorts. They say he had a strange look about him – short but somehow aristocratic, with black hair and extraordinary eyes. No one knows where he came from, or his clan, but there is nothing to say that he was not from these parts. They also say that he performed unspeakable deeds to appease the Evil One himself – and that many of his spells were uttered over a wizard's potion of untold power, boiling in a kettle.'

Silje could not stop herself looking at the kettle he had placed on the hearth earlier. It looked quite safe. Tengel smiled a knowing smile and carried on.

'After he had entered his pact with Satan, my ancestor

buried the kettle, with all its evils still inside, and placed a curse upon the ground where it lay. He then told the people that a chosen few of his descendants would inherit the gifts that he himself had been given – and that one of his kin would be granted greater supernatural powers than mankind had ever seen. The curse – for curse it is, Silje – could only be revoked if the kettle was found and dug up.'

'And has it been found?' she asked quietly, trying to meet his eyes in the darkness beyond the smoke and the dancing flames of the fire.

'No, because nobody knows where he may have buried it. He was away for thirty days and thirty nights, from one full moon to another, when he sought out Satan. He might have been high up in the mountains or even beyond – far beyond. It is said that after the terrible meeting he returned looking quite different from before: shrunken, shorter and broader – do you know what I mean? He became ugly and evil, and horrible to look at.'

'Do you believe these things?'

'Some of them,' he answered hesitantly. 'In any event, I believe that he did carry out the deed and that he tried in every way he knew to contact Satan. Yes, I do believe that. Whether he truly met with the Prince of Darkness, nobody will ever know, but I sincerely doubt it. He maintained that he had, but I imagine him to be someone who enjoyed scaring and misleading folk. It may be that he really did believe he had met the Evil One. There are many more devout people than him who claim to have done so. I think he made up the part about his descendants inheriting his powers. He probably knew that there had always been members of his kin who had passed on "occult powers" from generation to generation. I think he just wanted to show that he could prophesy the future. In other words it was a bluff. That he became smaller in stature and uglier is not to be wondered at either. It happens to us all as we grow older, and if someone is evil through and through, this will surely show in the person's face as well. One thing is certain, however, that he, the one whose name I bear, knew many things that were secret and untold. But no, the story about the pact with Satan is just that – a story, nothing more. There is no such creature as Satan.'

Silje was appalled. 'You must not say that! That is the same as denying Our Lord's existence.'

'Is it? Don't be naïve, Silje. I thought you were a sensible girl, despite your youth and background. But now you speak like any other foolish uneducated woman. I see Satan as a very convenient invention of humans who need someone to blame when they do not want to take responsibility for their own misdeeds – and who can say how much the priesthood has relied on a belief in Satan to gain power over the people.'

'Sire! You blaspheme!' she gasped.

'Oh, be quiet! If you accept that there is a Satan, then you condemn me to eternal torment. Is that your wish?'

'No, of course it isn't!'

He leaned forward. 'If it is true that the first Tengel sold his soul to Satan, then he likewise sold mine. For I am of the same blood, the same seed, the same soul and the curse rests upon all of us who have inherited his powers. Can you understand this? I refuse to acknowledge Satan, but I do believe there is a gentle and forgiving God who will have mercy on an accursed child of humanity.'

Silje had a lump in her throat. 'The way you explain it, I begin to believe that you may be right, and that the Evil One has been invented by people. But I do not believe that you are cursed, you who are …'

127

'Look at me!' he yelled. 'Do humans look like me? When I see my reflection on the surface of a pool it repels me. Look at these burning eyes, slanted and narrow, like those of a cat. The predator's jaw with powerful teeth and this coarse hair, better suited to a horse's mane. Have you ever seen anything so hateful?'

Silje's voice trembled slightly. 'I will admit that I was frightened by your appearance at first, but now, for some reason I cannot explain, I find you very … well, I just cannot explain it. I enjoy looking at you. I look forward to seeing you when you are away. Besides, you have been very good to the children and me…'

He stood up suddenly, saying, 'Ha! I am not always an angel.'

Her words had obviously disturbed him. He walked restlessly to the other end of the room, stood for a moment before opening a cupboard door for no apparent reason, then slammed it shut and returned to his seat again. Silje sat quite still, ashamed of her forthrightness. He must surely be in a rage because of that.

For a long time he sat with his hands clasped tightly on his knees, looking as though he did not know what to say. When the silence became too much to bear, Silje, in a quiet voice, asked, 'And are you sure that among your kin, you are one of the chosen ones? The power to heal – has that also been passed down from him?'

'Call it sorcery, magic, for that is what it is! Yes, it is passed on with frightening certainty – not to all, but at least one in every generation is afflicted. It is always the swarthy unusual-looking cat-eyed ones who are the victims.'

'You say "victims". Is that because this is a heavy burden to carry?'

'Yes, it is more difficult than you can ever know.'

'You also said there would be one who would inherit greater supernatural powers than man had ever seen. Do you believe that is you?'

He threw his head back and gave a dejected laugh. 'Me? Oh, no! I am not so tainted; my powers are few. All I have is the ability to sense tension and emotion in people, and my healing hands. No, there are others of my kin, unspeakable creatures whose very existence you would not think possible. I feel powerless when I see all the disgusting things they can bring themselves to do. But no, the greatest chosen one has not yet been born, and I intend to see that he never will be!'

She continued to look at him inquisitively.

'I have sworn to myself that the evil bloodline shall die with me,' he said at last. 'I shall never lie in the embrace of a woman, lest the dangerous seed I carry within me should be passed on.'

Silje looked down, not wanting him to read her thoughts, to see the vibrant hope within her at that moment. That he had been so reluctant to let her come up to the cottage, could that be because he might ...? No, of course not! Feeling quite indignant now, she was determined to ask one more question.

'If you believe in the possibility of the *greatest* chosen one being born, do you not also believe in the power of the first Tengel to foretell the future?'

The wolf-like grin flashed in irritation. 'Not really, I think my ancestor made it up, like many others who carry the dream of being a Messiah – even though he was the very opposite of the benevolent Messiah. But the inheritance alone is so much to bear that I do not want to pass it on.'

'Are you the only one in your generation, sire?'

'Yes. For some time we thought that my sister had been cursed with the inheritance, but happily it was not so. She left the mountains, Silje. Left them when she found love, and settled with her husband in Trondheim without daring to reveal that she was born of the Ice People. You see, Silje, anyone found to be of the Ice People is killed on the spot, their body burned and the ash buried deep in the earth, so it can no longer spread its sorcery. We heard that my sister has two small daughters, Angelica and Leonarda. I was going to visit her that night when you and I first met. We were worried for her and the children – but I never did find them.'

Silje suddenly became very still on her seat.

'What are you thinking?' he asked. 'You are very tense.'

'How old were her little daughters?'

'Very small – the youngest just newborn. I think she was called "Nadda" – Leonarda?'

'Tengel!' said Silje breathlessly.

'Well, at last you call me by name.' He was mumbling, which was unusual for him, but Silje was so agitated she did not notice.

'Tengel! My God, I think …'

'Come on. What?'

'I think your sister is dead.'

He froze. 'Why do you think that?'

'You know how I found Sol, don't you? Beside her mother's dead body – an incredibly beautiful woman, with dark curly hair and dark eyes. Later, when Sol and I heard the infant crying in the woods, she urged me to go to it, pulling me and repeating "Nadda, Nadda" over and over. At the time I thought perhaps she had a little brother or sister with such a name, another child who had surely died of the plague.'

130

'Leonarda? Dear God,' whispered Tengel. 'I'm sure you're right, Silje. I saw it on Sol's face – she has the character of the Ice People. But I would never have thought ...'

Suddenly, it was as though everything had become too much for him. He found it hard to remain composed; but there was more to come.

'Oh, Tengel!' Silje cried in despair. 'I am scared that ... that Sol carries the evil inheritance within her! I see her unruly behaviour and her weird moods. She can be impossible to understand. But most of all, I fear the strange absent look that comes upon her sometimes.'

'Yes!' he exclaimed. 'That is one of the first signs. Oh, Dear Lord, that poor child! Can that little girl Sol really be my niece Angelica? I cannot believe it – or that my poor sister is dead.'

Cracks had begun to appear in his hard shell of hostility. Silje waited patiently, while he tried to come to terms with all the tragic things he had just learned. She would gladly have gone over to him and thrown her arms around him to show that she understood his feelings, but she knew that it would not be advisable. It was not easy for her to see the mighty Tengel so hurt.

His eyes showed his anger; his voice reflected his feelings. 'If I were but strong enough, I would kill her right now, before she is old enough to understand. It is a corrupt seed that the evil Tengel has placed within us. Corrupt!'

As he spoke, his face looked less human than ever it had, but at the same time Silje saw that his eyes expressed more sadness, more pain, than she had ever seen.

In horror, she pleaded, 'No! You must not kill her!'

'No, of course not – but my heart bleeds in despair for her future. Oh, Silje, you can never know what a living nightmare it is to have these traits! Some of my ancestors have revelled in them, been proud of them and become evil wizards and witches. They have announced to the world that they were the greatest chosen one, with more powers than anyone before them – I hate those qualities.' Then he lowered his voice. 'But I shall keep my oath never to touch a woman. My seed shall bear no fruit, even though little Sol may continue our accursed lineage. We must pray to the Merciful Father that she has not been given the depraved nature of some of our forebears – those who chose to serve evil. I try to keep myself on the side of good.'

He straightened suddenly, as if listening to a voice from within himself.

'What is it?' wondered Silje.

'Do you recall when I came to your room, when I tried to save Sol from the plague?'

'Yes, I do remember that you hesitated for a moment. You started to say something and then stopped.'

'Yes, exactly. I had a fleeting feeling that I *ought not* to save her. Now I know why. She is one of the afflicted. I did not know it then, but something in me felt that she should not live her life. Well, there is nothing that can be done about it now. Nonetheless, I shall never take a woman.'

Silje sat fighting her tears. As always, he could feel her sorrow, but this time he became even more irritated than before. He stood up again.

'I have never found it difficult to avoid women. Not, that is, until … Ah! The water's boiling.'

She had hoped he would finish what he was about to say, but then she realised he was talking about the water in the kettle that had probably been boiling unnoticed, for some time. She opened the box, while he brought out utensils for eating and drinking.

For her part, Silje was proud to provide so much fine food, and was pleased to see his eyes following every movement she made. How wonderful it was for her to do something in return for all that he had done for her!

Meantime, Tengel was finding it difficult to regain his composure.

'I should have left here long since,' he said angrily, throwing a couple of wooden spoons onto the table. 'I don't know why I haven't.'

'I am pleased that you did not,' she replied. 'The knowledge that you were near has made me feel safe. You have been good to the children and me, sire. You are not an evil person.'

'Aha, it's "sire" now again, is it?' he muttered.

'I'm sorry. I forgot.'

'You say that I am not evil – yet all are afraid of me.'

'Is it not good that they show you respect?' She tried to make it a joke, but the laughter stuck in her throat.

'They believe me to be a three-hundred-year-old spirit, Silje! Yet I am but a normal living human, with the same desire for companionship as anyone – except that I have some special powers I have never wished for.'

He saw the look of complete empathy in Silje's eyes, and he had to turn away.

'But all those things about herbs and such-like – you must have been taught that.'

'The Ice People are *born* with this knowledge and learn more from their mothers. Something that I could not do. My mother died giving birth to me, and yet people still think of me as a wraith! But it was probably a blessing for her – she was spared from seeing the creature she had brought forth into the world!'

'Tengel!' she implored sadly, 'don't say things like that.'

'Well there is something else you should know about, Silje,' he said, his back to her as he stood by the cupboard. 'Another reason why I must live alone, I mean. Have you noticed my shoulders?'

'Yes. Was it an injury?' she asked quietly.

'No, not an injury. I was born like this and that is what took my mother's life. She bled to death.'

'Oh, how terrible!' she groaned, her sympathy heartfelt.

'And I do not want that to happen to any other woman,' he added quickly.

'Are you saying that this too is inherited?'

'One can never know these things.'

He turned back and continued arranging the table. Soon they had laid out a wonderful meal.

'Our Christmas feast, Tengel,' said Silje, smiling despite the sadness she felt for him.

They sat down facing each other over the old rough-hewn tabletop. Tengel, steadfastly refusing to look at her, poured out some of Benedikt's home-made *brännvin*. She hesitated.

'I never usually take such strong drink. I have no desire to behave wantonly.'

'This is Christmas, Silje, and now you know that you need have no fear that I will molest you.'

'Yes, I do know that – it's not your feelings I am afraid of, but my own …' she stopped, alarmed at her words.

He set down the flask firmly, saying, 'You are a surprising girl – a mixture of virtue and strong sensuality, together with a bold daring streak. I do not know which is the real you.'

Silje considered this. Hearing him say 'strong sensuality' had made her cheeks colour. She felt very warm, but decided not to pursue the subject.

'I should love to have someone to speak to – about myself,

I mean. In truth I have no one. Master Benedikt is very easy to talk to, but he's mostly interested in his art and himself.'

For the first time since she had arrived, a wry smile appeared on his face. Perhaps the festive atmosphere of the meal had softened his mood. 'You can speak to me.'

'Would you want to listen, sire, really?' she asked shyly.

'I am sure that I would.'

She felt he was sincere in what he said. She began to rationalise her thoughts and went on, 'I think it is like this. By nature I am very shy, almost wanting to avoid company. My upbringing made me more so. My father was very strict and my mother religious and they condemned everything to do with love and that other thing you mentioned.'

'Sensuality?'

'Yes, that,' she mumbled quickly. 'Everything was sin, sin, sin! This left its mark on me. On our farm there were one or two occasions when young men tried to approach me, but I fled in horror and disgust before they managed to touch me. Then I was left on my own, after that awful time when everyone died and – I still cannot think about it lest I break down in tears.'

She paused to take a breath and recover the thread of her story. Tengel sat with his elbows on the table holding his mug, unmoving and attentive, watching her closely. He had not even had time to take a drink.

'When I was driven out and left to wander the countryside, I was often accosted, especially in Trondheim. As you know, I had nowhere to live and walked about aimlessly, sleeping in the open or in the most wretched of hideaways. I learned how to defend myself and I am still a virgin, Tengel, please do not think otherwise.'

He roused himself and raising his mug to his lips, he emptied it in one swallow.

'I never would,' he muttered, pouring himself more *brännvin*.

'I found out how tough life can be – the good and the bad – and became hardened to it in order to survive. Although it is not in my nature to be like that – perhaps this is where I found the daring you see in me. I saw and heard so many terrible things that confounded my natural instincts. I was in turmoil! Then – no, I can't tell you any more.'

'Yes, go on. This is important.'

'No, I cannot.'

He grew impatient, 'You said that you would confide in me.'

Looking away she said, 'Your manner today has not strengthened my confidence.'

With some effort, he controlled his impatience.

'Your words are safe with me. I *want* to hear your story.'

Silje realised that she felt very warm. Was it from the fire in the room or just within her? No, there was something else, something unbelievably powerful, which did not come from her. At least, not entirely.

'It is very difficult, Tengel,' she said, fidgeting awkwardly. 'It's about the ... my sensuality.'

'Yes, I realised that.'

'How it has been ... awakened. I never knew that I could have such ... well ... such desires.'

His eyes seemed aflame as he looked at her. The shadows made his face appear narrower and his teeth shone as he drew back his lips. His smile put her in mind of a wild beast about to pounce.

'I've said enough. I shall speak no more of it,' she muttered.

'No! Has someone tried to ... entice you? Tried to take you to his bed? Excite you?'

'No, no!' she answered, frightened. 'No, it is *you*, and you know it full well.'

There, now she had said it! Too late, she realised that she had fallen into his trap. Oh, how she wished the ground would swallow her up! She was overcome with a childish desire to creep under the table and hide.

An uncomfortable silence filled the room. Neither of them moved for some time. Something was being offered to her, but in her embarrassment she had not been fully aware of it. He was holding a mug of *brännvin* for her. He urged her to drink. She coughed and pulled a face at the raw taste, but it warmed her. She noticed that his hand trembled as he held the mug.

'Riding together on the horse?' he said in a quiet voice.

She gave him a scared look. 'Why do you think that?'

'You couldn't sit still.'

Silje felt so ashamed. She shook her head. 'No. It began long before that.'

He paused, and then said thoughtfully, 'Ah, yes. The painting in the church …'

'Don't speak of it!' she shouted and burst into tears. Between sobs she continued, 'I had two horrible dreams and I will not tell you about them, no matter how much you want me to. What are you trying to do? First you berate me for coming, then you humiliate me in this way!'

He breathed out heavily and she realised that he had been holding his breath for some time.

'You must not feel humiliated, Silje. That was not my intention. I have been acting selfishly. I see that now, but in my loneliness I needed to hear what you had to say. Neither am I used to women's emotions. Without meaning to, I have treated you badly. Thank you for coming, but now I had better see you back through the woods.'

'But we have not finished our meal!'

He had already stood up.

'It is best that you go home. At once.'

She looked up and saw self-control etched in every line on his face. She felt delight race anew through her veins. She understood.

'Thank you,' she spoke with ambiguity, still a little confused by her feelings.

Then, together, they went outside. After the murky light in the cottage they were both taken aback by the bright sunshine.

Not a word passed between them as they tramped the snowy downhill path. Silje threw furtive glances in the direction of the fascinating creature walking at her side. He had not taken his fur and was wearing only a short smock, gathered by his belt. She mused how the wide square shoulders made his hips look almost too narrow and out of proportion. He had a determined look about him, although he was lost in thought.

She decided to hazard a question. 'Tengel, what is your connection with Heming, the bailiff-killer?'

'Heming? Have you not realised? He is also of the Ice People.'

'Is he? But you are so different.'

'You must understand that he is not of the evil Tengel's kin. There were several families at the beginning. Heming's family had never wanted to be mixed with ours. They have always found their women and husbands from outside our clan, or from "pure" families amongst our folk.'

'You once told me that he was valuable to you. That was when I believed him to be one of the rebels. I believed the same of you.'

'Heming is the son of the Ice People's chieftain. Yes, even in our small world we have one.'

Silje showed surprised. 'I thought *you* were their chieftain.'

'A descendant of Tengel can never be chieftain. We are too unpredictable. No. When I went out to search for my sister, Heming's father told me to watch over his errant son.'

'So when you said that he could betray you all, it was the Ice People you spoke of not the rebels?'

'Partly – to save his life he might have informed on the whole rebel movement, and by so doing reveal the secret tracks and pathways to my people's hiding-place.'

'He is afraid of you.' It was a statement of fact.

'Of course! He thinks I have the power to destroy him, and I will let him continue in that belief.'

'And is it true?'

'I have no wish to find out.'

How torn your emotions must be, she thought. Then she exclaimed, 'But does he have cause to believe any such thing?'

Through clenched teeth he muttered, 'If you had seen the others of my kin, then you would not ask that.'

Silje merely shook her head, resignedly. 'Then tell me,' she continued, 'why you and Heming are so ... learned? You know many words. How is that possible?'

'Much like you,' he smiled weakly. 'I was educated second-hand.'

'How do you know about me?'

'Benedikt.'

Silje sighed, 'He is like a sieve, that man.'

'He has spoken quite a lot about you,' admitted Tengel.

'And did you listen?'

He didn't reply.

'Well, anyway,' she went on, 'how were you able to learn?'

'One of our men left the mountain about fifty years ago and studied in Trondheim. He was very wise. Then when he grew old he returned to us, and since that time we have had a – what shall I call it – a tradition of learning. He taught me many things himself, because he believed I had talent.'

'I am sure that he was right.'

'And Heming, as the son of a chieftain, must have learning. The old man had died by this time and his pupils taught Heming. I have tried to remember his teachings and to use the beauty of our language. Not all of the Ice People do this.'

'How old are you then, really?' Silje's heart was beating fast. This was something she badly wanted to know.

'Is it important?'

'Maybe not. But it is something I have wondered about many times. It is not easy to guess your age.'

'I am – well, in truth I am not sure. Between thirty and thirty-five I think. Thirty-two would be a good guess, perhaps thirty-three.'

'And I am just seventeen now,' she said quickly.

He turned away, so that she could not see his face. They fell silent again and shortly afterwards reached the edge of the forest, where they stopped. They both looked down across the valley, neither one wanting to meet the other's gaze, neither one wanting to leave.

'Silje, I must return to my people soon ...'

'No! You cannot go!' She spoke without thinking and immediately regretted her words.

'But I must. I have been away for too long and when the ice melts and the spring floods start, all the tracks become impassable. I must be there before then. However, I was thinking about your situation and Benedikt. Maybe you should wed him anyway. You are fond of him and you cannot deny that it would safeguard you and the children for as long as you live. I would feel at ease, knowing you were safe. He is an old man and would never ask of you anything that you did not feel able to do.'

'But that is what he has done!' she exclaimed.

'What?'

'He is a wonderful man when he is sober. But he was drunk … and tried …'

'To come into your bed?'

'Yes.' She felt ashamed.

Tengel did not realise that his hand was gripping his belt so tightly that his knuckles had turned white. He stood staring at the farm below, his lips barely parted. Now, more than ever there was something of the beast in his expression.

'Tengel, I shall make sure that it does not happen again,' she said in a worried tone. 'And Master Benedikt is not aware that he did anything at all; he has forgotten everything. He was so very drunk. But I could not marry him.'

'No, you can't,' he said hotly. 'And that woman has arrived – and I'm concerned about Sol, my niece. I should like to stay, but I must leave. Look after Sol for me Silje. It will be better for her to be with you than with me. Will you keep her?'

Silje nodded.

'Thank you,' he said simply. 'I shall return in the autumn to visit you all.'

'It's a long time till then,' she said in a trembling voice.

'You are safe at Benedikt's farm and he will sort out that old witch, just you see. Benedikt has never been a servant to anyone. He knows his own mind.'

'Will you go at once?'

'No, I want to see what happens with that woman. In spite of everything, I am concerned about what she plans for Sol … and Dag. I will be around for a few more days.'

'May I come and …'

'No, you cannot. It was bad enough that you came today.'

The patch of snow where they were standing had been trampled hard. Silje stamped the snow awkwardly and, although her feet were beginning to feel chilled, she still did not want to leave. Not yet.

'Silje, those dreams,' he said quietly without looking at her, 'were they really as terrible as you said?'

The silence surrounding them was immense.

'What is your answer?' he demanded.

'I shook my head,' she mumbled.

He turned to look at her. Her head was bowed, her cheeks crimson.

'Well I couldn't hear *that*, you silly thing,' he said, laughing, and she thought she heard a sign of happiness in his voice. But was he just mocking her?

Without daring to touch him, without even saying farewell, she turned suddenly and ran away, down towards the valley. When she had come some distance across the pasture, she turned to look back. He was still there, powerful and unmoving, like a heathen character from a bygone age.

She waved quickly to him and he raised an arm in reply. For a long time they stood looking at each other, before finally she turned and continued homeward.

Chapter 9

On the farm, things continued to go from bad to worse. Abelone had begun regular visits to the neighbouring farms and, sometime between Christmas and the New Year, she found out that the children might have been baptised.

'Silje's baptism in the forest?' she yelled at Benedikt. 'What good is that? A young hussy like her, having the gall to conduct a holy rite – and *my* children have been living under the same roof as two *heathen* brats!'

'It doesn't seem to have done them any harm,' he remarked with a sidelong glance at her two well-nourished offspring.

Abelone half-closed her eyes. 'As you know very well my dear friend, there are two trillion, 665 billion, 866 million and 746,664 lesser devils. Can you imag ...'

'And you manage to keep that number in your head all the time!' Benedikt butted in. 'Do you look in all the corners every day? What happens if you lose one? Or count one of them twice?'

Abelone would not be interrupted, 'Can you imagine how many of those lesser devils have been able to enter this farm freely through those two children? They might be anywhere, they can …'

'Don't let yourself get hysterical. Your face turns awfully red when you do that.'

'They must both leave – immediately!'

'Never!' said Benedikt turning towards her threateningly. 'And, for all we know, the little girl was christened a long while ago.'

'We know nothing at all about her. She was found in the street, was she not? The woman was most surely immoral.'

Silje protested angrily at this accusation against Tengel's unfortunate sister.

'Still your tongue!' commanded Abelone. 'It is common knowledge what you are after. So that's all there is to it! They shall be baptised at once.'

'We do not yet have a new pastor,' objected Marie.

'Then we shall fetch the one from the next parish. Good Heavens! How did you manage your poor lives before I came? I happen to know that the Bekkemarken family is expecting him to visit today. They have a sick elderly relative who is close to death. The farmhand can go and fetch him.'

And so it was. The children were smartly dressed for the occasion. Dag was wrapped in his gold-embroidered shawl, the sight of which caused Abelone's eyes to widen with envy. Little Sol was tremendously proud of the fine dress that Grete had woven, sewn and almost finished embroidering for her.

Nobody could have called the baptism a success. They had made a beautiful setting in the main parlour, with a white tablecloth, tallow candles and the best silver dish to serve as a font – but Dag screamed all the time and Sol kicked and butted like a foal in its first harness at the sight of the pastor, who invoked terror in her with his long black cloak and cold air of dignity. In due course they persuaded her to stand close enough to him so that he could flick some water in her general direction and hurriedly baptise her 'Sol Angelica'. It had been Silje who had insisted that she should have both names and because 'Angelica' was a beautiful name, and Christian too, everyone agreed. Silje did not breathe a word about the girl being one of the Ice People.

Sol was determined that Dag should also be given two names and Silje, having in mind the initials 'C.M.', gave him the most noble name she could think of. He was baptised 'Dag Christian'.

The worst was yet to come. As they led Sol from the room she was heard to say, in a loud clear voice, 'That damned priest chucked water all over me!'

Luckily her words were still difficult to understand – and Dag began to scream again in timely fashion – but Silje, Benedikt and Marie, the proud godmother, all heard her.

Marie was shocked. 'It's that awful farmhand,' she muttered. 'Sol copies everything he says and does.'

Silje was also taken aback. Only Benedikt found it hard to keep a straight face. At least the children had been placed in the hands of the church and Abelone could sleep easily again. There would be no more devils beneath anyone's bed.

****

All this was not enough for Abelone, however. Everyone on the farm knew it was her intention to be rid of Silje and the children. Her son had even said it out loud for all to hear. At the time, he had been sitting in the parlour and he shouted for more ale. When Silje went in carrying the jug, followed by Sol, he was cutting himself large pieces of meat from the Christmas ham. He watched her like a hawk because, as everyone knew, the jug was prone to drip. Sure enough, when she poured some ale for him a small drop landed on the table and he rose up in a fury.

'Be careful, you slut. Are you trying to damage my table?'

'Forgive me,' muttered Silje, fighting back the anger that threatened to erupt from within her.

'I should think so! You had better not have any ideas about all this becoming yours. Is that what you're planning? Worming your way into the affections of an old man whom you can twist around your little finger, is that it?'

They were the words of his mother, thought Silje.

'I promise you this – you and those little bastards will soon be out of here. Faster than you think! Oh – ouch!'

With a scream of pain, he grasped his left hand – blood was seeping from between his fingers and, on seeing this, Sol left the room quickly.

'Have you cut yourself?' Silje said, concerned.

'I? I did nothing,' he whined. 'It was her fault – that little witch Sol willed it to happen. I saw it – I saw it!'

'Ridiculous!' said Silje, now quite pale. 'The girl was standing in the doorway. She was a long way from you.'

'Yes, but it was her, I know it was. She just looked at me and the knife slipped.'

'What rubbish!' Silje's anger boiled over. 'Grete, come and see to this injured hero – before he faints! He's screaming like a stuck … well, you know what he looks like.'

Grete came in as Silje left the room. Silje ran after Sol and found her in another part of the house, kneeling on a bench by a window. Sol turned as she entered and Silje shuddered when she saw the girl's eyes. They shone green with hatred and something else as well – something she had never seen before and hoped never to see again. Sol looked at her and the expression was gone immediately, as she stretched out her arms to her friend. Silje picked her up and cuddled her.

'Sol,' she whispered, tight-lipped, full of anger and horror. 'Dearest Sol, you must never, never do that again.'

'Do what?' she asked innocently. 'I do nothing. Man silly!'

'Yes, he was, but …'

In her distinctive childish voice, Sol continued, 'I don't want him live here any more. Strange ladies not live here more too.'

'None of us want them here, dearest, but that is how it is. Promise to be nice to them, Sol. Promise!'

The girl threw her arms round Silje's neck.

'Sol be good.' she said with a happy and beguiling smile.

Silje's thoughts were of Tengel. Dear God, how she needed to talk to him now. Then again, it was probably better that he did not know about this. She wondered what she should do. Trying to raise this unfortunate little child would be a monumental task, she decided. When he heard about the matter, Benedikt was extremely depressed. Not even the church painting could lift his spirits.

'I shall kill that bitch,' he was heard to mutter on more than one occasion. 'I swear I'll kill her!'

One day in a fit of rage he had tried to get rid of Abelone and her children, going so far as to throw all their belongings into the yard, yelling, 'Out! Out!' so loudly that it disturbed the cattle in the barn. As it was, Abelone was able to master him by threatening to tell the bailiff that he was in league with the rebels. Although she plucked the accusation out of thin air, it was enough. Benedikt knew that he would not be able to defy close scrutiny on that score, so they stayed.

The three of them alone consumed copious amounts of food and their appetites were never satisfied. The farm's larder was running low, life was miserable and everyone felt helpless. Eventually, on New Year's Eve, Benedikt broached the subject that Silje had been expecting for some time.

They were sitting alone in the kitchen, when he said, 'Marry me, Silje.' His distress showed in his eyes. 'We would solve so many problems. That old hag and her spawn would have to leave and the future would be safe for the children and you.'

Silje reached out across the table and took his hand gently in her own. 'I'm very grateful for your offer. It's very kind, and you know how fond I am of you. But it wouldn't work.'

'Whyever not? I won't live many more years and I would not … I would not want to have physical …'

She stopped him from saying more. She felt she had to tell him about the night he had come into her room. When she had finished, he whispered, 'Oh God. I thought it was nothing but a dream.' Then, with a sigh, 'I suppose I really must be honest with you. I have lied. Foolish old man that I am, I have found myself attracted to you, but I was sure I could hold back my desires. Obviously the *brännvin* plays games with me and maybe I have hoped, secretly, that you would want me. I see that now. I suppose that you could not consider sharing my bed?'

There were tears in Silje's eyes. 'Oh, I cherish you so very, very much, Master Benedikt, but not in that way. No – because it worries me that we would lose our wonderful friendship and find only bitterness and heartache instead. I wouldn't want that for anything in the world.'

'Neither would I. At least nobody can ever accuse you of wanting to get hold of my possessions and my riches! Other women would have hidden their disgust and jumped into bed with an old man to get their hands on his worldly goods, but not you. And in some ways I would have been disappointed in you if you had said "yes". The true artist does not sacrifice his principles just for the sake of convenience.'

At this point he began an oration about the artist's noble vocation. It was his true passion. Finally he sighed, saying, 'Oh, Silje this is all so tedious. Everything is tedious.'

'Yes, and I am scared, Master Benedikt. For everyone – but most of all for the children.'

****

As the Old Year ended, Silje reflected on the many changes that had occurred and wondered what the New Year of 1582 would have in store for her. As it happened, she did not have to wait long to find out. Three days later, Abelone made her move and it was a cruel and crushing blow. The farm lad had come running, out of breath and wide-eyed, into the kitchen where the 'real' people of the house were eating.

'Something awful is going to happen,' he gasped. 'She, that *woman*! She's ordered me to take her and her children for a drive in the carriage – but I heard her whisper to the daughter that they would be going to the bailiff to report Silje.'

Benedikt jumped up. 'What for? Why on earth?'

'She has heard from one of the old women in the parish that Silje was seen riding with Tengel of the Ice People!'

'Oh, dear Father of God,' said Benedikt quietly. 'Then Silje will be accused of giving herself to the Devil's disciple, the undying Tengel!'

'But that's not true,' shouted Silje. 'Tengel is not undying – and I am still a virgin. I will prove it if I must.'

'My dear child,' said Benedikt, 'no one's virginity will help us now. If the bailiff's soldiers lay their hands on you, then you will most certainly die! They will torture you – slowly and with great pleasure – until you are dead, but not before they have forced you to tell all you know of Tengel and the Ice People. You will bring misfortune on others as well. And yes, I expect they will take the children too. They will say that you or Tengel have ravaged them or put a hex on them. The authorities will treat you as a witch of the first order because of your association with the beast-man. And you know how much they enjoy punishing witches.'

'But what are we to do?' she asked.

'I don't know.' His voice was tired. 'I really do not know. Of course we must get you away from here, but how? And where to? To think that bitch will get her way in the end!' He turned to the farmhand. 'You must go back outside at once before she begins to suspect anything. Then drive as slowly as you can so that Silje and the children have time to get away.'

The lad nodded and walked towards the door, but Silje ran to him and gave him a farewell hug. He put his arms around her, tears welling in his eyes. Quietly, so that Sol would not start to fuss, he bade goodbye to the children as well.

'Please be gone by the time I return,' begged the farm lad. 'You must!'

Feverish activity began as soon as the carriage had left the yard. All that Silje and the children owned was strapped into two rolls and the others packed the best of the food and clothes they could find in the house. Benedikt brought her a glazed mosaic in wonderful colours that he had made.

It would impossible for her to take it with her, but Silje could not take her eyes off it. Secretly, he gave her a little book that he had bound himself. The pages were glossy and he told her it was a sketchbook, for when she felt the need to draw. There was a fine-tipped pen and some charcoals as well. She tried to thank him, but they were both so filled with emotion that all they managed was a tearful hug. The old sisters cried helplessly, alternately cuddling the children and packing their belongings. Sol, not understanding what was happening, cried in sympathy.

'However is Silje going to carry all this?' asked Benedikt, alarmed when he saw the enormous pile of goods.

They all stopped and stared, and Silje put her hand to her mouth. 'If all this wasn't so serious and frightful, I should laugh,' she said with a dejected look at the enormous heap. Grete and Marie started to giggle and soon they were all chuckling. The mood had changed, but no one wanted to start sorting through the things again.

'But where is the poor lass to go?' moaned Grete.

Silje hesitated. 'Tengel was close by here at Christmas. He was the one I visited on Christmas Eve, but I will not tell you where, so that you know nothing if you are questioned. I think he may have left – I have not seen any signs of life for days.'

Silje drew a deep breath to control her emotions. The thought of his not being there was making her empty and cold inside.

'Can't you and the children take refuge there, alone?' asked Marie.

Silje looked outside. 'I too had that thought, but I fear they would track us through the snow.'

'Yes, you are right. Oh, God, what are we to do? Can we hide you somewhere?'

'And if young Dag should start to cry, what then?' asked Grete.

They all heard the sound at once and were rooted to the spot. Moments later, a rider on horseback came into the yard at a furious pace.

Marie screamed, 'Are they here already? Hide yourselves – hide yourselves!'

'No,' said Benedikt relieved. 'It's not them.'

Tengel jumped down from his horse and met them as they came running out of the house. This time the old women had completely forgotten their fear of the Ice People's ghost.

'What is going on here?' he asked.

'Did you sense something?' wondered Silje breathlessly, beaming with pleasure at seeing him again.

He gave a crooked smile.

'It was more down to earth than that this time. I was just riding down from the ridge to go south, but I stopped to consider whether I should come here to see you and say farewell once again. I couldn't decide whether I should or not, but then I saw all the activity in the yard and dread filled my heart.'

Benedikt explained quickly what had happened. He finished with, 'You have been sent by heaven', forgetting that this guest apparently owed his allegiance to another dominion entirely.

The colour had drained from Tengel's face. He looked around at the drawn tear-stained expressions – his gaze lingering on Sol a little longer before finally resting on Silje's face.

'Yes, thank God I decided to come this way,' he said.

Marie took a breath and crossed herself. Tengel's temper flared, 'Is it not even allowed for one who is excommunicated to speak His name? Do you want me exiled to the depths of darkness? What can you know of my soul? You think I do not have one, is that it?'

Marie and Grete lowered their heads in shame.

Tengel composed himself again and said to Benedikt, 'A wagon awaits me further south, down the valley, if only we can get there. But Silje, me and two children – not forgetting their bundles – will be too much for my horse.'

'That harridan took our only good carriage and there's not enough snow for the sled,' said Benedikt. 'You can take the other mare. Leave her at the farm far down by the bridge. The lad can bring her home.'

'That's agreed then,' said Tengel.

'But what will happen to all of *you*, Master Benedikt?' asked Silje, full of concern. 'They won't arrest you for this, will they?'

'No – of course not.'

'So where are we to go?'

The two men looked at each other for some moments before Tengel said, 'There is only one way to save Silje.'

'Yes, I agree,' nodded Benedikt. 'And I dare not have the children here any longer, no matter how much it breaks all our hearts to see them leave. No one knows what that evil cow Abelone and her gluttonous offspring might get up to. I must hand the children over to your care, Tengel.'

The big man nodded. Both horses would be carrying more than was usual and he packed the awkward glazed mosaic on his own horse, but unbelievably they managed to take everything. It was a small miracle.

A swift heart-rending round of goodbyes was said. One by one Silje thanked them each with a hug for all their kindness. Grete held Dag closely, as if she would never let go, but then handed him up to Tengel, who was already astride his horse. Marie stood beside Silje's mount urging Sol not to forget her and said that they must all come and visit again. Then it was time to leave. They would have to ride as fast as they could, because the soldiers would be sure to follow them. Every moment counted.

Silje was glad that Tengel had taken the boy, because she was not an experienced rider and an infant would be difficult to manage. There was no sidesaddle on the farm, so she sat astride the horse. Grete and Marie had quickly covered her knees with her cape, while Tengel had discretely looked away. Silje was sure she saw him smile. 'You rascal!' she thought.

As they came out onto the highway they both glanced northward, but there was no sign of soldiers. This made them both feel more at ease. Saying farewell to such kind people had proved painful and Silje found herself drying her eyes from time to time. The threat of danger, however, and the effort of holding Sol in the saddle, soon took all her attention. The countryside was completely quiet as they rode on southwards along the country highway. The only sign of life was the smoke that billowed lazily around the roofs of the houses, but Silje had already discovered the hard way that eyes were watching every stranger who travelled the roads.

Tengel was impatient and drove them on. Silje and the old mare did their best, but it was not enough for him. 'We are only about an hour ahead of them,' he called to her, 'and soldiers ride fast when they set their minds to it.'

Silje was starting to get cramp from holding onto the girl and guiding the horse, as well as keeping herself and her bundles in the saddle. Decency had long been lost, as her cape had blown back from her legs soon after they started, exposing her uncovered knees. Best forget about it, she thought, and let Tengel think what he liked.

Sol, on the other hand, seemed to be enjoying the excitement and the wild ride. She sat in front of Silje, with bright eyes and an enormous smile. Silje noticed how Tengel kept looking at her, both with affection and concern. He is a good man, she thought. No matter what they say about him or the names they give him, despite his fearful looks and his occasional temper – deep down he is a good man. But no one could deny that he did look like a demon from the underworld as he rode on ahead of her – a noble, attractive and fascinating demon, if such a thing existed.

Silje had realised for some time that she had overreacted to Sol's strange behaviour towards Abelone's son on the day he had cut his hand. But his reaction had also been uncalled for. Of course, Sol had been angry with him, and when she was in such a mood, her eyes really could be frightening. The boy had been distracted and possibly scared by the hatred felt towards him, and the knife had slipped. How easy it was then to blame another! It was as simple as that – her outburst had been exaggerated.

They had now left the parish behind them and were riding through the forest on their way to the next village. They had slowed the pace in order to spare the horses. It was still early in the day, and Tengel had told her they had a long way to travel and *must* arrive before nightfall.

'There are wolves in the mountains,' he added. 'We will not be able to fend them off in darkness.'

Silje tried to hide the anxiety his words had caused her. She knew full well where they were going, but was trying hard not to think about it. Subconsciously, though, the thoughts kept nagging at her. In a way, things had come full circle. All her fantasies and her nightmares had been a preparation for the time when something preordained would happen – and that time had arrived.

'Is it really so dangerous for us to stay down here in the valley?' she asked, trying hard to make Sol sit still.

'It is now,' he answered bitterly. 'Your dealings with me have put you outside the law.'

'Oh, what an evil woman,' she grumbled. 'Poor Master Benedikt and the others will have to put up with those awful people, perhaps for the rest of their lives.' She hesitated for a moment, then continued, 'You were right, you know. Master Benedikt did ask me to marry him. I thanked him, but said 'no'. Perhaps I should have accepted his offer and we could have avoided all this upset.'

'I fear a marriage would not have saved you now,' said Tengel. 'Think of all the wives of clergymen they have taken for witchcraft and sorcery! It did them no good, even when the priests vouched for them. Once you have been accused of being a witch, your fate is sealed.' After a short pause he added cautiously, 'Master Benedikt has asked me to return as soon as I can. He wants me to help him with his visitors.'

'But isn't it dangerous for you to be among humans?' As soon as she had uttered the words she realised that she had fallen into the same trap as Benedikt once had. 'Among humans' – how insulting it sounded.

He replied simply, 'Yes, it is. But I've survived until now.'

Silje reflected for a moment, then asked, 'What sort of help does he want?'

'Oh, he believes I have the power to destroy them.'

'On this occasion I almost wish that you could,' she said in a low voice.

'No, I shan't do anything like that. I have no desire to awaken any evil that may be lurking deep within me. But I will go back to him, not least because he was kind and took you in at my behest, although I know that he *certainly* has

156

no regrets about that. They have all come to love you and the children greatly, you know that, don't you, Silje?'

'Yes, and it's a very comforting thought. I want you to try to help them. They are all good kind-hearted people, all four of them, and they do not deserve this.'

'I agree. They truly do not. It is hard to accept that evil should triumph so easily in this world.'

This should have been the time for her to tell him about Sol and the signs of the powers she might have within her. Silje said nothing, however, certain in her own mind that she had exaggerated the whole episode.

Tengel urged the horses along faster once again. They were leaving the forest and open countryside, dotted with farms, lay before them below the ridge. The direction of the valley had changed, and it was clear they were heading towards the foothills of the Barren Mountains – apparently one side of them could be climbed. A little further on Tengel turned off the road onto a farm track. Silje followed.

'Wee-wee,' said Sol.

'What a time to choose,' said Silje. 'Tengel, can you help her down? I don't want her to wet us both.'

'Wait until we reach that stand of trees over there. We don't want the whole parish to see us.'

'I hope she can wait,' muttered Silje.

They made it to the trees without mishap. Tengel dismounted, helped Sol down and, as he put his strong hands around Silje's waist, she looked steadfastly at the ground. She did not want to meet his gaze now, as she had done the first time he had helped her down. But the very nearness of him made her feel light-headed – overcome – and she had to fight the overwhelming urge to throw her arms around him to feel his warmth, her cheek pressing tightly against his.

Was she under some kind of spell? Had he enchanted her? 'Has he used his sorcery on you?' wasn't that what Master Benedikt had asked? Silje did not yet understand that affairs of the heart create their own magic.

When Sol was ready to move on again, Tengel checked their packs with one hand, holding the sleeping Dag gently against his shoulder with the other. As he helped Silje back into the saddle, this time he could not look at her either. He can see it in me, she thought. He feels it, he knows …

They rode off along the track and after a short while entered a very small farmyard that seemed all but deserted. To her surprise a man came out to greet them.

'Hello, man!' called Sol happily.

'Hello, you little charmer!' he called back with a grin.

What a memory the girl has, thought Silje. It was the wagon-master who had taken them from the execution ground to Benedikt's farm over three months earlier.

'Yes!' he said to Tengel, taking a sidelong look at the child, 'she's one of us right enough! She is the image of Sunniva.'

So Tengel had spoken about Sol to others. He was probably quite proud of his little niece.

'Are they coming with us – up to …?' asked the man.

'Indeed they are – only death awaits them down here. Well, for Silje anyway.'

'Fine, I'm ready. Everything is prepared.'

Tengel told him about the bailiff's soldiers, who would no doubt be on their heels before long.

The man nodded, 'My horses are well rested.'

'I must stay behind,' said Tengel, turning to face both Silje and the man. 'I have to leave the mare at the bridge, as promised, but I am also sworn to bring Heming home. I know where he is, close by here in the valley, and this time he will be coming with me. I shall drag him by that mane of pretty blond hair, or tear him away from the arms of a woman if I have to! So you get going at once – I'll follow you later.'

'Please, please come with us,' Silje begged anxiously. 'Don't stay, come with us now.'

'I'll soon catch up with you. Now go – hurry!'

Her heart sank as they parted once again, but he had made up his mind. Soon their belongings were packed on the wagon and they were travelling up a hidden forest track.

'He takes so many terrible risks,' she complained to the wagoner.

'Don't worry about Tengel,' he replied. 'It is best we do not ask about some of the things he can do.'

'No, I don't believe you. People think ill of him, but he isn't like that – really.'

'My dear Mistress Silje,' said the wagoner turning to her, 'how do you think he has survived down here for so long, taking chances the way he does?'

'Do you mean that he …?'

'Look, I cannot say if he can make people see things or if he uses some other wizardry, but I do know that this is the first time he has stayed among humans for more than a few weeks.'

He said 'among humans' as well, thought Silje, shaken.

'Well, why does he put himself in such danger?'

'I hadn't expected that question from you, Mistress Silje,' he mumbled and turned back to face the road.

Dag began to cry loudly, shifting Silje's attention to their present needs. Whether he was hungry or needed a change, she wasn't sure – probably both. She couldn't do anything with him on the wagon. His milk was ice-cold and to undress him would be madness. All she could do was to hold him close to her cheek and rock him, until finally he stopped crying and slept. Bless him, she thought to herself.

The horses pulling the wagon were powerful. The steep track twisted and turned, with a sheer drop on one side, and they were climbing all the while. Every time she looked down over the valley, the river and the houses appeared smaller and smaller, until finally they were no bigger than toy houses and the river just a rivulet running through them. Eventually they disappeared from view.

Dag was warmly cradled in her arm, still sleeping, while Sol stood behind the driver's seat, shouting encouragement to the horses. Silje held tightly to Sol's leg in case she should fall. Occasionally she looked across at the window mosaic that was wedged against the side of the wagon. She had never possessed anything quite so beautiful and she wondered if she would ever have use for it. What sort of home would they live in? Whatever it might be, she would give the mosaic pride of place, hanging on a wall perhaps. But what if they all lived in wooden huts up there?

She ran her fingers across the sketchbook Benedikt had given her. She could feel the woven binding along its spine. How kind of him to part with it! It would have cost a lot, in both time and money, to make. What neither she nor Benedikt knew, however, was that she held something in her hands at that moment which would become of the utmost importance, something that one day would help to solve the riddle of the Ice People – but, for now, it was no more than a few sheets of home-made parchment, bound together.

She looked again at the pale, well-formed features of the little boy sleeping in her arms. His hair had grown and some wispy strands had escaped from under his fur hood. She wondered what his mother would have said if she had seen him like this, on his way to the realm of fear and cold – on his way to the Land of Shadows! She had frequently wondered about Dag's mother. What would the woman have been feeling? Relief, perhaps? No – not that. Silje's instinctive understanding of the human spirit answered her question. There was one small item that had persuaded her more than any other – a small wooden pot with a lid, filled with milk and carefully placed at the side of the abandoned baby. Surely this was the pathetic cry of a lone mother's despair.

Chapter 10

A pensive Charlotte Meiden sat looking through her window at the run-down remains of Nidaros Cathedral. Since the fire of 1531, which had caused extensive damage, no one seemed to have made any effort to repair the enormous building. The country had suffered the effects of the Reformation, followed by famine and countless outbreaks of plague and there was little energy for any activity beyond sheer survival. Only some small parts of the cathedral were being used; most of it still lay in ruins. She could see a small stretch of the River Nid as well, circling its way around the town so delicately and thus making it nearly impossible for an enemy to overrun. There was only one way in – the fortified western gates.

'Tell me, mother,' she said absent-mindedly, 'Whatever happened to the nuns' convent at Bakke? Is it still there?'

Taken aback, her mother looked up from her needlework. 'The Benedictine Order? No, they will not be there now. All that sort of thing was swept away by the Reformation, was it not? Yet in truth, I cannot say.'

'The Cistercians at Rein, then? Were they not also nuns?'

'I cannot believe that they are still there either. Did the land not become part of a large manor estate?'

Charlotte sighed. 'What about back home in Denmark?' she asked.

'I really do not know. But why such questions? This is a strange conversation and no mistake.'

'I am thinking of becoming a nun.'

'You! Have you gone mad? Why, you are not even of the Catholic faith!'

'Why should that matter? I shall convert.'

'No – whatever next! I'm sorry, Charlotte, but I will not allow such a thing. What would people say? And what of your father? Now listen, we are invited to attend the County Lieutenant's seasonal ball this Saturday. That will lift your spirits and soon you'll forget these silly notions. I am told there will be some agreeable young noblemen from Denmark present as well. There is, as we know, little to choose from hereabouts!'

Charlotte got up and, impatiently, without a word, left the room, watched by her anxious mother. She wondered whether it was nothing more than religious confusion and contemplation that had been troubling her daughter of late. But a Catholic convent! Well that was impossible, of course. If only they could get her married. Oh, why had they had not been blessed with a pretty child? The protruding nose – an inheritance from a long line of Danish aristocracy, including the royal family, of course – this was Charlotte's most unattractive feature, poor girl. There could be no doubt that she would be a problem.

Back in her room, Charlotte threw herself on her bed. She was well aware that she was no beauty. As a young girl she had been betrothed to the son of a count in Denmark, but after the first formal meeting, arranged at a ball, he had made a succession of lame excuses and stayed away. Eventually this breached the contract agreed between the parents and he had quickly found himself a bride, before anyone had a chance to protest. At the time she had felt terribly humiliated and shamed by the episode, but eventually she banished all thought of it from memory, as if it had never happened.

When a second charming young Dane had courted her, about a year ago, she had been easy prey for his attentive advances, deprived as she had been of male admiration. She had learnt to hide her natural shyness behind a hectic social façade, with glittering smiles and light-hearted conversation – not allowing anyone to see how ugly and clumsy she felt inside. The young man was an accomplished seducer and Charlotte's virtue proved no match for him. Afterwards, in a rush of euphoria, she had floated on air for days, until news reached her that he was already married – followed soon afterwards by the crushing discovery that she was expecting a child.

None of this mattered to her any longer, but she did still yearn to turn back the clock and hold the child in her arms once more. This was the constant unremitting notion that tormented her. Again and again panic tore at her when she thought of her baby, lying helpless and uncomprehending, abandoned in the forest, left for days without food or human affection.

Enough! She turned and buried her face in the pillow. If only she had somebody to talk to. Someone to whom she could unburden her woes – her pastor perhaps? No, he would not understand – merely judge her. Everyone would judge and condemn her. But deep down, was that not what she really wanted? Someone to condemn her, force her to her knees, whip her and beat her. That would never bring the infant back, of course – and yet another thought troubled her. The child was unchristened, cursed. She had left a *myling* in the forest. Should she go back there and read a prayer? No, never, *never* would she visit that place again! Could she ask the pastor? She could not bring herself to do that either. Was it cowardice –fear of what he might find out there? She was irredeemable, doomed. What sort of life would she have now?

****

At that moment the baby son Charlotte Meiden had abandoned so rashly was sleeping, snug in Silje's arms, as they travelled higher into the Barren Mountains. The track was ever steeper and Sol had begun to tire of the constant jolting of the wagon. She was hungry too. Silje brought out the bag of food she had been given and handed the girl two small bread baps.

'Give one to our driver, as well,' she asked her.

'Here, man,' said Sol eagerly.

With great aplomb, the driver took the roll.

'Why, thank you *so* much!' he said and then asked, 'Would you like to sit up here with me for a while?'

Sol didn't need to be asked twice. She has a way with men, thought Silje, amused. The farmhand had been her favourite, and now it was the turn of the wagon-driver. Sol, one hand on the reins, sat safely beside the driver, looking like a round bundle, parcelled up by Grete in layer upon layer of winter clothes. From time to time she turned to make sure that Silje was witnessing her achievements.

The landscape through which they passed was wild and frightening. They had left the view of the valley far behind and were now travelling between sheer black cliffs, where snow lay packed in the crevices. The 'track' had petered out long since, but the wagoner clearly knew where they were headed. Silje was worried by the deep ruts they were leaving in the snow – they would be easy to follow.

The wagon made its steady way alongside a large river, where it cut through the mountain. The high sides of the pass had shielded it from the worst of the snow, making lighter work for the horses, as the heavy wheels turned more easily. However, Silje was only too aware that the snow would be deeper the higher they climbed – and how high would that be in the end?

Wherever she looked lay a dismal wilderness. The wind whined as it blew relentlessly through the mountain pass, following the path of the river. The winter ice had created hideous shapes, which transformed and slowed the rushing torrent. They sucked and spurted the water from deep holes and blew cascades that froze in the air. In places the cutting was so narrow that it was like driving through the packed streets of Trondheim, with high dark buildings on either side. Here, though, there was not the slightest sign of human life, of any habitation – only the close menacing presence of the river. Now and then, as they bumped over the rugged surface or crept too close to the water's edge, she could not help a sudden rush of fear and tightened her hold on Dag. She noticed that the horses were also getting nervous.

Then, quite without warning, they were out of the pass and wide-open countryside lay before them. They had left the shelter of the mountains behind and now the wind buffeted them even more strongly. Freezing cold, it blew the snow into hard-packed drifts. Silje hurriedly pulled out a quilted blanket to warm the three of them, although Sol was reluctant to climb down from the driving seat to get beneath the covers. They huddled together under a small canopy, draped over them, Silje with one arm around Sol and the other holding Dag. She had seen to it that the driver was as warm as he could be in his exposed position up front. She pulled her shawl more tightly round her and wished that she had thicker mittens.

'Are we going to be all right in this weather?' she shouted to the driver as he sat with a large frozen dewdrop forming under his nose.

'This is good,' he shouted back, turning away from the wind. 'The snow will cover our tracks.'

She could not argue with that. Shortly afterwards he halted the wagon and jumped down.

'Have to put the runners on,' he yelled, while the scarf he had wound round his cap flapped about his ears. 'The snow is too deep. The wheels are cutting through it.'

Put on runners? What did that mean, wondered Silje. She watched as he locked the wheels with leather straps and, from the rear of the wagon, pulled out two long runners that had lain along the sides.

'Let me help you,' she called, jumping down into the snow. 'No, Sol, not you. The snow's too deep for you here.'

As the driver lifted the wagon, she pushed one of the runners under the wheels, where they fitted perfectly. He had no doubt done this many times before. While they were occupied, Sol shouted, 'Horses!'

They both looked up, a little surprised. There, far behind them at the edge of the heath, were two riders. On catching sight of them, the driver relaxed.

'It is all right,' he said, 'no need to worry.'

Silje's heart immediately began to pound with joy and expectation – she felt slightly embarrassed. It was Tengel and only now did she realise how afraid she had been that he might not return. She was cross that she could not control her emotions when he was near her, because he had never given any indication that he had feelings for her. Well, she consoled herself, not openly or directly.

Heming was with him. As they drew closer, she recognised the aristocratic-looking young man. As soon as they reached the wagon Sol began to jump up and down with joy, shamelessly demanding a hug from Tengel.

'Move away, Silje, we'll do this,' said Tengel. 'I see that you've managed very well.'

'She's made of stern stuff, that young lass,' said the driver.

'I'm aware of that,' mumbled Tengel.

'Did you catch sight of the soldiers?' asked Silje.

'Yes. They galloped past on the highway, going south. We're still well ahead of them. But the day is short.'

She saw then that the sky had begun to turn that deep blue colour that precedes dusk.

'Looks like it'll snow, too,' said Heming, as he lifted the wagon.

Silje did not want to look at him – rage still boiled inside her. Tengel turned to face her.

'Listen to me, Silje,' he said severely. 'I know that you have good reason to be angry at Heming, but we are going to be living together for a long time in a small community. There is enough ill-will here already – there is no place for more. *You* at least can show yourself to be wiser than the fools who scowl bitterly and drearily at each other.'

She said nothing. This was the first time he had looked at her since they had arrived, and the first thing he did was to scold her.

'Understand?' he asked threateningly.

'Yes, I understand. I shall contain my anger, but do not ask me to love him.'

'*That* is something I would never ask of you.'

Heming approached her, showing not the slightest sign of embarrassment, for although he was trying to put on a show of humility and regret, he could not hide that mocking twinkle in his eye.

'Silje, I beg forgiveness. You see, we desperately needed money for the rebel cause.'

'Don't dress it up,' muttered Tengel.

'Of course, I should have stolen your virtue instead,' he teased, ignoring Tengel's remark. 'It's probably a disappointment for you that ...'

Tengel had grabbed hold of his collar and thrust his face close to Heming's. Through clenched teeth he hissed, 'Are you trying to make things worse?'

'No – no!' said Heming, his voice one of complete innocence – but there was no escaping the worried look in his eyes.

He stretched out a conciliatory hand towards Silje. She hesitated before accepting it, but his charm was irresistible and she could not stop herself from giving him a little smile. She had forgiven him as she would forgive a child crushed by the guilt of some misdeed, not as a repentant adult.

'Get back up on the wagon again,' commanded Tengel, and he made sure that they were all well stowed. Feeling his hands tuck the quilted blanket round her and seeing the gentleness reflected in his expression made Silje feel quite secure.

Finally he said, 'Keep a lookout behind us, Silje.'

Then they were on their way once more, but this time with the riders leading the way. The wind stung her cheeks as they travelled upward, but the children were safe and sound. Dag had started to cry again and, after some difficult searching, Silje had found the piece of knotted rag that he chewed on to comfort himself. This time, however, it was not an acceptable substitute for proper food and they continued their cross-country journey to the accompaniment of his tiny angry cries.

The going was slow. Sometimes the snowdrifts were so deep that they had to go around them; sometimes they fought their way though them, Tengel and Heming riding beside the wagon horses, gripping the shafts to help pull the load. Silje felt she was just useless extra weight adding to the burden, but she knew that her place was with the children. Eventually they were forced to hitch all four horses to the wagon, using any straps or bindings they could find. With this accomplished, progress became easier.

The high featureless plain soon ended and they found themselves, once again, surrounded by mountain peaks. Silje tried to get her bearings, but it was impossible. She had never realised that the Barren Mountains stretched so far.

A little further on they reached a glacier that looked impassable. A cruel icy blast blew around them. With practised hands, the horses were steered down a steep slope to the bank of a river, which they followed into a narrow valley. Here the glacier spanned the river in a great vaulted arch. Silje held on tightly to the side of the wagon throughout this jolting, swaying journey. Wide-eyed she gazed at the mass of packed ice now soaring above their heads.

They had reached the secret mountain track to the home of the Ice People. The men removed the runners and unhitched the two extra horses. It was peaceful here, but eerie and cold – a strange subterranean world. The ceiling above them varied greatly in height. Sometimes Silje was forced to duck out of the way of outcrops of ice, yet in other places Dag's screams would echo in giant caverns.

It was not completely dark; the ice gave the caves and

tunnels an unusual, shimmering green-blue glow. The wagon made its way along, close to the bank of the river, as it crashed and gurgled on its way with an echoing roar, marking its passage under the glacial ice. Silje wondered why there were not more droplets of water from the ceiling, but then realised it was probably too cold to thaw.

At one point Sol's frightened face peered round the edge of the covers. 'Where are we?' she whispered.

'On the way to our new home,' answered Silje in a hushed, almost reverent tone, which the tunnel of ice seemed to inspire.

'Our new home' – the words she had spoken brought a tightness to her chest, as many emotions overwhelmed her. The most powerful of these was great sadness – followed by uncertainty.

'Marie not come too?'

'Not just now. We'll see them all later.'

Will we? She asked herself this, as she wondered about their future. It seemed bleak and forlorn, and she kept thinking back to those they had left behind. Perhaps it was just her hunger speaking.

The glacier was not as extensive as she had expected. Before the frosty mists rising from the surface of the river had begun to penetrate her clothes, the way ahead lightened and suddenly they were in the open again. The wintry dusk was filled with flurries of snow, which was settling over the plain that spread before them.

Putting Dag down, Silje removed some of the blankets and coverings that had been wrapped about them. She and Sol stood up in the wagon to look around. Tengel had reined in his horse and rode alongside her. Now he waited nervously for her reaction.

This is his homeland, thought Silje. He will have strong

ties to it and love it dearly, just as one always loves the secret haunts of childhood, every stream and forest glen. Above all she was lost in amazement, for they had entered an oval-shaped valley, completely surrounded by mountains. There was a lake in the centre, the outfall of which they were now passing, and on the southern slopes stood cottages, nestling among thinly wooded areas of birch. It was remarkable that there was so little snow up here – the sun must be very strong and the mountains would protect the valley.

'Tengel!' she said in amazement, 'there's a whole village!'

He gave a wry smile. 'The Ice People number many more souls than folk would have you believe.'

Heming said quietly, 'Don't say "souls" when you speak of the Ice People. They are damned – the spawn of ice and darkness and evil.'

Silje understood that Heming was most unwilling to be counted among the Ice People and it did not surprise her. This isolated community would hardly be able to offer much to one of the world's great explorers! On the other hand, he was safe here. Outside the valley there was a price on his head.

Tengel retorted, 'A few of those who live here are fugitives like you, on the run from the injustice of the authorities. They cannot be counted as belonging to the true Ice People, the first ones.'

She felt his eyes on her. He was still waiting for her verdict on the scene before them. This man, considered by many not to be human, was willing her to like what she saw, afraid that she would be indifferent, or worse – reject it.

Silje swallowed hard. The desolation, the silent mountains and the loneliness she felt inside were beginning to affect her. 'It is so very lovely here,' she said softly. 'I am a little afraid of the strangeness of it all, but it has great beauty.'

He breathed out at last and gave her a wide smile. Silje was pleased that she was able to tell him honestly of her fears, but also that he should understand how much the wild landscape impressed her. Looking around she counted ten or fifteen cottages.

'Do you keep animals here as well?' she asked.

'But, of course! We must be able to provide for ourselves. This place is no different from any other village in Tröndelag. It's just more remote that's all.'

Heming snorted, 'Just like any other village? Silje, this is the most godforsaken place on earth!'

'Is there no church?' she asked worriedly.

'Did you really think there would be?' replied Tengel. 'We hold Sunday prayers in our homes, each family in turn. The chieftain is our preacher.'

She detected bitterness in his tone and could not help wondering where one such as Tengel would stand on the matter of religion.

They were coming to a farmstead that stood like a gatehouse by the icy entrance. As they approached, a man came out to welcome them.

'It's good to see you again,' he shouted. 'We'd almost given up hope and begun to count you among the dear departed. Your father will be pleased, Heming,' and turning to the driver, he said, 'and so will your wife.'

No one it seemed was waiting for Tengel, who asked, 'Is everyone accounted for?'

'Everyone is back for the winter, yes.'

'Good! Then we must block the entrance.'

With an eye on Silje, the man said, 'Newcomers?'

It was both a question and a statement of fact.

'Yes – on the run from the bailiff's men.'

'Your woman, Heming?'

The young upstart gave Tengel a quick nervous glance. 'No – no!' he said at once.

The man didn't ask if she was Tengel's woman. That thought didn't seem to occur to him. Though of course she wasn't strictly speaking his woman. He had simply shown her friendliness and consideration, and she could not ask for more than that. She gave a gentle sigh. She owed him a great debt of gratitude.

Heming joined the driver and the man from the farm as they tended the horses. One had almost lost a shoe in the icy tunnel and they wanted to take a closer look at it. Sol decided that it was much too cold and cuddled down under the covers again, arranging everything properly and tidily in the special way that only a self-confident young girl can.

'Where do you live, Tengel?' Silje asked bashfully.

He was still standing beside her, holding his horse. He pointed towards a farm some way off, up on the slopes. 'That is my childhood home.' He was smiling sadly as he spoke.

It seemed impossible that Tengel had been a child. She couldn't imagine him as one – she thought of him as always having been big and strong since birth. 'And, er … where shall the children and, um … I be staying?'

'Over there – on my farm.'

Silje's heart beat a little faster, making it hard to breathe.

Then he added quickly, 'I will live in my uncle's cottage. It is not used. It lies at the far end of the valley – you cannot see it from here.'

'But is it not better that *we* live there? Otherwise we shall be taking your home from you.'

'The cottage is not suitable for the children. My way is best.'

Silje could not get rid of the gloomy feeling that seemed to have overcome her since they entered the 'fortifications'. She could not explain it to herself either.

'Are you the only one in your family?' she asked quietly. 'Apart from Sol, I mean.'

'No. I have a cousin. She lives in the cottage next to mine, but because I am often away she has taken over all the livestock. Her name is Eldrid and she is a good deal older than I.'

Silje sat and reflected over the silhouette of this man, outlined against the lake in the failing evening light. She felt irresistibly drawn to him and she gripped tightly on the side of the wagon to allay her feelings.

Tengel felt her gaze and slowly turned to face her. He had a sad whimsical look in his narrow eyes, but then a slow suggestive smile began to trace across his lips. Her heart beat even faster and she looked away at once.

'Aren't you going to ask me where *I* live then?' said Heming, as he strode back from looking at the horses.

She grinned. 'So where do you live, Heming?'

'Can it be so hard to know?'

She had already noticed a farm down by the lake that appeared to be grander than the others.

'Down there?' she asked.

'Well, how *did* you guess?' he replied in mock surprise.

The others were ready and the driver urged the horses on again. Slowly the wagon began to trundle forward. Silje was looking around at all the new sights the valley held for her. The homes of the Ice People – how long she had dreamt about them – imagining deformed castles, where deep pits led down to the underworld, buildings continually bathed in moonlight, full of mystery and evil. Then to find this! A perfectly normal settlement, protected by the mountains.

Yet, try as she might, she still could not shake off a sense of anxiety, almost panic. What was it that was so frightening about this peaceful place? Its reputation, perhaps? Or something else, something in the silence, the way the buildings stood, crouching, as if ready to pounce like wild animals?

No, Silje thought she knew. She sensed deep melancholy in the wind that swept down the valley. The air was overwhelmed with the harsh memories of bygone centuries – everything that had ever occurred here – famine, poverty, extreme winters, loneliness; the tragedies and drama of life; sickness and misfortune. Who could say? But, worse by far was the curse that one man had placed on his people, which lay like a heavy yoke upon them still, after three hundred years.

Although Silje did not believe that the evil Tengel had ever met with Satan, it was enough that he had spread uncertainty and suspicion, sowing the seeds of fear among simple folk. That had been his evil legacy, especially in this place, so desolate and damned by the world outside. A heavy feeling of despair overcame her and she tried to reach out instinctively for Tengel's hand. He was riding slightly in front of her, lost in thought, and did not notice her gesture. Besides, judging by his expression, his thoughts also seemed to be negative.

Darkness began to close in around them and pale yellow lights lit the windows of one or two cottages. The Ice People were retiring for the night. Then, from behind the slow-moving procession, they heard a roar that echoed and reverberated down the valley, before it slowly died away.

'The way to the outside is now closed,' said Tengel. 'Only the spring thaw will open it again.'

She winced at the thought, but was comforted when he added, 'You are safe here, Silje. No one can reach you or the children.'

She glanced down at the little ones, resting in a pile of blankets and furs, and felt immense gratitude.

They carried on without speaking, listening to the wheels grinding and squeaking after the long journey. Suddenly Silje felt as though a dark shadow had fallen across her, clutching her heart with a vice-like grip.

'Tengel,' she gasped, 'what was that?'

Reaching out over the side of the wagon he took her outstretched hand in his. His eyes seemed to have taken on a dull glow. 'What is wrong, Silje?'

'I was so afraid. There is something … something watching – something evil, close by. I feel I am being stared at.'

'You do? Then you are more perceptive than I thought.'

His strong hand squeezed hers. Her eyes followed his gaze down below the track to a hollow where an ancient building lay hidden. In the gathering darkness it appeared to be cowering low, watching and brooding.

'Don't *ever* go there, Silje,' he said slowly. 'Not ever!'

'Is it …'

'One of the evil Tengel's descendants? Yes. Two, in fact. My mother's cousin and my grandfather's sister.' The last few words were in a whisper, as though they were difficult for him to utter.

'Your grandfather's sister?' Silje's tone was one of disbelief. 'She must be awfully old.'

'Yes. She is, very.'

Somehow that simple reply filled her with untold dread.

'Stay with me, Tengel,' she pleaded in a hurried whisper. 'I dare not be alone, not this first night. Everything is new …'

'You will be all right, you'll see.'

'But are there many descendants of …Tengel.'

'No not many. Not now. Only very few can trace their line directly to him. The Black Death took many of them and nearly all the rest fell to the plague of 1565. There are those two down there – they are not mother and son, neither have they had offspring. No one will marry kin of Tengel the Evil, as you know. His kinsmen take the women they desire and force them to live with them. The women of my family are raped and then cast aside, with their children, to care for themselves. Only my sister was properly wed, but she never revealed where she came from. Because of this there are not many children in our family – and that is not a bad thing.'

'Please do not be so bitter, Tengel. It saddens me so.'

'I'm sorry. Let me tell you more about my kin. There are two old men, unmarried and very amiable with no terrifying powers. There is also a disagreeable old woman living in that hovel over by the lake, but she keeps herself to herself and you won't meet her. Finally, of course, there is Sol. So now you see that, until we found her, I was the last one who could carry our evil line forward.'

'Yes, but you knew that your sister had two daughters in Trondheim, so the line would not have died with you.'

'I only found out about the daughters last autumn, when my brother-in-law, whom I had never met, died from the plague. I rode out at once to see if I could find my sister, Sunniva, and be of help. But, may God forgive me, Silje, I wish the plague had taken the little girls too!'

She said nothing for a moment, then asked, 'Do you still wish it?'

He sighed deeply. 'No, I know the whole thing is very confused, but Sol fills me with a tenderness I cannot put into words. I am responsible for her now.'

Softly she said, 'I do understand.' Then she paused. 'So you are descended from the first Tengel on your mother's side?'

'Yes. She was never wed. My sister and I had different fathers and they both left our mother to fend for herself.'

'So what became of you both after she died giving birth to you?'

'Her father took care of us. It is his farm I have inherited.'

'Oh, Tengel!' she said gently. 'It hurts me so to hear this. If only I could ... help you somehow. Show you the tenderness you have missed!'

'Don't say that!' he exclaimed savagely. 'No one need concern themselves over me, and you should *know* that!'

A pitiful 'I'm sorry' was all she could say.

They had emerged onto a plain above the valley. It was lighter here and the anxiety she had felt a little earlier left her. Nevertheless, Silje held resolutely fast to Tengel's hand, pulling him to her, but with practised ease he rode close alongside the wagon. He was her tower of strength and, if he had asked, she would gladly have placed her whole life in his hands.

By now she had grown tired of this difficult and long journey – pummelled by the incessant shaking of the wagon, aching for food, warmth and rest – and she longed to wash herself and tidy her hair. She could not help feeling a little despondent at not knowing what she had let herself in for. Then she let out a short harsh chuckle.

His keen senses did not miss it.

'What are you thinking?' he asked sternly.

'All about the dreams for the future that I had as a child.'

'I do not expect they've come true, have they?'

'No, but I did have one great desire.'

'What was that? Tell me,' he urged.

'Well, on the estate where I lived, and where my father worked, the owners had a painting in the hall that portrayed an avenue lined with linden trees. It was the most elegant thing I had ever set eyes on. There was a real avenue up to the manor of course, but it was lined with maples. I would follow the changing seasons by it. The misty light-green leaves of spring that became so tightly packed together in the summer. Come the autumn, the sticky touch of their fruit. I saw the leaves changing colour and the naked boughs of winter that turned bluish-lilac as they began to bud once more. Then one day they chopped them all down. They said they were too old and took too much out of the earth. But oh, how I missed them. I was still most fond of the linden trees in the picture, though. Naturally I did not know what trees they were at the time, but I found out later, and then I promised myself that when I was grown up I should have an avenue of lindens leading to my home. Yes, a childish dream for one of my position in society, of course, especially as linden trees will not grow in Tröndelag.'

Tengel was silent for a while. 'No, I'm afraid you will probably never have your avenue.'

'No.' she replied. Then, shaking off her reverie, she tried to catch his eye in the dim light. 'But I have something of greater worth – the tenderness and trust of another. Thank you, Tengel, I do not know if I can find the words to tell you how I feel. Such words of affection do not exist.'

He let go of her hand gently and spurred his horse forward. He neither spoke nor turned to look at her as he rode on ahead again.

Chapter 11

Silje lay awake for a long time during that first night in the valley of the Ice People, listening for noises outside – but all was quiet. Yet, because she was so on edge, even the silence felt sinister. Was there something on the other side of the wall, something unutterably awful, waiting for her almost to fall asleep, so that it could bang on the wall and frighten her to death?

These fears gripped her even though, as soon as they arrived, she had secretly blessed the house in every way she knew. She had placed the wooden spoons on the bench in a cross, drawn a cross above the door and then formed one more cross from some kindling to put beside the fire – any evil spirit trying to enter through the flue would be blinded by it straight away.

The children had been given food and dry clothes. They lay asleep close to her, warmed by the fire in the main room, its embers still aglow on the hearth in the middle of the floor. Sol's rapid breathing was easy to hear, but Dag always slept so quietly that, just like any natural mother, she listened all the time to make sure he was still alive.

What did she know about this cottage? How many

people had died here and had any souls remained to haunt it? She was still frightened. Quite simply, she was scared of the darkness and all it hid in this cottage and the valley. All these people she did not know – how would they welcome her, an outsider? There was the penetrating cold of the mountains and the children's uncertain future – all these concerns and more whirled around in her exhausted mind, making her restless and unable to sleep.

How she wished that Tengel was with her now! He had told her that he would have to leave for the sake of her honour. Oh, what did she care that people should gossip? She needed him close to her – to feel safe, as a child needs the comforting embrace of its father. Then she allowed herself a little embarrassed smile. Perhaps it had been better that he had gone, after all. She knew how he made her feel and that she could not hide these emotions from him. Were he to put his arms around her, he would release passions that a daughter would never have for her father. Nonetheless, her loneliness bore down on her. She was homesick for Benedikt's farm, as it had been before Abelone arrived and Benedikt had come to her room – before so much had gone wrong.

Heming had gone back to his home, where he would no doubt have been greeted with great disapproval by his father, the chieftain. She thought that Tengel had sent him on his way, for he had shown no eagerness to leave them. The wagon-driver had remained behind for a while, helping Tengel to arrange things as best they could in the chilly deserted rooms. At first Silje had been unable to do much more than stand in the middle of the floor, frozen and awkward, just watching, while they lit a fire and prepared the beds. Then the children began to whine, dragging her slowly back to her senses, and she started to help.

It was an old farm, nowhere near as large as Benedikt's, but it certainly appeared now to be warm and well built. The single storey cottage had a room at one end that was used for preparing food and eating meals, beyond which lay the dairy and a barn, all connected in one row. At the other end of the cottage were two small rooms, and it was in one of these that Silje and the children now lay, leaving the door to the main room open. There was no glass in the windows of course, and Silje thought briefly of the leaded light that Benedikt had given her. No, she decided, it would not find its rightful place in this house.

She wondered what Tengel was doing at that moment. Was he now heating and tidying up in another cottage, or some run-down hovel? He must surely have been as tired as she was. She had wanted to suggest that he stayed the night at the home of the wagon-driver, but as there seemed to be no hinting of this from the man himself, she suspected that Tengel was not welcome in the dwellings of others. Once again the pain of sadness and compassion for him lay heavy on her heart.

He had stayed behind until long after the driver had left, putting things in their place – almost not wanting to go. Silje had carried on talking feverishly to keep him there longer. She had asked him again to stay, for his own sake, not wanting him to suffer any discomfort now that she had taken over his home. He had merely shaken his head and, finally, there was nothing more left to do and no more left to say.

Her arms felt empty. Could this be just because she had been holding Dag for so many long hours? Restlessly she turned onto her side and tried to sleep once more, still filled with worry about the day to come, when she would stand face to face with the others of the Ice People. Sleep would not come, however hard she tried. Instead, thoughts and images that she had tried to banish assailed her mind – memories of the unbearable days when the plague reached the manor.

Fear and anxiety had taken hold of everyone when one of the servants was the first to fall ill. There had been silence at mealtimes, the watchful eyes of the others looking all the time for the signs and symptoms. She remembered her brother, sweating with fever, and her mother's hysterical screams; his funeral, when her youngest sister stood weakly, leaning on her at the graveside, before collapsing; then the sister's own funeral – there were many more dead by then.

On that occasion the pastor held the burial service in front of four coffins. One of them contained the master's own son, the boy she had looked after and through whom she had received so much education. Silje had grieved for him, but she was so numbed by the death of her siblings that she had been in a daze. She could still hear the anguished cry of the master, 'Why *me*, why *me*?' Did he not see that the plague had no respect for social boundaries, taking the highest and the lowest as it pleased? That the servants should die was perfectly normal and nothing for him to concern himself over, but one of his own family, well!

Then her mother and father fell sick, almost at the same time, and Silje cared for them on her own. No one had the courage to enter the homes of the sick and offer succour any longer. She remembered how she had fumbled around in a haze of tears – and how her prayers begging that they should not leave her had finally gone unanswered. Her baby brother had been coughing, choking, crying. She was all alone with him. That had been the worst day of all.

There had been three coffins on that day, the last ones

from the blacksmith's little cottage. The foreman had come to the door that very same day, not daring to enter. A curt 'You are to clear out, Silje. The master needs the cottage for the new blacksmith' was all that was said. Nobody gave a thought to where she would go.

A sound from across the lake brought her back from her sad contemplation. Was it the bark of a fox – or was it the scream of a tormented soul echoing down the valley? No, there it was again and it did sound more like a fox. But still she prayed it was nothing worse. In any case the interruption was welcome, because she was starting to feel her sadness take over again. She must stop reflecting on the past before it sapped all her strength – especially now that she needed all the energy she could muster.

She relaxed slowly, and took long deep breaths of the strange smells and aromas of the cottage: birch-wood smoke, the dry straw of the mattresses, branches of juniper on the floor. Nothing nasty at all, she decided.

Tengel had been so different when he left them and had told her to fasten the door. He had not wanted to see the desperate pleading expression on her face, her fear of being left on her own – and yes, her deep-felt desire for him to stay close to her.

He had waited, holding the latch before he said, awkwardly, 'It's good that you are here, Silje – you and the children. It is easier for me.' Then just as he closed the door, he added softly, 'But also more difficult.'

Tengel … Silje was trying to imagine his face close to hers, but couldn't. Instead she saw an image of him outlined in the doorway, just as she had last seen him, his wolf-skin hood thrown back and his straight black hair reaching to his shoulders. This giant figure, with his broad upper body and shoulders, seemed so out of proportion that he resembled a proud forest animal, more like a stag or great bear with a large black mane. The wolf-skin did nothing to lessen this image. His legs were long and hips narrow; she had glimpsed beneath his shirt and noticed a profusion of chest hair, exactly like an animal's. 'Beast-man' is what she had called him when she first saw him, and she was not the only person to use that description.

How was she able to feel such a strong attraction to one so frightening? What were all these feelings that she had for him – loyalty, tenderness, warmth, belonging, sympathy, shy admiration and a burning, agonising sensual desire. No, she would not dwell on such thoughts again – she knew from experience that she would never get to sleep if she did. She curled up on the crumpled straw-filled mattress and finally fell into a slumber.

****

The woman who lived in the next cottage, Tengel's relative, was a great help to Silje during her first days in this strange valley. Eldrid was a very down-to-earth sort of person, sharing neither Tengel's demonic looks, nor his dead sister's beauty. A farming woman, she was hard-working and reliable. Although she had remained unwed, because nobody dared marry any descendant of the evil Tengel, she knew so much more than Silje about housekeeping and small children. Tengel had allowed her to take over all his livestock and, despite Silje's protests, she arrived with fresh milk every morning. Although Silje felt that she should be fetching it herself, Eldrid insisted on bringing the milk for them all.

Silje did her best to keep the cottage in good order and perform all the usual household tasks. She had to do everything herself; fetch water from a nearly frozen well;

chop and bring in firewood; build a fire in the icy chill of morning; grind grain for bread-making; wash the children's clothes; mend the split in Sol's winter boots; try to fashion a sewing needle from a fishbone, because in their haste they had forgotten to pack the sewing things and she found none in the cottage, and much more besides.

One thing that Silje had never quite realised was just how much Marie and Grete had done to reduce the burden on her of caring for the children. Now she was left to do everything herself. To her disappointment, she began to see that she would not be able to manage. An infant with a sore bottom after the long journey and a very unruly two year-old were driving her to distraction. She felt completely useless.

Eldrid saw what was happening. 'You are only seventeen, lass, and you've had two strange children dropped in your lap. I'm not sure you're the homely sort either, are you? You've made it look very pretty here and you're working every hour there is, but still the dust piles high in the corners.'

Disheartened, Silje dried her eyes. 'I know. I thought I could at least manage the children, but I lack the patience.'

Sol had been smacked for kicking burning embers over the floor for no other reason than that Silje had told her not to, and she was showing the world how badly she had been treated by screaming from the end room, even drowning out Dag's continual whining. One by one, the bread cakes Silje had been trying to bake had been burnt to a cinder because of Sol's unruliness.

'Let me take the children for a few days, until you get settled,' said Eldrid. 'There have not been many children in my home, but Sol is my cousin's daughter.'

Silje hesitated. She was tempted, but on the other hand, being so fond of them, she wanted to keep them with her.

'Thank you very much,' she answered, 'but I think we should talk to Tengel first. He has placed them in my hands and I should seek his advice.'

'I understand, of course, but you are completely worn out and that will do you no good at all. Grown mothers with their own children can despair at times – and many give up for less. Tengel has told me what you have been through, about how you cared for the children and your friendliness towards him – and that is something he is unaccustomed to. You mean so well, Silje, yet you are no more than a young girl.'

Embarrassed by this praise, Silje grinned. 'I am so worried about Dag,' she said. 'His tiny bottom is red raw and no matter what I do to try to make it better, he screams almost all the time.'

'May I take a look at the boy?'

Eldrid's work-worn hands held the babe with easy confidence.

'Goodness me,' she exclaimed, shocked by what she uncovered. 'Why have you said nothing to Tengel? He can have this cleared up in a few days.'

'Babies' sore bottoms?' Silje grinned in spite of her concerns. 'I find that hard to believe.'

'I meant illness and discomfort in general.'

'Well, I have not seen Tengel since the night we arrived, ten days ago.'

Eldrid gazed thoughtfully at her. 'That's just like him! He comes to me every day to hear how you are settling in and to give me new orders. His regard for you is without bounds, Silje. Well, he is not at home just now, he is on the mountain getting things ready for winter, but I shall tell him. He may come to see you tonight. There is something else – I wondered if you would join us in our prayers tomorrow? Then you can meet the other people who live in the valley and not sit here shut in with the children.'

'But who will look after the little ones?'

'Tengel can do it. He is not allowed to attend the service, anyway.'

'Whyever not?'

Eldrid pulled a face. 'They say he carries a shadow with him – one of you-know-who. It is so foolish and cruel. They are all suffering from the results of centuries of inbreeding, yet they look down on us.'

'Do they despise you?' asked Silje in disbelief.

'No, not despise. Fear.'

'But in fact it is your kin that have the purest lineage here, isn't it?'

'Yes indeed! The others are completely inbred with one another, something that has to be expected after several hundred years of isolation – some of the consequences have been very unfortunate.'

'And do they let you attend their prayers from a feeling of compassion?'

'Yes. I am not scarred by the inheritance of the first Tengel. I am "normal" in their eyes.'

Silje looked long and hard at the children in the end room.

'I should like to come with you, for I have been acting like a heathen of late. But can we really leave them with Tengel? The boy cries so much.'

'He will just have to put up with it. Now, let me help you with the baking.'

As soon as Eldrid had gone, Silje ran into the room where the children were and lifted Sol from the floor.

'Tengel is a-coming, Tengel is a-coming,' she sang, as she danced round with the girl.

Sol joined in wholeheartedly, whirling round and round, and by doing so granted Silje a pardon for all the hardship she had inflicted!

'We must make everything spick-and-span,' said Silje excitedly. 'If you sweep then I shall clean the bowls.'

'Pretty skirt?' inquired Sol.

'Oh yes! You will wear your finest skirt, but we must wait until evening. First there is work to do.'

They set the table with the nicest things they had and, when Tengel finally arrived, they had been waiting patiently, dressed in their best clothes, for a long time. Sol rushed up to him, throwing her arms around his knees in welcome. He lifted her up and admired her dress, then looked at Silje.

'You had some trouble with the children, I heard.'

That wonderful, deep voice of his, drawing her to him, made her go hot and cold at the same time.

'No, it's not that …'

'I was given a real telling-off by Eldrid,' he interrupted. 'She told me that I had no understanding of what it meant to keep house and care for two children alone – especially for one as young and impractical as you. So tell me, what's wrong with them.'

'Well,' she stammered, finding it hard to utter the words while he watched her so seriously. 'Dag first of all,' and she undressed the infant again. It was a tedious, awkward process.

'Tengel looked at him. 'Did I not give you an ointment once – for your foot?'

'You did, but can it be used for this as well? I did not dare try it.'

'Hmm, no! I have something better,' he replied, taking out a small pouch.

In a soft voice, with memories of his last healing fresh in her mind, she asked 'Do you need to be alone with him?'

There was almost a smile as he said, 'I don't invoke chants and incantations for such a little rump as this!'

So that was what he did – incantations! Silje felt a cold chill run down her spine. Tengel read her thoughts.

'For so long as I use my powers in the cause of good, I see no reason for you to find fault with me.'

'I would not do that,' she replied, blushing, feeling ashamed. 'It's simply that you scare me at times.'

'Have I given you cause to fear me?' His voice was low, remorseful, and the words tore at her heart.

'Sille dance – dance,' shouted Sol suddenly, changing the mood.

Tengel turned to her, 'What's that you say? Was Silje dancing?'

'Sill an' Sol dance roundanroundanroun – like this,' she showed him, adding, 'Sing'd *Tengel commin, Tengel commin.*'

'Tell-tale,' muttered Silje through clenched teeth.

Then Sol stopped her whirling, hopping dance and said, 'Sill cry – in bed, cry!'

Tengel was serious once more. 'Do you, Silje?'

'No – she makes too much of things. Pay her no heed.'

Then Sol remembered how badly she had been treated, the insult she had suffered, earlier in the day. 'Sill *hit* me, *hit* me,' she announced wide-eyed, sensing the importance of this message.

'Oh yes! I did hear that a young lady had scattered hot coals all around the hearth – and I cannot think that Silje would hit you very hard.'

Once they had tended to Dag and wrapped him up again, they sat down to eat. Sol was delighted to be awake at such a late hour.

'I think the boy's skin rash may be caused by the milk he is getting,' said Tengel. 'At this time of year our cows are being fed on turnips and their milk may be too strong for him. I will tell Eldrid to feed one cow on hay and see if it helps. We must be a bit careful with him, because he never fed on his mother's milk.'

Silje was fascinated. 'How do you know so much? I have never heard anyone speak like that before. I mean – what the cows *eat*!'

'Ah, we know many things in our family.' There was some bitterness in his voice. Then he said, 'I agree with Eldrid that you must have some help. You have dark rings under your eyes.'

'There is not much time to sleep that's true, what with Dag crying all the time. But there is something I should like, Tengel.'

'Yes?'

'The old loom in the back room. I should love to weave on it, if I may.'

'Of course you can!' he said gleefully. 'I shall ask Eldrid to help you set it up. I wonder if she has any yarn.'

'I can spin my own – there are piles of wool in there. I am good at things like that, Tengel. It will help stop me from feeling so useless, so helpless.'

'Why on earth do you feel like that?'

Sol had fallen asleep on the bench, still wearing her best dress. She was not used to being up so late, but had wanted so much to see Tengel again and, as the most obstinate child in all of Norway, she had got her way.

'Well, because I *am* useless,' she retorted. 'The only things I am good at are things nobody needs to know. Benedikt told me that as well.'

'Benedikt said that you were a little artist, a creative

soul, and that one should not overburden such folk with mundane tasks or their nerves will suffer. That is what has happened to you.'

'But I feel so ashamed by it.'

Tengel had never touched a woman. Now, instinctively, he reached out and gently stroked her cheek. Silje gasped and turned her head slightly and her lips kissed his hand. He took some of her hair in a strong grip and gave a deep trembling sigh. Then abruptly he rose and stood away from the table. 'I must leave now.'

'But you will come back soon, won't you?' She stood there waiting for his answer. He didn't move. He just looked at her.

'I cannot say. I shall try not to but ...'

'But what?'

'Ever since Eldrid came to fetch me today, telling me that I should come here, I feel as though I have been struck by fever. Yes, I will come back, but never alone. I just ... would not be able to do that. But I will look after the children tomorrow.'

Then he turned quickly and left.

Once she had put Sol to bed and tidied everything away for the night, Silje began slowly to undress. Usually she would sleep wearing her shift, not wanting to take off all her clothes; she was a little prudish about such things. Tonight was different, however, and she sat on the edge of the bed, bathed in the glow from the fire in the main room, and slowly, very slowly pulled her shift over her head and placed it beside her. Without daring to look down, she lightly touched her skin, letting her hands play across her body and down towards the curve of her waist. She knew she was slim and well developed, with breasts that were firm and nicely rounded. She placed her hands on her belly to feel how flat it was and only then, feeling a little bit ashamed, did she look down at herself.

He would like her body, she thought. There was nothing displeasing about it. If only he had wanted it ... then she snapped out of the fantasy and her courage left her, to be replaced by shame once more. Picking up her shift, she pulled it back on as fast as she could.

****

The prayer meeting was held at the home of Heming's father, the chieftain. Silje walked there with Eldrid, nervous and anxious, but excited at the same time. Tengel had arrived to take care of the children and his swift, almost unseen smile was enough for her to live on for a whole week, or so she thought.

They had come to a magnificent house, not quite as large as Benedikt's, perhaps, but it offered all that one could ask for in this isolated place. It boasted woodcarvings and patterns that would be hard to find anywhere. Every doorpost and ceiling beam had been worked in the most artistic fashion. Silje was so impressed by it all that she completely forgot to curtsey and greet her host properly.

'Yes, they are rather fine, aren't they?' Heming's father was every inch the chieftain, with his long beard and lean noble bearing.

Coming back to reality, Silje looked down from the beam she had been admiring.

'So unbelievably beautiful,' she exclaimed. 'Who has done such fine work?'

'Ah – it is very old, a couple of hundred years, I think. One of my ancestors did it. Anyway, I expect you must be Silje. Heming has spoken of you and how you helped to decorate a church. So you understand this sort of thing?'

This last question was followed by a patronising chuckle, as if to confirm that a woman would know nothing of art.

Silje remembered her manners and gave a low curtsey. Heming was there in the hall, with that mocking smile of his, but he said nothing and his father continued, 'I had been told that you saved the life of my errant son. For that you have my heartfelt thanks.'

'I did not do very much,' she said humbly. 'Tengel did most of it.'

He cast a curious glance at her. Something about the way she had spoken Tengel's name – with reverence, breathlessly – had surprised him.

They were taken into the great hall, where the rest of the Ice People had congregated, with the exception of those who had most right to call themselves Ice People: the poor accursed descendants of Tengel the Evil One. Silje felt very uncomfortable in front of the many inquisitive faces of those watching her entrance. Benches had been set up on either side of a long table, one for men and one for women. Both sides seemed to be equally critical in regarding the newcomer, but Eldrid had prepared her for this. Silje had lived on the outside with those they feared most. Who would dare do such a thing? What sort of person would she be?

Not a word was spoken. She did the only thing she could – curtsey to them and wait by the door. She could see at once, however, evidence of everything she had ever been told about in-breeding. There were two cretins, their mouths agape, one other who was clearly mad and a pair of very dangerous-looking individuals. Yet they were all accepted for what they were, and Silje found that touching. She just could not understand why a good person like Tengel should be shunned.

They showed her to a place on the women's bench and the service began. She found it hard to concentrate, no matter how she tried. Although she knew full well that she ought to be listening to the words of God, she could feel the artful glances of the others; the eyes that were averted as soon as she looked in their direction.

Most of the people there seemed friendly, but that didn't make them any less critical or curious; almost the opposite, in fact. Worst of them all were two young boys who simply sat and stared at her all the time, without once pretending to look away. One of them was probably not as normal as other folk, but this was not easy to see from his appearance. There was something about him – she couldn't describe it – his eyes had a wildness in them, uncontrolled, that told her she had better be wary of him.

When the prayers were finished and everyone rose to their feet, she saw to her dismay that many of those whose minds were disturbed were wearing chains. So this was how they were kept safe! Their plight saddened her, but could it be that there was no other way to control them?

She walked home with a heavy heart, full of compassion for all in the valley, disturbed and far from strengthened by God's word. Something Eldrid had said earlier came back to her – that, in many cases, those pious faces were just for show. For behind the low narrow doors of their homes, people bowed before different gods – the invisible forces of nature, supernatural spirits that one didn't even dare to name. It was not only the kin of the first Tengel who were immersed in such things, although they were the only ones with powers. It was not surprising that *all* the Ice People were feared, excommunicated and hunted down by the worldly authorities outside.

They had been walking in silence for a while when her

curiosity prompted her to ask, 'There is a dwelling close to the outflow of the lake that Tengel showed me when we came. He said two of his relatives lived there and that I should never go near it. Were they at the meeting today?'

'Hanna and Grimar? No – are you mad?' replied Eldrid, crossing herself as she spoke.

'Are they the … *worst* ones?'

'Oh, yes!' said Eldrid drawing a deep breath. 'Nobody goes there. Not ever!'

'Why not?'

The older woman's voice became a whisper. 'They can cast sickness upon you, make you see things, make you lame or blind your eyes, put a curse on the cows and stop them milking – all that is evil is within their grasp. It is they who have cursed this valley with so many simpletons.'

'That cannot be!' said Silje decisively. 'In my learning I was told that even the families of nobility were not permitted to marry into each other too many times, for there would be bad blood. So I do not think Hanna or Grimar can be blamed for that.'

Eldrid said nothing as they walked on.

'Who looks after them?' asked Silje, 'who knows if they have food?'

'Ah, they take care of themselves.'

Silje persisted. 'But I thought they were old, the woman anyway.'

'They are both old. But we will have no dealings with them – and you will do well to heed Tengel's words and keep away from them!'

Tengel was waiting at the door. Eagerly he met Silje's gaze, as though he had been waiting all day for that very moment, and it seemed to calm him.

'Well, how was it? You seem disturbed,' he said to Silje.

'Is that so surprising,' Eldrid butted in as she entered the room, 'with that congregation? Their eyes were devouring the lass. Especially those Bratteng lads!'

Tengel followed them in, a worried look on his face.

'Do you think there is any danger?'

'Well, if you ask me, *someone* should stay here with her,' answered Eldrid, 'and you are not living in the best of places at the moment either. Still, did things go well with the children?'

'Sol has so much energy, she has run me ragged,' he said with a smile, 'and the boy has been holding concert as usual. He is sleeping just now – at last! Silje, I do not know how you have managed all this. Why did you not ask for help sooner?'

'I would have been ashamed of myself,' she replied. 'Think of all those mothers with a dozen children or more – and who also live in great poverty! I am well looked after – should I not be able to take care of just two?'

Tengel laughed, 'I would say Sol on her own is the equal of any five!'

Silje thought she sensed a nervousness about him. He was unsure of himself and, for the first time ever since she had met him, somehow inept. Now he avoided looking directly at her, turning away with a melancholy expression.

Eldrid decided to take Sol with her to fetch some milk and they were left alone. They stood facing each other, neither one knowing what to say.

Silje broke the silence, 'Tell me what's wrong, Tengel.'

He didn't answer at first, then slowly he said, 'You should not have done that last night.'

'Done what?'

'When I … caressed your cheek.'

He meant when she had kissed his hand. She looked at

the floor, hoping that the bright red glow of embarrassment would be less visible. 'I couldn't help myself, Tengel. It just happened. And it was you who put temptation in my way.'

Sad eyes stared at her for a few moments.

'Please don't make fun of me, Silje. I couldn't bear it!'

'I am *not* making fun of you at all,' she retorted.

'My dear girl, do you not think I am aware of my looks? Deformed, disfigured, like some wild animal – reviled by one and all.'

'Not by me,' her whisper was as gentle as a passing breeze.

He stood perfectly still. He could almost have stopped breathing.

Silje swallowed hard. 'Surely my feelings come as no surprise to you?'

Without a word, in one fluid movement he crouched down beside the fire and began to prod at it with a stick.

'Then tell me about your dreams, Silje.'

'About my – oh, you mean *those*.'

'Yes, you say that I understand your feelings, but I don't. It is not easy to read the difference between – well, what you once described as loyalty to me – and sympathy.'

With some trepidation she crouched down beside him. 'I do not know whether I dare tell. I have been brought up to be chaste, as well you know.'

'I do. But now I need to hear them. Many things are difficult for me just now, and I need to find out whether I am alone or if there is another who understands my emotions. A person who …'

'Who is fond of you? You know that there is – but you ask too much of me, Tengel. How can I describe in words all that I felt in my dreams?'

'If you are able to do this, then I shall tell you all that I have dreamt about you.'

She began to feel very hot and self-conscious beside him. She went and sat on a low stool, but the hard unpadded seat was uncomfortable and she changed her position slowly, with a painful sensual movement that he could plainly see. He turned back to the fire.

'Please try to understand why I am asking this. I need something to *nourish* my life! Now I have plenty to live *for* – you and the children – but I have nothing to live *on* when I am alone. Grant me that, Silje. My life has been filled with many hours of solitude. I know nothing but loneliness.'

She understood what he meant and, plucking up the courage, she began in a whisper, 'I have always had dreams about your mountains. I used to call them the Land of Shadows and they were the lair of terrible demons that would rise up, fly towards my home and frighten me. But then, in my special dream, something different happened.'

She stopped, and Tengel gave her a sidelong look. He was unusually tense.

'Carry on,' he said. 'Do you mean the sensual part?'

'Yes! Tengel, I can't say more. This isn't right.'

'I beg you,' he whispered to her, his hands shaking as they grasped the stick.

The atmosphere in the room had changed. The air itself was quaking, trembling in some strange way.

Silje gave a moan of despair and then said, 'The demons were not the same as they had been. They were different – grown, lustful men – and they desired me. I lay naked in a pasture. I was waiting for a special one.'

Tengel's stern expression stayed fixed.

'At last the demon I was waited for appeared, but he remained a long way off above the mountain ridge. But I could see it was you, and my body began to … become excited with an unbearable fire inside. With that I awoke. That was the first dream.'

She covered her face with her hands. Gently Tengel pulled them away. 'And the other one?'

'No, I cannot tell you that one!'

'Did it come to a … conclusion?'

'No, it ended as the first one had done, at the moment of decision. But I behaved shamelessly in my dream, Tengel. I wanted to see your body and feel it touching mine – and both times, when I woke up … No, how can I tell you this?'

'You awoke filled with lust and desire?' he asked without looking at her.

Her silence told him what he already knew.

'It is nothing to be ashamed of,' he said. 'It happens to most people. I think that, despite your upbringing and your shyness, you have very strong …' he paused, searching for a word, 'urges, and I have known this since I first saw you. It is in your eyes – and your expression.'

'But it is only for …' she began loudly, then realising the significance of her admission, finished quietly with 'you'.

She saw at once by his smile that she had made him very happy. He tried, without success, to conceal it.

'And now it is your turn,' she said covered in embarrassment. 'You promised to tell me your dreams.'

The warmth in the room was almost intolerable, and Silje knew that it did not come from the fire in the hearth.

'It will not be easy.'

'I said that too, but you would have me tell you anyway.'

'It will not be easy, Silje, because my dreams are waking dreams. When I sleep, I sleep. Nothing more.'

She felt a sensation of excitement flowing through her. She moved slightly on the stool again. 'Waking dreams?'

'Yes! I have been with you, Silje. Every evening, even when you were at Benedikt's house, I knew what your room looked like. I remembered the time when I put my hands on your foot, but then I let them move up under your skirts. I, who have never allowed myself even to think of women. In agonies of delight, I have undressed you and gazed at you lying there and …'

Silje was gasping for breath – terrified by the feelings his words had evoked.

'And my hands were still around your waist, long after I had helped you down from the horse. I can still feel exactly how it was and, in my thoughts, I let my hands reach inside your clothing and hold your breasts. I have touched your soft warm skin …'

A whimper from Silje urged him on.

Quickly he said, 'But I have never dared to come to you, not even in my thoughts – that is too sacred, unassailable. I realise that it can never be real – I must never allow a child to be born into the same misery that I suffer. But I offer you my deepest, most heartfelt thanks for daring to tell me of your dreams. You have given me the strength to carry on.'

'But has this made it easier for you?'

'No,' he replied quietly.

'And not for me either.'

He placed a hand on hers.

'Silje,' was all he said, but in that one word she could hear *everything* he felt for her – body and soul.

Overwhelmed with the tenderness and warmth, she said, 'We will never speak of these things again, do you agree?'

'Yes,' he nodded.

They remained sitting in front of the fire, deep in thought, each aware that the presence of the other brought a sense of belonging as well as sadness.

Eventually, it was the sound of Sol's joyful voice outside that broke the mood. Tengel stood up at once and pulled Silje to her feet. A fleeting smile, gentle but sad, brightened his face for an instant. Then together they walked to the door to meet the others.

Chapter 12

Next morning Eldrid came to collect the children. It had been agreed they would stay with her for a few days. Dag had managed to sleep a little during the night and Silje thought that his bottom was not as red and sore as it had been. Perhaps it was just her imagination. The previous day Tengel had asked them to loosen 'that terrible swaddling', a request that Eldrid had argued strenuously against. Everyone knew that a child not securely bound in swaddling would be deformed. One had to make sure that the infant's legs grew straight. Had he taken leave of his senses?

Silje decided to loosen the binding nonetheless, as soon as the boy was returned to her. She had already been doing so while they were living with Benedikt and now her unfailing belief in Tengel served to reinforce her decision.

As soon as Eldrid had left, taking the children with her, Silje busied herself filling a basket with food. She was full of nerves as she got ready to go out, wearing the beautiful velvet cloak Tengel had given her. Following little-used paths in the hope she would not be seen, she walked through the woods of birch growing on the hillside to the far side of the valley, closer to where the outflow joined the glacier.

It would surely snow before long. The mountain peaks had disappeared into the low heavy grey clouds and the few slopes that were visible were completely covered in snow. This day was far colder than recent days had been and icy winds cut noisily through the trees, rattling at the few leaves left clinging to their branches.

Silje knew she would have to cross the road at some point, and hoped she would be able to do so unseen, but it was not to be. As she stepped into the road, she saw a woman walking towards her, but to Silje's great surprise, the stranger immediately leapt into the woods at the side of the road and hid. She remembered how she'd noticed similar behaviour before in this valley, where people who had lived closed in and isolated for so many generations were intensely fearful of *any* outsider. Quite simply the woman was scared of Silje, possibly even believing her to be a dangerous threat. Silje chuckled to herself and walked on her way.

As soon she saw the old low-roofed building in the hollow, her heart began to pound and her hands started to tremble. Should she dare go on? The cottage showed no sign of life. The sound of an axe biting into wood came from far-off, down the valley. She wondered if it was Tengel working and found comfort in the thought. There were no tracks in the snow where she now stood, even though the last snowfall had been a week earlier. How long had it been since any neighbour had been to visit?

'*Nobody goes there. They can take care of themselves.*'

They could have been dead for weeks, she thought. Then she recalled the tremendous sense of dread she felt in passing this place when she first came to the valley – the feeling that someone was watching her. She walked on up to the cottage, with uncertainty eating at every fibre of her body. Every step became harder as fear began to take control.

The cottage had a stable door, skewed on its hinges, with snow lying deep up against the lower half of it. Her fingers were shaking so badly that her first attempt to knock made no sound at all. Her heart fluttering like a sparrow's, she tried again. By now she was scared out of her wits.

Shivering slightly she waited, straining her ears, but there was no sound. She had still heard nothing when the top half of the door swung open, making her jump. In the darkness beyond glowed, cat-like, the eyes of an old man. Silje curtsied as the suspicious gnarled old face – which bore a striking resemblance to Tengel's – came into view.

While she was still trying to find words that seemed to have vanished into thin air, a clear ironic voice from inside the room called out, 'It's Tengel's woman! Let her in, Grimar!'

At this, the lower half of the door opened and Silje stepped over a high threshold onto the earth floor inside. The most awful smell met her – the reeking consequence of dirt, old age and the years of wood smoke that had impregnated every inch of the place. There was very little daylight in the room, because the cover over the smoke-hole in the roof was blackened with soot, and although there was a glow from the primitive hearth on the floor, it was so weak that it shed almost no light on anything.

It took a little while for Silje's eyes to adjust to the soot-laden smoke-filled atmosphere, but eventually she was able to distinguish a figure sitting up in a short bed over in one corner. She curtsied low once again, wondering if the usual greeting of 'God bless your home' would be appropriate here.

Instead she said, 'Good day, Mother Hanna! I am Silje and, because you are both Tengel's closest kin, I took it upon myself to call on you. I brought some things for you that I hope you will do me the honour of accepting.'

Could they hear how her voice trembled, she wondered? The old woman grunted something. Silje could barely see her face, hidden as it was in deep shadow. She had only a sense of seeing something ancient, half-eaten by decay, but which was looking at her with eyes that pierced her soul. Grimar had closed the door and come across the room to stand close behind her. She could feel his breath on her neck.

For one awful moment she was almost overcome by wild panic and wanted to flee the cottage. The silence in the room and the disgusting sour odour mixed with smoke – but above all else, something lurking in the very air itself, something undefined, a hex she could not describe – made her blood run cold. She stood straight and turned to look at Grimar.

'Can I leave these somewhere? I must take the basket back with me. It belongs to the house where I am staying.'

When Grimar put his hand on her arm she nearly screamed out loud, before realising that he was just showing her to the table. She unpacked the food – bread, cured ham, Yule sausages, butter and cheese – most of which she had been given when she left Benedikt's farm. The old woman had sat up straighter in the bed and craned forward.

Silje spoke to her directly, knowing that she held sway in this home, 'If there is anything I can do for you then you must tell me. I can help to clean and tidy. I can ask Tengel to fetch firewood.'

'Tengel!' sniggered the old woman in her strange clear voice. 'Tengel is a fool! He has the power, but will not use it. He prefers to destroy it! I do not want Tengel here – and what task would you do here? You have no heart for such work.'

The old crone's anger was beginning to frighten Silje.

'Tengel has been very good to me,' she said in a soft voice, determined to defend him, even though this might provoke the woman further.

'But he will not make you with child!' Hanna exploded. 'Only he can pass on the power, yet he would rather see it die with him!'

'How can she know all this?' wondered Silje. She just lies here; she sees no one.

'He is not the only one,' she argued. 'There is Sol as well.'

'Sol will not pass on our true inheritance! You, girl! You are the one who will pass on the heritage of the first, the Great Tengel. You, only you, can change the mind of his obstinate kin. You!'

Her eyes fixed on the floor, Silje answered, 'You know well that I want to, old mother. You read my feelings, do you not?'

'Oh, yes!' she replied harshly. 'I can read your feelings and I know what flames burn inside you, girl. There is no doubt you are Tengel's woman. It is more than just the desire to be in the arms of the other that binds you. I shall prepare a potion for you that will change his ...'

'No!' Silje said forcefully. 'Love that is brought about by sorcery is worth nothing to me. If I cannot win him without such things, then I am not worthy of him.'

'You are the bravest little creature I have met in many years,' said Hanna softly and slowly, 'and you have pride, too. Beware your pride, Silje, it is a dangerous burden you carry.' Then she laughed, but this was no normal laugh. 'You dare to refuse my help! This is because you are new in the valley and know nothing of our powers. Do you know that I can destroy you without even touching you?'

'I have been told of your powers – but I was more worried that you were here in need and alone.'

Hanna leaned back against the bed-head again.

'You are *indeed* Tengel's woman,' she said sounding satisfied. 'Do what you can, and it will be as you desire. He will come to you. But tell me, have you seen it yet?'

'Seen what?' she asked, unthinkingly.

The old witch lying on the bed cackled again.

'I saw him as a newborn baby. I thought to myself at the time that, if only they knew, women would stand in line for him when he became a man. But it will not be good for a young virgin!'

Suddenly Silje realised what the old crone was talking about! Her cheeks turned bright red and she felt a sense of repulsion and was overcome with embarrassment.

'You'll see. You'll see,' the old hag gloated. 'Oh, yes, you'll see.'

With great effort Silje managed to regain her self-control. Hesitating slightly, she asked, 'Are you …? Can you tell me what my future holds?'

Silence lay heavy in the room.

'I could do so. Tengel's fate I cannot see, because he shares my powers and prevents me from seeing it. I cannot say if your future lies with him, but you will be blessed with child – though I cannot see who will be the father, because that tiresome stubborn nephew of mine shields it from me. Go home and talk sense into him, Silje. Ensnare him with your youth and your tenderness – then before he knows it, he will have sown his seed in you!'

Silje curtsied, her cheeks more flushed than they had been, and picked up the empty basket. Grimar followed her to the door. Without any words of farewell he saw her out and, as soon as she had made her way back into the woods where she could not be seen, she stopped and covered her face with her hands. Her whole body shook violently from the fear and shame, her teeth chattered and her breath came in short rasping coughs.

But there was one thing she had learned from this meeting – as long as there was a chance that she could produce an heir to Tengel, she would have nothing to fear from the evil Hanna. She resolved to tell no one of her visit to the old ones. She did not dare.

****

The worst months of winter passed slowly, bringing icy winds that howled around the corners of the buildings, slippery paths in the yard and snowdrifts packed hard against the door, making it almost impossible to open nearly every morning. Silje regained her strength and took the children back to live with her and life in the cottage went more smoothly. Dag was healed and Sol was chirpy and happy – as long as things went her way!

There were times when the two children wore each other down of course. They could not go out for days at a time because of the cold and, as a result, the big room sometimes looked like a battleground or a rubbish tip; but with a little effort Silje managed to keep things running reasonably well.

When she had spun some yarn, they set up the loom. The time Silje spent weaving gave her the energy to tackle the more mundane jobs in the cottage. In no time her neighbours had learned of her talent for producing beautiful cloth and, overcoming their fears, started to visit her. Although welcome, these visits caused Silje some anxiety, because she did not know what refreshment to offer them. Her bread cakes were always a little singed at the edges, her cheeses too soft or too hard and her pieces of dried fish cut badly or flaking.

The village wives gave her sound advice on the use of the loom, while she taught them different techniques and showed them new patterns. No matter how she tried, though, Silje was dismayed by how narrow-minded and limited their topics of discussion could be. The language was miserable and the vocabulary exceedingly small. Conversations were limited to a few subjects: other peoples' happiness and woes – mostly the latter – and the care of their homes and farms. That was all. If Silje tried to talk in general about something else, history, art or religion for example, they regarded her with suspicion and were silent as the grave. They knew nothing of life outside the valley and cared little for it either. It seemed their whole world consisted of nothing but the valley of the Ice People.

She saw Tengel very rarely. He only made a visit when absolutely necessary, to do the heavy work that she could not manage and to ensure that they wanted for nothing. He tried never to look at her directly and, because she knew his reasons, she accepted his absences.

There were moments, of course, when their eyes met, each holding the other's gaze, and when this happened they became joined in a strange trance-like silence. They both knew that nothing had changed between them – or had it? Had their longing and desire become in some way more vivid, so intense that eventually it would reach breaking point? Silje was frightened that it might and kept out of his way as much as she could.

Tengel, for his part, had been speaking with their chieftain. They had been out together on the frozen lake, trying to catch some fish to eke out the food stocks. Using their axes, each had made a hole in the ice which, because of the intense cold, they had to keep clearing to prevent them from re-freezing. Although the biting wind pulled at them, there was an occasional mildness, a sign that a new spring was waiting.

The chieftain was one of the few people who did not shun Tengel and, when they spoke, it was as equals.

'So what are you going to do with Silje?' he asked suddenly, without warning, as they fished side by side.

Tengel was confused by the question. 'How do you mean?'

'She is a distraction for the lads. They watch where she lives – and they fight over her.'

'I did not know of this.' Concern was etched on Tengel's brow.

'Don't worry. They dare not interfere at the moment, but one day something will happen. You must get her married off – and quickly! A maiden living all alone, well, it's too much of a temptation for any young man.'

There was a knot in Tengel's stomach. 'I don't know – I cannot simply wed her off against her will.'

'Of course you can, man! Is that not our custom? It is not expected that a girl should decide these things. You shall speak to her. She will have feelings for some young lad, I expect. She is a good-looking woman and very able. I suspect that even Heming is interested in her and I would not say "No" to such a daughter in wedlock.'

'She will bring two children into a marriage.' Tengel pointed out.

'You or Eldrid will take care of the girl. She is of your blood. The little boy on the other hand can be of use in the house. The strength of an extra man means a lot on a farm.

You talk to her and find out what her feelings are and remember – Heming is not a bad catch!'

After that, Tengel had lost all heart in the fishing and went back home. He did not tell Silje of the conversation and this proved to be a mistake. The very next day, things about which the chieftain had spoken began to occur.

Tengel came back from an unsuccessful day on the slopes, hunting grouse. He was aware that Heming had also been out hunting and, as he reached the narrow deep river close to Silje's cottage, he caught sight of him. He was standing on a ledge above the rushing waters, watching something. Tengel edged forward with some foreboding. Heming saw him and waved him over. There was an arrogant smirk on the face of the chieftain's son.

'Look over there,' he urged.

Tengel looked down at the river, where Silje had obviously been rinsing out clothes in the ice-cold water. An unpleasant scene was unfolding in front of them on the opposite bank. She had laid out her washing on the rocks and one of the Bratteng brothers was crawling along, obviously planning to come at Silje from behind. It was the nastier one of the boys and his intentions were clear.

Tengel shouted a warning, but the noise of the water drowned out his cry. The riverbank was too high for him to get across at this point – and Heming just stood grinning! Tengel was looking around urgently for a stone to throw, when Heming, with a look of admiration, grabbed his arm and pointed.

At the same instant that the Bratteng boy attacked Silje, she turned and they watched as she did something so incredible and so fast that neither of them could believe their eyes. With lightning speed, Silje grabbed a fistful of the boy's hair, pulling him forward, so that he raised his hands to break free. At that moment she hit him hard under the chin with her other fist, after which she drove her knee up into the most sensitive part of his body. The boy fell to the ground and remained lying there, writhing in agony. Silje quickly gathered her washing and ran from the river up towards the cottage.

Tengel and Heming looked at each other.

'God help me,' panted Heming. 'I don't think I'll try my luck there!'

'She said she'd learned how to take care of herself,' said Tengel weakly. 'I never thought she meant like that!'

They walked on down to find a crossing point. The Bratteng boy had got to his feet and left, swaying unsteadily. He would be unlikely to try *that* again.

'I'll go and see how she is,' mumbled Tengel when they had crossed and they went their separate ways.

Tengel found Silje outside, hanging up her washing. Even from some distance he could see she was upset and he hurried to her. 'I saw everything that happened.'

Dropping her linen in the snow she ran to him, throwing herself in his arms, forgetting that it might not be what he wanted. 'Oh, Tengel, Tengel! Why can't you be here always?' she whispered, trembling. 'I am so helpless without you. So unprotected.'

'Not from what I saw just now,' he answered, surprised by his own faltering voice.

It had been hard for him to stand on that ledge unable to do anything to help.

They had not mentioned the sensitive subject of their relationship since the day they had confided their feelings to each other. That had been nearly two months earlier.

'Where are the children?' he muttered, his lips pressing against her hair.

'With Eldrid. I did not want to take them to the water.'

Tengel did not want to let her out of his arms and she was certainly not making any attempt to free herself.

'And Dag is well?' he asked, for no other reason than to make the wonderful giddy moment last a little longer.

'I do not think he is very strong, but that may be because he has never had a mother's milk, as you said. But he can sit up – with help.'

'Silje, I have often meant to say something to you about Dag, but whenever we meet there are other things to occupy us.'

She gave him a quick understanding smile. His fingers played with a lock of her hair that had come loose while she was working. Her head rested against his chest, turned towards his shoulder so that she could look dreamily out over the farm. Her hands lay on his back.

'Do you recall the letters C.M. on the cloth you found Dag wrapped in?' he asked.

'I could never forget them.'

'You know that you found the boy not far from the city gates and also that the cloth carried the emblem of a nobleman's crown. I sent a man – it was the wagon-driver – to try and find the child's mother. We believe he may have done so. I just didn't have the time to tell you before we had to flee and, since then, as I have already said, I forgot about it.'

'How could you forget such a thing?' she asked reproachfully, with a severe look on her face. 'You know how much thought I have given to Dag's background! Well, what did your man find out?'

Tengel tried not to let himself be overcome by the magic in her lovely clear eyes.

'There is one Baron Meiden who has a palace quite

close to the city gates. He has a daughter, Charlotte, who it is said is neither one of the youngest nor most beautiful.'

Silje stood in his arms, unmoving, forgetting he was there.

'So now the unknown woman has become flesh and blood – Charlotte Meiden. It is sad, somehow, to know at last who our little boy belongs to.'

Tengel noticed that she had said 'our little boy'. It touched him deeply. In a gentle voice he said, 'She has no rights, Silje, and she can hardly want him either. But I do understand your feelings.'

Charlotte Meiden – the name kept running through her head. She felt sympathy as well, no matter how unwarranted it might be, for this woman who had left her child out in the cold to die – but Silje felt there must be more to the story than this.

'Wake up, Silje,' his soft voice urged her. 'Your thoughts were far, far away.'

She turned her attention back from Trondheim to this poor mountain farm. In the yard, smoke still rose from the fire beneath the washtub that stood by the tree.

A great tit twittered cheerfully in readiness for spring, but Tengel noticed none of this. He saw only Silje, feeling her in his embrace, exactly as he had always dreamt.

'Silje,' he whispered, 'I have lived every day in torment. Every night has been twice as bad.'

'For me as well,' she said softly, looking up at his face, as though she had only just noticed he was there.

'And just now, when I saw that young whelp at the riverbank – I thought I would fall apart.'

Slowly a smile lit up her face. The intoxicating realisation that she had been in Tengel's arms for such a long time began to surge through her, warming every part of her body. Her hands were trembling as she touched his distinctive face as gently as the wings of a butterfly beat the air.

Tengel drew a quick breath – he might almost have sobbed – and pulled Silje closer to him. Tighter and tighter she felt his arms around her, her cheek against his. When his lips touched the soft skin of her neck, she threw back her head in expectation. His warm breath excited her as his mouth gently brushed the curve of her throat and, with a languid joyful smile on her face, she pressed her body even closer to his. Tengel's mouth moved slowly up to her face and he gently kissed her cheek, her forehead, her eyes, her other cheek and then … her mouth.

At first their kiss was soft and sensitive, but in seconds it became passionate and all-consuming, as her pulse started to race, her body responding to the release of pent-up emotions. Again and again he kissed her, feeding from her passion like the hungry man he was – dizzy, possessed – yet so full of love that Silje welcomed every kiss with a surge of delight, as her world reeled and swayed and she soared upwards, borne aloft by gentle clouds of desire.

Suddenly she found that her fingers were clawing into his shoulders like talons and that she was slowly moving her body against his, leaving him in no doubt about her feelings. Breathing heavily, he relaxed his hold on her and looked down into her face, seeing the sensuous happy smile that still played on her lips. He had a distant look about him, as if he was unsure where he was.

'What will become of us, Silje?' he whispered. There was regret in his voice. 'I should not be alive – it would be better I were dead!'

'No!' she wailed. 'I could not be in this world without you! Without you I am nothing. Come – come with me. Look, we'll stand with the bottom half of the door closed between us – you outside and I will be inside – and then we can talk together, but please, you must not leave!'

She rambled on and on, hoping her words would keep him there. Reluctantly he gave in to her somewhat silly idea, feeling a little bit foolish standing on the outside of the stable door, although he did understand why she had suggested it.

She talked without stopping, 'We need each other in so many different ways, Tengel, every moment of every day – to talk to each other and solve our problems together, to share happiness and worry.'

'I know,' he interrupted sadly. 'We are made for each other, to share our lives together. We are like a tree split in two – if the parts are not bound together to heal, the tree will die.'

She looked at him – breathless. She had been expecting him to say something else as well. When he did not, she decided it was time for her to say it for him.

'Then why do we not try? Do we *have* to have children?'

As he looked at her, his gleaming wolf-like teeth shining through his warm smile, he said, 'I think we are both hot-blooded creatures. Don't you think we would forget ourselves?'

'Yes,' she said a little ashamed, 'forgive my lack of modesty!'

He placed his hand on hers where it rested on the top of the door. 'You need never beg forgiveness from me, Silje! Do you not think I understand you? You give voice to those feelings that I also share. But now I must leave.'

She tried desperately to find more to talk about. 'I have often wondered …'

He stopped, waiting expectantly and watching her face.

'I have often wondered about that night we first met.

218

You had many men with you – soldiers who obeyed. Who were they?'

'Kinsmen,' he smiled. 'Our chieftain had sent us all out to find Heming, you see. We had heard that he had been captured and his father thought I needed more men with me to free him. They all came back here shortly afterwards. Now farewell, Silje, and take good care of yourself!'

He left and there was nothing more she could do to make him stay. From then on his visits became more frequent. He called in every day to make sure all was well and that none of the young men had been back to trouble her.

****

Silje found she was heartily glad that winter was coming to an end. Others told her that it had been mild – but she couldn't agree. At least they had been spared the attentions of wild animals; it wasn't uncommon for packs of wolves to cross the glacier during the winter months, causing all kinds of problems in the valley – but not this year. Thanks to the help she had been given by Eldrid and Tengel, the winter had not taken too much out of Silje. She needed nearly all her energy to manage Sol, who could be a handful, and to keep the infant Dag alive – he was still not as strong as he needed to be for this hard mountain life.

Eldrid was worried, too. The fodder was running out and she herself was exhausted from years of working this large farm on her own. Silje had taken to helping her in the barn every afternoon, to ease her load, and the two women became very close. One day, while Sol was scurrying to and fro among the calves and kittens, and Dag lay sleeping in a basket in one of the empty stalls, Silje found herself confiding in Eldrid her feelings for Tengel.

'Tengel is so foolish,' said Eldrid. 'Just think what a good life he could have with you! But I can also understand why he is the way he is. I have seen far more of our evil inheritance than you – enough to make me not want to bring a child into the world.'

'But I have never really been able to believe in this evil heritage, Eldrid. I don't believe people can conjure up magic and I don't think there are witches. I refuse to believe in them.'

Eldrid stood up straight, a faraway dreamy look on her face. 'You are right in some ways. It is not witchcraft and sorcery that hold the greatest dangers in the power they possess. It is the will to do harm. The belief that they are able to injure folk and animals is the ruin of so many of our kin. That is what Tengel fights against.'

'I do not think he needs to worry,' Silje butted in quickly. 'I'm sure he has none of that power – except the power in his hands to heal, for that I have seen with my own eyes. What evil can there be in helping others?'

Eldrid looked at her with the same strange expression, 'Tengel? You should be glad he is the way he is! I have watched him do things, as a child and a youth, but something scared him – I know not what – and after that he tried to put it all behind him. Hanna would rage at him, saying that he could have great gifts. But no, I think Tengel knows his own mind, when he says he will not settle with a woman.'

Silje kept looking at her, but Eldrid said no more and turned to start milking one of the cows. She was so rough and heavy-handed that the animal started kicking angrily. Silje felt there was no hope in sight.

****

The thaws came. Rivers and streams broke their banks, while the compacted snow became porous and slowly melted away. The pack ice that had dammed the outflow of the lake broke up and the river roared as it flowed under the glacier, almost filling the tunnel to the brim. The walls of the cottage gave off the scent of sun-warmed tar. Sol's face soon turned dark brown, because she was always playing outside, most often in the rivulets of melted snow in the yard. Spring had arrived sooner than expected. Eventually the torrent of water subsided and the way to the outside was open once again. Eldrid's hopes began to rise. Perhaps the fodder would last until they could put the cattle out to pasture.

Then one day Silje received a visitor – Heming. She did not particularly welcome this intrusion, because she was alone with Dag, while Sol was out with Eldrid. Heming, sly young scoundrel that he was, could still appeal to her a little with his handsome good looks and natural charm, in the same way that he would appeal to almost any woman on earth. Silje, though, could never have any fondness for him – she considered him to be an irresponsible, incompetent young man who would exploit all those around him. Still, she could not stop herself from admiring the way he looked – the gleaming smile and the eyes that told a girl that she was the one who meant something special to him. He was a dangerous visitor to have in the home.

If she had known the real reason behind his visit, Silje would have had even more cause for concern. On the previous evening, Heming had been feasting with the other young men of the valley and, drunk as they were from too much ale, they started to talk about Silje. It seemed that the Bratteng boy had not been the first to get ideas about her and, although they had not been as daring, a couple of the others had been spying on her. They had decided that she was one girl that they would get nowhere with.

Heming took up the challenge at once. 'I could have had her once,' he told them, slurring his words and emboldened by the ale, 'only I offended her. I chose to take her valuables instead of her virginity – but I can still get her on her back whenever I want.'

None of them believed him. So now, to prove his point, he was here with her while the others waited in the woods above, excitedly watching to see what happened down in the farmyard.

They quickly saw that Heming had been invited in. Getting that far was a good start, they thought, and then crept closer to hide behind the corner of the outhouse. While they were giggling amongst themselves, one of them stood accidentally in the remains of an icy pile of snow. The noise from outside made Silje realise what Heming's true intentions were and she immediately asked him to leave. For his father's sake and for the sake of their friendship, she did not want any fuss.

His sly grin mocked her. He didn't believe her for a minute. When she walked towards the door to open it for him to leave, he jumped to his feet. He would not allow the other lads to see her throwing him out. Remembering how she had fought off the Bratteng boy, he grabbed her and held tightly onto her arms. He had intended to seduce her slowly using the power of persuasion, for he disdained violence where women were concerned – he had never needed to resort to it before with any woman. Now he was panicking at the thought of the others listening outside.

Silje was stronger than he had expected, and she was in a fury. She sank her teeth into his arm and made him yell, but he wasn't going to give up. He pushed her down onto the floor in the full knowledge that many girls would become aroused by such domination and readily submit to him. A near-silent and determined battle was ensuing and, because he was so sure he would win, Heming had started to prepare himself for the final assault. At this point Silje lay still for an instant and took a deep breath and, just as she was about to scream, he put his hand across her mouth. Silje now had one arm free, as she had planned, and she used all her strength to hurt him in that most sensitive part of a man's body. Heming let go of her with a terrible cry of pain – and at that same moment Tengel stepped through the door.

The young men had scattered in all directions like startled rabbits, as his enormous frightening form came striding across the yard. At first he was of a mind to run after them, but then he heard Heming's shout of agony, followed by the screams made by Dag, as he woke up.

Tengel burst through the door and understood in an instant what was happening. His arm reached out and he dragged Heming to his feet by the collar of his tunic, almost throttling him in the process. Shaking and close to tears, Silje got to her feet. She brushed the dirt from the earthen floor off her skirts and pushed her hair back.

Tengel's rage was terrifying. Never before had she seen such a hateful expression on his face. Heming screamed in fear. 'Please don't destroy me, Tengel!' he whimpered. 'Don't put a curse on me, please. It was only in fun – I just …'

'What do you prefer,' Tengel said violently, his face drained of colour, 'Shall I beat you or use other powers?'

'Beat me, beat me! For God's sake, beat me if you must – but I never meant to do anything …'

'Then fasten your leggings and trews,' hissed Tengel.

Heming quickly did as he was told and then, as Tengel took hold of him again, he began to scream in fear once more. 'No, no, don't hit me. Please don't. She's not worth it. She's just a …'

Tengel's fist struck out hard. Not just once, but again and again in a blind frenzy until he felt Silje's hand on his arm and her voice begging him to show mercy. Heming fell to the floor in a whimpering blood-soaked heap. Tengel lifted him up, carried him to the door and threw him bodily into the yard.

'Take him away with you!' he yelled at the lads who had hidden, terrified, in the trees at the edge of the woods and then he went back into the cottage. 'Are you hurt, Silje?' he asked, still breathing heavily. 'Did he do anything to you?'

She stood leaning on the cupboard, her back to him, her whole body in tremors.

'No – no, he never had time. Thank you, I'm so glad you came! You have a habit of arriving whenever I need you.'

'Well something made me uneasy, so I left home a bit earlier today. Don't cry, little one, it's over now.'

I'm not crying,' she said, taking a deep breath. 'Not really. I just didn't like the way you – kept hitting him. I know he deserved it, but I don't like to see you beat anybody.'

Tengel closed his eyes. 'I have been waiting for this moment for a long time, Silje. Not only me, but everyone in the valley as well, I should think. Sooner or later someone had to put a stop to his ruthless, arrogant behaviour. I'm sorry it had to be me, but I lost my temper. Forgive me, Silje, I did not want you to see such a thing.'

'I see,' she muttered. 'Dag needs me,' she added quickly – she knew that she must not fall into Tengel's arms at that moment.

She picked up Dag and began to comfort him. Tengel went over to the window and took off the shutters. He could see the lads dragging the limp unsteady form of Heming away with them.

'You should let in more daylight,' he said as he fitted the shutters back in place and looked indecisively around the room. Knowing that he had upset her by what he had done had caused him to lose confidence.

'I see you've hung your lovely leaded light over there. What if I were to saw up ...' He stood running the tips of his fingers over Benedikt's glasswork, which she had placed above a cupboard.

'No-o,' he said slowly.

'What do you mean?' asked Silje.

'No, this light does not belong here.'

'I don't understand.'

'It is destined for another wall, in a home far grander than this,' he replied.

'Do you mean that we should not keep it, then?'

'Of course you should keep it – it was a gift to you,' he said, perplexed by her question.

He moved his hand away from the glass.

'Did you see into the future just then?' she asked quietly, trembling.

'Yes – I did. Something forceful was telling me not to fix the glass here.'

At this they both fell silent for a while.

Then suddenly he seemed more cheerful. 'Let me help you with your chores. I shall fetch water and firewood.'

'That would be good. I must see to Dag and change his clothing.'

Tengel picked up the pail and went outside. When Eldrid returned with Sol a little later, everything was as before. Neither of them ever said a word to her about the incident with Heming.

Chapter 13

After Tengel and Eldrid had left, Silje took out the sketchbook that Benedikt had given her and ran her hand gently across the cover, on which she had made a careful drawing of the valley of the Ice People. She had told no one what she was using it for, not even Tengel. She had been keeping a diary of sorts – making occasional entries when she thought something special or interesting had happened. Now, in her elegant handwriting, but with so many spelling mistakes the teacher at home on the estate would have been reduced to tears – had he not already been long dead – she began to write, 'Today I witnessed yet another of Tengel's hidden powers. He placed his hand on my glazed mosaic and saw into the future.'

She continued for some time, recording other recent events that she thought were worthy of note, then closed the book and replaced it in its hiding-place. At last, exhausted and still a little distraught, she climbed into her lonely bed.

Tengel did not go back to his home that night. Instead he wandered aimlessly along the mountain paths, restless and confused, his mind in turmoil. The moon had risen, shedding a pale light over the valley. He stopped and covered his face with both hands, in supplication.

'Dear God,' he prayed, 'Merciful Father, look upon me, your wretched child. Help me! Counsel me! Give me a sign! What am I to do? I love her so much that I cannot bear to be without her and you know, Lord, that she and the children need my help. I am the one who brought them to this wilderness and, without me, no one will protect them. I could not leave her on the outside, but I sense, I know that she is not completely happy here. Dear God, all this is too much for me, show me what to do. I want only what is best for her.'

The vast firmament above him remained silent. There was no answer, so he turned and began to trudge back down the path, his feet heavy and tired. In the distance he could make out the rooftops reflected in the moonlight. In his agonising distress, Tengel strayed from the track and across the frozen surface of the river. Soon the ice gave way beneath him and he cried out in fear and surprise. The next moment he was almost paralysed by the cold of the swirling waters, which started to drag him under, down into their depths.

Instinctively his hands reached out for something to hold onto, but the crumbling rim of the ice was his only support. He grasped hold with all his strength.

'Is this your sign?' he shouted at the night sky. 'Is this what you wish to tell me – that my life is worthless and she will fare better without me? That there will never, *never* be any mercy shown to a wretch with the blood of the evil Tengel flowing in his veins?'

In exhaustion, he bowed his head and rested it on his already frozen arm.

****

Tengel did not come to visit Silje the following day – or the next. When she had not seen him for three days, she left the children with Eldrid and set out for his house, far down the valley. She had never been there before; had only seen it from a distance and thought how run-down it looked. She felt anxious as she approached it now – there was no smoke coming from the flue and that frightened her.

The cottage was very small and one gable had started to lean dangerously, looking as if it would collapse at any moment. She dared not knock too hard on the door, for it too looked ready to fall apart.

'Come in.' That was Tengel's voice, but it sounded unusual. No matter, just hearing him was enough to make her heart skip a beat. She realised how concerned she had been these last few days at his absence.

Silje went in, certain that he would be angry with her for this intrusion. Perhaps he had just wanted to be alone and expected her to have sense enough to understand that.

'Silje!' his voice was very hoarse and he was struggling to sit up in bed. 'I'm sorry you should find me like this – and everything is in such a muddle!'

That he should be worried about what she thought was very touching.

'Oh, Tengel, I don't care whether it's tidy or not, you know well that I am hardly the neatest person on earth, but you are living in hardly more than a woodshed – one that is ready to fall down! It doesn't even keep out the weather – I can see through cracks in the walls!'

'I tried to patch them with moss and tow, but there were too many.' His voice made a throaty rasping sound as he spoke.

Silje was upset by how weak he looked. The face she loved had been changed by the dark shadows under his eyes and his sickly pallor contrasted with the flushed colour of his hollow cheeks.

'You are ill!' she said sitting down on the edge of his bed, and becoming even more concerned, as she felt how hot the fever was making him. 'Why have you not told anyone?'

He turned his face away from her.

'Don't sit too close, Silje. I must look awful – I only want to look my best when I am near you.'

'What foolish talk – you are too vain!' she said with a smile. 'How long have you been sick?'

'The day that Heming came to you I was enraged and so unsure about our future that I spent the whole evening walking the mountain. I fell through the ice on a stream and ended up in the water.'

Tengel was overcome by a fit of coughing just as he finished speaking.

'But you might have died!' she shouted at him.

'True! But never in my life have I felt so forsaken by the world, and even by God. You were angry with me too, because I fought with Heming.' He stopped while another bout of coughing took hold. 'But I had to see you at least once more – and that gave me the strength to pull myself out of the water. The next day I was too weak to get up from my bed.'

'Well, thank God you managed to get back here,' she muttered. 'How do you feel now?'

'I am better, I think, but still a little weak.'

She pushed her hand inside his shirt and rested it on his chest. She could not stop a certain excitement from within, but she knew that she must concentrate and ignore the arousal she felt from just touching him. She could feel the rattle of his breathing against the palm of her hand.

'I know that it has gone to my chest,' he said weakly. 'I have tried to cure it myself but ...'

She stopped him. 'You need to be warm – this place is as

cold as ice! And you need nourishment as well. You are coming to stay with us, and I will not hear a single word against it!'

'Well, at least you can be sure I will pose no risk to your virtue in this condition,' he smiled and lay back down again.

'Your horse – has it been fed?'

'That was the other most important thing on my mind – I have almost had to crawl to the stable to feed him.'

'So you will be able to ride – which of us was first in your thoughts, the horse or me?'

'Quiet, Silje. You know the answer to that very well.'

Her heart began to pound with happiness. At last he had agreed to come and stay with her. Now she would do all she could to make sure that he never moved back here again. Sometimes she frightened herself when she noticed how wilful and determined she had become. Had she always been that way? She could not say. Perhaps her own will had been suppressed by her strict upbringing – she suspected that this was the case.

Until now she had not wanted to admit, even to herself, that she had made a decision about her life some time ago. The old woman, Hanna, had promised her that she would be with child. Silje would be sure that it was with Tengel and no one else. She had no fear of the evil legacy. If they were all like him, what was there to fear?

Silje managed to help Tengel onto his horse. He sat bolt upright, but his head hung forward, as though he was sleeping. She proudly led the animal, so happy that she felt as if she were part of a triumphal procession. They passed Eldrid's farmyard on the way and she called out from a distance. Eldrid and the children joined them and they all made their way back to the cottage together.

Tengel lay on Silje's bed, watching trance-like as they eagerly prepared a place for him to sleep in the main room. Sol was helping, as happy as the others that he had come to stay. Silje wanted to give him the best she could offer and so she cooked and cleaned with boundless energy, happier than she had ever been. Tengel found all this very touching. He was not used to living with other people. No one had ever cared for him so tenderly before – no one had ever taken such pleasure in his company.

Thanks to Silje's devoted attention, his condition slowly improved. They all thought it was wonderful to have a man in the house, especially Sol, who joyfully jumped onto his bed every morning. Even Dag seemed to know that something exciting had happened, as he grinned delightedly at the big man, proudly showing his first his two teeth. For Silje, life had become perfect in every respect. She happily fussed over Tengel in every possible way. She kept everything neat and prepared the best food she could – and Eldrid couldn't help smiling to herself.

'You deserve to be spoilt, Tengel,' she told him. 'Your life has been harsh and without love. You could have moved here long ago.'

He didn't answer her, but he realised how enjoyable life was becoming. He wondered if anyone could fail to be anything but a good person when surrounded by these warm-hearted folk?

Word reached them that Heming had left the valley as soon as the way was open. They all knew that Silje's rejection and the beating he had received from Tengel had damaged his pride and reputation far too much for him to stay, but Silje could tell from Tengel's furrowed brow that the news concerned him. He explained that he was always apprehensive when Heming was at large, because a reckless fool like him might easily be captured – and there would not always be a Silje to get him out of trouble. The most worrying aspect was that, if he were tortured or threatened, Heming would gladly betray his own family in order to save his skin.

'I shall get up today,' Tengel announced unexpectedly one morning

'Stay in bed for one more day, just to be certain you are completely well,' Silje pleaded.

'But I *am* well,' he insisted.

Indeed, he was looking much better, but she was adamant. 'One more day, that's all.'

With a sigh, he resigned himself to her wishes – for a few hours anyway. When she returned later in the afternoon, after helping Eldrid with her chores, she found him dressed, but still lying on the bed.

'Where is Sol?' he wondered.

'She wanted to stay and play with the kittens at Eldrid's. I will fetch her later. Tengel! You should not …'

'No, I shouldn't! You have been bossing me about for quite long enough. It's time I showed you who is master in this house – and tomorrow I shall move back to mine.'

'No!' she shouted in alarm, 'I won't let you return to that cold bleak shack.'

She had stepped over to the bed and put her hands on his shoulders, pushing him down to make him stay. His strong fingers wrapped themselves around hers.

'You know that this cannot go on,' he said softly. 'What do you think it's been like for me these past nights? You in the next room and me here knowing that you lay under the bedcovers – imagining your shape, your warmth and your soft mouth, which I have felt against mine but once, and never forgotten.'

His words had made her feel quite weak and she sat down beside him.

'I know,' she whispered. 'I have had the same thoughts. Staring into the darkness I have thought of you leaving your bed – walking across the floor – standing at the doorway with your wide shoulders outlined in the glow of the fire – coming to me. But you never did.'

'I have done so in my thoughts.'

His eyes shimmered like never before with their strange green and yellow glow, as if on fire.

'Have you not been happy here?' she asked desperately.

'Never have I felt so at home – I would give anything to stay.'

His hand stroked her neck and shoulder. She unlaced her blouse a little, so that he could touch her skin. His hand was hot and his fingers trembled.

'Let me see you,' he whispered. 'Just once.'

'No,' she whispered back, 'but you may touch me.'

She undid her blouse a little further, so that his hand could caress her breast. His breathing told her that he was becoming more and more excited. Suddenly, he withdrew his hand. She looked down at the fearful face that she held so dear and felt the sting of tears welling up in her eyes. With a deep sob she threw herself down onto his chest.

'I couldn't bear to lose you again,' she whispered, muffled by the pillow. 'Please don't go back!'

Tengel had put his arms around her. Touching her so intimately had not been good for either of them.

'Dearest, dearest Silje,' he muttered, coughing slightly. 'It hurts me so much that you too must suffer for the sins of my forefathers.'

Then, with his hand under her chin, he turned her face to his and kissed her – softly and gently, yet with a wild, restrained passion that set her lips on fire! Slowly he took his mouth from hers.

'It is best that you get up now,' he told her.

'Then let go of me,' she whispered, but his arms continued to hold her tightly to him.

'Dear God, this is madness, Silje!' He was breathless and anxious now. 'Please get up.'

'I can't – you are still holding me.'

Without a word being spoken, but with wild passion in his eyes, he pulled her right up to him on the bed and started to feel for the seam of her clothes. He pulled at her apron and threw it to the floor, then did the same with her leggings. Tengel was a man possessed, overwhelmed by that most primitive of instincts, so carefully under control until this very moment. Now he was no longer a man able to suppress his passion – he was at the mercy of his primal desires.

Silje rose to her knees and tore open his shirt. She had no need for pretence with him any longer and modesty had been driven from her by his undisguised lust. Tengel sat up higher on the bed as he unhooked the waistband of her skirts, his hands shaking in haste and his teeth bared in a fixed grin as he looked at her. She let her hands roam over his firm chest with gentle rhythmic movements before pushing them under his arms and round to his back. Impatiently, she touched the supple, throbbing muscles from his shoulders to his waist, noticing how his body was becoming aroused – heavy – warm and moist.

She felt her dress fall from her shoulders and then took off her blouse and underclothes herself. Wild and crazed with desire, she heard him gasp as she revealed her naked body to him – this man who had never been with a woman – and he threw her down onto the bed. She lay beneath him, waiting, looking up at him. His expression was not focused; he was looking into the distance as though he was no longer aware of what he was doing.

She ran her hands over his shoulders and for the first time felt how they were deformed – but she loved the feel of them as she loved everything about this man. Hands lower now, she touched his narrow hips and then his thighs, which were hairy and faun-like. He shifted his weight slightly to lift her knees, and at that moment she caught her first sight of his manhood – the size of it! How shall I be able to … she thought, just as she felt he had found his way to her. Every fibre in her body was aching for him – she was ready.

Although she had realised that it was going to be difficult to take him, she was not expecting the sea of pain that drowned her senses at that moment. She bit deep into his shoulder to stop from crying out. She wanted to get away, she fought him, but it was too late. The only thing she could do was to close out the pain and let him give her everything, yes, everything they had both wanted almost since their first moment of meeting. His hand was resting on hers – his touch gentle and loving. He did not mean to hurt her, but feeling his distress she opened her eyes and forced herself to smile so that he would know that she understood and wanted him to go on.

Quite naturally, and to Silje's relief, he did not take long. She watched his expression turn to one of unbridled ecstasy and at that same instant her pain began to subside and was replaced by a warm glow from knowing that she had given him such pleasure. Tengel, his lust exhausted, sank down beside her. Only the sound of their heavy breathing could be heard in the room.

After a short while he broke the silence, 'And you

imagine that you and I can live together without having children?' he whispered. She heard both joy and sadness in his voice.

'Not any more,' she answered, savouring her own complete contentment. She remained on her back, shamelessly, letting his seed find its way deeper and deeper into her.

'Do you know what I want, Tengel?'

'No.'

'I want you again!'

He laughed a gentle laugh that showed his happiness and his regret.

'You are mad, Silje, and I understand why. But this was too … selfish of me. It was not how I had planned it to be.' He lay on his back, his forearm covering his eyes. 'What have we done, Silje? God, what have we done?'

'The inevitable,' she replied slowly.

'Yes, it was bound to happen sooner or later.'

'Do you regret it?'

Raising himself onto his elbow he said, ' Of course I regret it! But never in my life have I been so overcome with joy. What are we going to do now, Silje?'

Her expression hardened and she said sombrely, 'Well, I suppose you could always move out again and hope that no damage has been done!'

'No!' He was shocked and felt guilty as he realised how much his words had hurt her. 'No, that wasn't what I meant. I wanted to say that we have burned all our bridges and I cannot for one moment think of leaving you. That will not happen. I love you and I know that you and I must be together. No, my thoughts were not for us, but for our children.'

'You told me yourself that only a few are cursed with the legacy of Tengel – and, even though you have inherited it, you are the finest person I have ever met, so it is not always bad, this power. Anyway, if *I* have to keep begging and proposing to *you*, I shall hit you, Tengel. Are you deliberately humiliating me?'

He hid his grin in her hair.

'Silje Arngrimsdotter, I reverently ask for your hand in wedlock. Will you, dare you, be my wife?'

'Yes, yes for heaven's sake, yes! And it was about time you asked, too!'

She laughed loudly as he put his arms around her in a great bear hug.

Hanna, she thought, I have taken the first step!

****

They lay together that night, talking in whispers while the children slept. They did not make love again because Silje was still in pain; the smallest movement making her gasp in agony.

'Tell me, Silje, do you like it here?' he asked at one point. 'Sometimes I think that you don't.'

She thought carefully before answering.

'I enjoy being here because you are here – and all I want is to be with you. I am safe here; only fear and danger await on the outside. It is a beautiful valley, I have started to put down roots and Eldrid is a good friend, although I have little to say to the others. But I have to tell you that sometimes I feel fearful and cut off from the world – I long for the freedom of the open countryside. I have thought many times of Benedikt and Grete, Marie and the farm boy, and worried about them too. And I have thought a lot about Charlotte Meiden; not because I want to meet her, but because I wonder what her life must be like, poor woman.'

'That is something that I can't begin to understand, but

it is no doubt because you are a woman and more sympathetic to the way another woman feels.'

'Has my answer displeased you?'

'No, it was what I expected.'

'And what about you, Tengel? Are you happy here?'

He sighed.

'Since I brought you here I have felt more settled and it is, of course, the place where I grew up. But now that we are to be one, I can admit to you that I have always wanted to leave, ever since I was a boy. I have this impatient way with me, you see. I want to *be* something, not just a mountain farmer all my life. But there is little hope for one such as I, so long as the authorities suspect I am a sorcerer – and even if they do not, then I am still damned for my appearance. Last year they hanged a man just because he had a clubfoot. They said it was a sign of the Devil.'

'Oh, please don't tell me of such things. You know how it hurts me to think of these poor creatures. My heart bleeds for them!'

'I'm sorry, I will remember. But you have to understand that other things cause my impatience as well. Something inside me makes me believe I am destined for a future other than the one this valley can offer. I really can make something of myself – be a great person.'

Silje snuggled closer to him, relishing his warmth. 'Is this something you just know? Like you did with my glass mosaic?'

'It is, and the strange thing is that you …'

'Go on. Why did you stop?'

'No,' he said. 'It is wrong for me to put ideas into your head.'

She turned over and leaned on her elbows, staring at him in the darkness.

'Come on, Tengel!' she implored.

'All right,' he said with a smile. 'Your destiny will also be a special one – one we cannot as yet comprehend.'

'Away from here?'

'I am sure that it will be, but at the moment I feel it would be dangerous to leave the valley.'

'You know so many things.'

'I don't really – not as Hanna does. She can foretell most things. I just have vague sensations – premonitions – from time to time. I have learnt to listen and be guided by them, but otherwise I am not so special.

Silje didn't quite believe this.

'Eldrid says that you did things as a child that she didn't like to think about.'

'Eldrid shouldn't speak about such things! Yes, I recall that sometimes I would be angry with people and that if I concentrated hard enough on hurting them … Silje, what's wrong? Why did you sob like that?'

'Oh, Tengel, I was not going to tell you this! Something happened at Benedikt's farm.'

'What do you mean?' he asked in a fearful whisper.

Reluctantly, she told him all about Sol's rage towards Abelone's son on the day he had threatened to throw them out. How Sol had stood, defiant, in the doorway then rushed away as soon as he had cut himself – and his accusation that Sol had willed it to happen. She described the look in Sol's eyes when she eventually found her.

Silje felt Tengel become more and more tense. When he spoke, his voice was cold.

'Why have you not told me of this before?'

'I did not want to distress you without cause, because I was not sure of it myself. What do *you* think?'

'Think?' his voice sounded tired. 'I did something very similar as a child. I thought it was exciting and fun …'

239

'But you changed your mind and stopped causing such things, didn't you?'

'Yes, we can only pray that Sol does likewise.'

Silje lay back and stared up at the roof timbers. Sol was completely different from Tengel. She had none of his considerate, serious nature. She could often seemingly be nasty – hateful – even evil! But she is still only a very little child, thought Silje, trying to be fair.

'There are two of us now, Tengel,' she said at last in a forthright voice. 'Together we will cope with it.'

'Thank God I have you, Silje,' he whispered, 'you are a great blessing.'

Chapter 14

With the arrival of summer, Silje was able to appreciate the valley of the Ice People in all its glory. She realised for the first time how truly wonderful it all was and learned to love the mountains, the sunsets, the forests of mountain birch and the lake – every little thing interested her.

Her happiness was boundless. They had been wed in a simple ceremony, performed by the chieftain, who had been surprised – not to say shocked – by her choice of husband. He assumed that, since Heming had left the valley, she must have taken Tengel in desperation. The chieftain had never learned the true reason for Heming's departure – no one had dared tell him. In this way, indirectly, the people of the valley had shown their loyalty to Tengel. He drew a certain comfort from that knowledge.

So Silje was now Tengel's wife. Everyone was in good health and their future together looked bright. She found that doing chores in the home had become far more rewarding since he had moved in and she in turn had joined him, cheerfully lending a hand, when he ploughed and sowed the fields in the spring, and cut the grass in the home fields and distant pastures. They decided to keep no livestock – the barns were so badly in need of repair, and Silje had enough to do in looking after the children. It was better that they all helped Eldrid instead. Sol had been allowed to have one of Eldrid's kittens and Tengel was more than a little worried when she chose the one that was blacker than pitch and would have no other. This and Tengel's horse were their only animals.

Tengel also seemed to be very happy with life. Despite this, Silje often had to wake him from nightmares – he who had once said he could not dream! As was the custom for wedded couples, they slept naked beneath the bedcovers and when he woke, bathed in sweat, he would straight away fumble to touch her face to make sure she was there.

'Silje, Silje,' he would moan, his eyes wide and full of fear. 'Never leave me! Don't ever leave me!'

She would promise never to go and then take him in her arms to calm him and stop the nightmare. Sometimes, when he was very distressed and his whole body quaked, she would open herself and let him plunge into her – even when he had lain with her earlier the same night – because this seemed to quieten him. She was saddened a little when this happened, because, like most women, she knew that a closeness of spirit between two people is just as important as any physical bond.

However at these times he always managed to lift her to the dizzy heights of fulfilment – and when he noticed that he was pleasing her, wildly taking her with him, all his demons and dark imaginings would vanish and he would sleep soundly in her arms. Silje found this very uncomfortable at times and she had great difficulty in getting him to move over far enough for her to have even a small part of the bed to herself.

This is almost as it was in my dreams, she thought to

herself with some irony. I use my womanly sensuality to turn a man's evil thoughts to something else – but why must it always be sexual? What is this dark obsession within me that always draws me back to that? Should I not be more than an object to be desired by men? Is it my own lack of confidence, not wanting to reach out for other things? Whatever it is, it's very frustrating!

They found themselves in the company of the other Ice People more often now. Since the wedding, much of their fear of Tengel had abated and the farmers would now more happily discuss matters with him, sharing a joke or two. But there was always the tiniest hint of apprehension in their faces – the thought that they must be ready to flee without warning.

Eldrid's life began anew. Encouraged by Silje's bravery in marrying a descendant of the Ice People's evil spirit, a man who had for some time had his eye on Eldrid – and her large farm – finally plucked up the courage to ask for her hand. He and Eldrid were married at the feast of Saint Hans around the midsummer solstice. The man was one of those who had fled from the bailiff's soldiers and sought refuge in the valley a few years earlier. Silje was pleased for Eldrid's sake. Now she would not have to work so hard and would have a companion in her later years. She was beyond the age of having children, so they would not have to live with the worry of bringing yet another descendant of the Evil Tengel into the world.

Silje had so much to occupy her that she had no time for her weaving, and although she missed this, she had so many other new and exciting things to do instead. Tengel took her and the children with him to see all his most cherished places and being out of doors all the time helped them keep the hazelnut-brown tan given to them by the first warm rays of spring sunshine on the last snow. They were all in the best of health. Tengel carried Dag in a haversack and Sol, at his side, had her kitten in a basket. Silje and Tengel noticed that her cruel tendencies were less frequent, possibly as a result of living among people who loved her and wanted only the best for her – but she could still frighten them occasionally.

There was the time when they came to a waterfall and her eyes seemed to mist over.

'Lady dead,' she said.

Tengel was startled. 'How could she know that? A woman threw herself into the falls just here about – oh, it must be twenty years ago now.'

There were other unexplained occurrences too. On one occasion, while they were walking in the foothills, she came rushing towards them shouting, 'Home!' Her eyes were wide with terror. 'Danger – man under tree! Home!'

They would always follow her wishes when these things happened, but never found any explanations for them.

As autumn drew closer, Silje became very out of sorts. Her appetite vanished, she lost weight and her skin became very pale and covered in brown blotches. Tengel had thought of riding out of the valley to see how things were with Benedikt and his household, but decided against it. He sent the wagon-driver instead and the man returned after a few days with news that, while they wanted for nothing at the farm, Abelone was still living there and making their lives a misery. They were pleased to hear all about Tengel and Silje's little family and sent back a large parcel with food and clothes for the youngsters.

Silje was very touched by their generosity. 'If only we could do something for them,' she said. 'Rid them of those unwelcome parasites, for instance!'

'Yes, I agree,' Tengel replied, 'but my place is with you now. I cannot do anything for them.'

****

Silje stood at the door one day and looked out into the yard where the first frost had already set in. Then with a sigh she closed the door to keep in the warmth and sat down.

'I'm afraid, Tengel. What is wrong with me?'

He looked thoughtfully at her, not wanting to laugh at her ignorance. 'It's been a long while since you have refused me for womanly reasons, has it not?'

She considered this, 'Yes, yes it was a while ago. I've had so many things to do that I have given it no thought. Oh, Tengel!' she sat up, panic-stricken. 'Of course – naturally! When nothing happened straight away last spring, I thought maybe it never would. I put it from my mind, you see?'

Tengel was looking resolute. 'I have been wondering about this for some time, but I haven't had the courage to speak to you. When do you think?'

Silje started to count, but it wasn't easy because she had not been paying any heed to herself, no longer expecting anything to happen, not considering the possibility of motherhood. 'In April,' she said hesitantly.

Now he looked at her sombrely for a long, long time. 'I have the power to stop it – a potion …'

She shot to her feet, angry and confused. 'You wouldn't dare!'

'But what if it is a monstrosity?'

Tears welled up in her eyes.

'Monstrosity!' she sniffed. 'Are *you* a monstrosity? Is Sol? Is Eldrid? Or was your sister, Sunniva? I have seen others of your kin in this valley, yes I have, and do you think I'm afraid of them? If you take away my child, you will never see me again.'

She exaggerated, of course, but she wanted to make sure he was in no doubt about how she felt.

Tengel closed his eyes and sighed.

'It will be as you wish,' he said, but he seemed far from happy about it.

Tengel in fact, as the days passed, was distinctly apprehensive about the baby they were expecting. He lay awake with worry, heaving great aching sighs and making Silje feel so guilty that she began to doubt she had done the right thing. However, when she examined her own heart, she knew quite clearly – she was sure that she wanted this baby.

In the days leading to Christmas, she went to Hanna and Grimar's cottage with some bits of food that they barely were able to spare. She simply knocked at the door and placed the basket on the step, then left, but not before she turned to see Grimar picking up the food. He stared at her, she thought, as if noticing suddenly that she was with child.

Throughout this period, Tengel became withdrawn and quiet and, to make things worse, Silje's health continued to wane. He knew that she was suffering a great deal, although she never complained. She liked him to rest his warming hands on the small of her back – it soothed the constant nagging pains. This is the price I must pay for not being pear-shaped, she thought, smiling at how indignant she had been when Benedikt drew his picture of her on the church wall. She imagined that women with broad hips must have a much easier time when carrying a child.

On top of all else, a harsh winter brought bitter weather. The snows came early and remained throughout Yuletide. Everyone stayed inside their homes, as the drifts piled up as high as the roofs. The only way out was to dig tunnels through the packed snow to reach outhouses and barns. The cold caused a great deal of suffering – one old man was discovered frozen to death just outside his house. They could not bury him, but kept his corpse on a litter in the woodshed to wait for spring. A young lad who had been out hunting suffered frostbite on both legs and Tengel was sent for. He was very upset when he returned from the lad's home, but never revealed what he had done there.

Their stocks of food did not seem enough to last until spring, so Tengel and Silje used them as sparingly as they could. This was bad news, because Silje now needed good nourishment. Dag had started to crawl and, by holding on to walls and furniture, he was able to get everywhere. Although he was not as lively as Sol, he was very clever at pulling things to the floor wherever and whenever they came within reach. Silje felt she could no longer leave the children with Eldrid, as they were too difficult for her to watch now. Despite the swaddling, Dag's legs had not grown completely straight and Silje blamed herself for this, because she had so often loosened his covering. Tengel, knowing more than most people, said that it was caused at birth or by a lack of some vital life-giving element.

Silje found it hard to hide the fact that she was beginning to grow tired of the valley. It was not because of their hardships – she and her beloved Tengel shared them all – but she became overwhelmed by a frightening sense of helplessness when faced by the forces of nature. This was increased by the isolation and the cold, together with that intangible something in the valley that always troubled her, yet she was not able to define.

She had shared her feelings with Tengel on one occasion, explaining that it seemed as though the will to live was being drained out of her.

'I know,' he had said, 'it is something that old evil Tengel left behind him as a parting gift.'

But she hadn't truly believed him.

Then, late in March on a day bright with life-giving spring sunshine, her labour pains started. Eldrid took the children home with her and two of the neighbours' wives stayed with Silje.

It soon became clear to them all that it would not be an easy birth. Tengel did what he could to comfort Silje, and gave her a hot bitter drink that helped to relieve the pain. In great secrecy he read some of his incantations, but time wore on and, after two days of unyielding agony, everybody was getting anxious.

Silje could tell what Tengel was thinking – it was written all over his face. He had never been able to forget that it was his own deformed shoulders that had cost his mother her very life.

Silje lay exhausted on her bed, sweat glistening at her temples, her tired eyes dark and puffy. She no longer had the strength to sit in the specially built birthing chair. She looked up at everyone who stood at her bedside.

'May I have some water, please,' she asked. Her mouth was so dry. Loving hands lifted her head and a wooden cup was held to her lips. She sipped a little water then sank back on the bed. 'Get Hanna!' she whispered at last.

'Have you lost you mind?' Tengel exclaimed.

The women both crossed themselves.

'Is there another who can help my child now?' she asked. 'It is dying, Tengel!'

And so are you, was the unspoken feeling in the room.

'We shall wait a little longer,' he muttered. 'Perhaps it will be all right.'

But there was no change, other than Silje growing

weaker. As the evening came they lit the rarely used oil lamps and placed them around Silje's bed. It looked as though she was already dead and Tengel shuddered at the sight. He felt useless – he had done everything he could and nothing helped.

Then suddenly the door opened, startling everybody. There in the room stood the most grotesque likeness of a human that Silje had ever seen. The women screamed and fled into the children's room, closing and barring the door firmly behind them.

'Silje called for me,' said Hanna.

Tengel, too, took a step back from her.

'Go outside, foolish boy, you are of no use here!' muttered Hanna. 'And keep those worthless women out as well!'

Tengel walked to the door. Silje lay watching, horrified by the awful figure shuffling towards her on grossly swollen legs. She could never have imagined anything like it and the sight made her understand why Tengel had objected so strongly to having children.

'Hello again, Mother Hanna,' she said.

Tengel turned as he reached the door. 'Again?' Had Silje been keeping something from him? But his thoughts were interrupted as Hanna waved him away impatiently. Consumed with regret and anxiety, he left the room, for he did not dare force Hanna to leave. She was the one person nobody would ever want to cross!

If Hanna had been in the world beyond this valley, she would have been burned at the stake long ago, Silje thought to herself, trying to stop trembling. Here was a witch, a sorceress of the worst kind. Her bulging eyes seemed to be on fire beneath matted tufts of dark grey hair and a demonic grin played on the lips of the almost toothless, sunken hollow that was her mouth. Her clothes were nothing but rags that hung about her, rotted and decayed. Silje could not escape the vile feeling that these were the clothes Hanna had been wearing when she died and was buried, long ago. The skin was a sickly yellow with blotches of grey and black – it had never been washed. Her eyes had the same colour as Tengel's, but they were rheumy and rimmed with skin that was far older, yet still they shone in a way that seemed to burn right into Silje. Hanna's head was thrust forward from between her hunched shoulders, giving her the appearance of an ill-tempered predator.

Silje felt a wave of nausea wash over her as Hanna drew nearer. How on earth would she hide her disgust for this woman? How could she remain civil to her?

Then, in that strangely clear voice of hers, Hanna said, 'Let Hanna have a look. We'll see if we can't bring this young lady into the world.'

'A girl?' asked Silje, amazed. 'You know?'

'Of course I do! No, do not be afraid. You have done favours for me, now I shall do one for you. Besides, we both want this youngster to be born alive, don't we?'

Silje nodded, but at that moment her body shuddered with a new bout of pain.

Seeing this, Hanna shook her ugly head. 'That is not good. First we must give you something to build your strength, for this will take all your energy, my girl! Oh – that man Tengel! He cost his mother her life, you know. He is harsh on his womenfolk, that one!'

She fumbled in the pockets of her clothing. Silje breathed out, trying to avoid the choking stench that this witch carried with her, trying not to look at the few crooked teeth, the blackened pores and the wrinkles.

'Here – do you have any water?'

Silje pointed. Hanna filled the wooden cup and gave Silje a white powder.

'That is just for your heart.'

Hands shaking, Silje lifted the cup to her lips and managed to swallow the powder. She looked up at Hanna with the eyes of a wounded animal.

'Help me,' she whispered.

The aged crone nodded, 'No one calls on Hanna in vain. We will make this right.'

Silje had begun to harbour doubts, but was reassured by the kind words. After waiting a while, Hanna took out another powder, this time grey-green in colour, with an odour that made Silje's nostrils twitch. Instinctively she pressed her head back into the pillow.

'Drink this down, it will soften your hardened bones.'

Silje dared not refuse, even though somewhere in her head a voice was telling her to ask what was in the powder. These would not be simple herbs!

'There, then!' said Hanna. 'Now we wait. You should have been in the chair, but I doubt you are strong enough.'

Silence filled the room.

'Aaah – no! No!' Silje's body was contorted with a terrible stomach pain. It felt as if she had eaten crushed glass or drunk burning acid. Hanna was mouthing words as her hands moved, making circles in the air above Silje's tortured body. Then there was a stab of pain so fierce that, as she screamed, everything around her went black.

I am going to die, Silje thought. Merciful God, I am dying. This child will be born – dead or alive – but I will die. This loathsome woman, this spawn of Satan, only wants the child. She has sacrificed me!

Then she felt the touch of Hanna's ghastly hands on her, and heard her muttering terrible incantations.

'*Belial, Athys, Kybele, Reba, Apollyon, Lupos Astaroth, Nema ...*'

To Silje's tired mind it sounded as if she was summoning demons. No, she thought, not demons, not now! I am in the Valley of the Ice People and I have seen the demons rise above the mountains. It is all my doing, this is all my fault and I am to be punished. I have made love with a demon! All this went through her mind – and then, nothing.

****

Slowly, very slowly, Silje climbed back out of a deep black well. She heard noises, faint at first, then more clearly. They were voices.

'She is so tiny and weak.' It was one of the farmer's wives.

'Slap her backside, you foolish woman, and put your finger in her mouth.' This was Hanna's strident voice.

Silje wondered what were they talking about. She felt a warm hand on her brow and heard Tengel's gentle voice, indistinct but close by. 'Silje, Silje. Come back to me!'

She fought to tell him that she was alive, but nothing in her body seemed to work. She heard a child's weak cry. Was that Dag? No, his cries were far louder. The *myling* in the forest had cried like that. A newborn – a newborn baby? A little girl for her and Tengel?

'So tiny,' said the farmer's wife. 'That little creature will never survive.'

At last Silje had regained the strength to open her eyes, but everything seemed shrouded in mist.

'Tengel,' she whispered.

'Thanks be to God,' she heard him whisper in reply. His hand lovingly stroked the hair from her temple. Part of her wanted to see her baby and part of her could not. She ought not to, not before she felt stronger.

'Hanna gave me something,' she said. 'It soon worked.'

'Well hardly "soon",' whispered Tengel, 'you were fighting for your life for a long time after that.'

She gave this some thought.

'It's very painful – has it torn me wide open?'

'I think it may have.'

Hanna, who was crouched by the fire like an animal about to pounce, turned to them.

'Your wife is not a good child-bearer, Tengel.'

'Do you mean that this will be our only one?' he asked.

'It should be,' the old crone replied with a nasty knowing grin, 'but you won't be able to keep away!'

Tengel and Silje exchanged a glance and tried to stifle a smile. He had tears in his eyes, something she had never seen before.

'These embers tell me strange and remarkable things,' said Hanna suddenly. 'From your kin there will be ...' She paused.

'There will be what?' Tengel asked at once, 'This evil we carry, will it continue?'

'It will – it will. But far stranger are the things of this world. You asked me once if I could see your future, Silje. I see it now. You are the Ice People – you and no others.'

'But that cannot be,' argued Tengel. 'All who live in this valley are the Ice People.'

Hanna smiled the smile of one who holds the oracle.

'It will be as I say. From the children you bring into this world, Silje, you will have great, great joy – and *one* great sadness. And then ... no, it doesn't matter. But this I don't understand. I see a double line of trees ...'

'An avenue of linden trees?' asked Silje. 'That cannot be possible.'

Hanna ignored them and turned her attention back to

the embers in the hearth. Tengel stood up to take the swaddled baby from the farmer's wife.

'Do you want to see her?' he asked Silje with genuine fatherly pride.

Silje closed her eyes, 'Is it …?'

Before she had finished the question, Hanna, without looking up from the fire, answered, 'You need not be afraid of that one. She carries no powers.'

Quietly, Silje gave a sigh of relief. Looking up, she was dismayed to see how tiny and blue with cold the poor little thing was. 'She is pretty,' she said unconvincingly. 'But will she have red hair?'

'No more than you, I expect,' replied Tengel.

He loves her already, she thought with surprise. He who had never wanted a child – while I, who fought so long for it, do not have the strength in me to feel anything.

Then the other farmer's wife, who had kept as far away as possible from Hanna, asked, 'What will you name her?'

Silje noticed that the old hand, which had been clutching a stick and turning the embers of the fire, stopped still. Although not looking towards them, Hanna was obviously listening intently.

Tengel answered, 'She is such a tiny, poor little thing. I have been thinking about the day you found Dag in the forest. You remember that you said you would have named him Liv, if he had been a girl?'

'I remember,' said Silje.

Beside the fire, Hanna's hunched shoulders dropped slightly.

'Then I would like her name to be "Liv",' said Tengel.

'Liv is a good name, but I want her to have a second one, just like the other children,' whispered Silje.

The fearful creature by the fire held her breath.

'I want her to be called "Liv Hanna",' added Silje in a stronger voice.

Tengel looked doubtful and a little scared, then he said loudly, 'Her name is Liv Hanna.'

Now the hideous crone again began to stir the embers excitedly. A strange whining, humming tune came from her lips. Silje didn't know what it was – spells, chants or tradition? Whatever it was, she could not deny that it held all the pride and joy that this sad, banished old woman now felt. She was obviously singing for the baby, yet there seemed to Silje to be no hint of evil in these strange heathen verses.

INTERNATIONAL BESTSELLER

Margit Sandemo

The Legend of the Ice People

Witch-hunt

ISBN: 978-1-903571-77-4

*Book 2 of The Legend of the Ice People
series, Witch-hunt, is to be published
on 7 August 2008*

Further Information

Publication for the first time in the English language of the novels of Margit Sandemo that begins with *Spellbound*, will continue during 2008, 2009 and beyond. The first six novels of *The Legend of the Ice People* are being published monthly up to Chrismas 2008 and further editions will appear throughout the following year.

The latest information about the new writing of Margit Sandemo and worldwide publication and other media plans are posted and updated on her new English language website at www.margitsandemo.co.uk along with details of her public appearances and special reader offers and forums.

All current Tagman fiction titles are listed on our website www.tagmanpress.co.uk and can be ordered online. Tagman publications are also available direct by post from: The Tagman Press, Media House, Burrel Road, St Ives, Huntingdon, Cambridgeshire, United Kingdom PE27 3LE.

For details of prices and special discounts for multiple orders, phone 0845 644 4186, fax 0845 644 4187 or e-mail sales@tagmanpress.co.uk